GHOST AGENTS

NITA DEBORDE

Ghost Agents

Nita DeBorde

Mabelonia Press

Acknowledgements

Thanks so much to everybody who has supported and encouraged me throughout this whole process.

I'd especially like to thank my mom for never failing to believe in me.
And, of course, a huge thank you to my beta readers – Sheri Carey, Ann Dolbee, Amanda Ponder, Georgia Ward, Rebecca Gardea, Lynn Craft, & Laura Ransom. Your feedback and input were invaluable in shaping this story!

GHOST AGENTS

The clouds shifted across the moon, intensifying the glow of the translucent form as he wavered among the grave markers. He had no clear destination. No plan except escape. But escape to where? He wasn't tethered to this cemetery, but it was still his home. He had made that choice long ago, for reasons that were no longer clear to him.

Nothing was clear anymore. Even the fear and sadness that had engulfed him only minutes before had begun to fade. A faint memory lingered. A vague feeling that something terrible had happened, but he struggled to remember what had happened and to whom.

The figure slowed his pace as he moved through the grave markers, eventually stopping next to a mausoleum, uncertain what to do next. He hovered listlessly, frowning at the cool stones glowing in the dim moonlight. Why had he been in such a hurry before?

A thrilling hum began to spread through his entire being, drawing his attention toward the far side of the cemetery. Compelled by the delicious tingle that was slowly overtaking his senses, he moved toward the source. He had never felt anything like it. The pull was irresistible, and it only intensified as he drew nearer.

He crossed the cemetery at lightning speed, his destination a clearing in the northwest corner. In the center of the clearing sat a dark, metallic object about the size and shape of a shoebox. Normally he would have found this odd, but the exquisite sensation coursing through his entire being clouded his senses. With an almost reverent awe, he approached the strange object, completely oblivious to the group of hooded figures standing only a few feet away.

He desperately wanted to touch the energy source but for some reason couldn't. Something held him in place, unable to move at all.

One of the hooded figures stepped into the center of the clearing and flipped a switch on the strange device. The warm pulse of delectable energy quickly disappeared, leaving the translucent being feeling listless and drugged. As the fog in his head slowly evaporated, he looked around the clearing, noticing the hooded figures for the first time. He instantly recognized the danger, but there was no means of escape. He was frozen in place, still completely unable to move.

A familiar humming noise started from somewhere nearby. The translucent figure closed his eyes, waiting for what would inevitably happen next. In a few moments, he would be gone, along with all memories of who he was in his previous life.

Chapter 1

"I believe in ghosts. I have to. It's in my job description."

Claire Abelard smiled at the woman who had just asked the most ridiculous question anyone could ever ask the leader of a ghost tour.

The final stragglers from the evening's tour group milled around the Gold Room, snapping photos. They all hoped to capture an image of Galveston Island's supernatural celebrity, Miss Bettie Brown, the famous ghost of Ashton Villa. Claire could sense Bettie was close by. She prayed the ghost would hold herself together a few more minutes until the house was clear.

"Claire!"

The energy in the hallway rippled as Bettie poked her translucent head around the corner. Claire cut a quick glance at the remaining tourists on the opposite side of the ornate formal living room which had been nicknamed "The Gold Room." They were admiring the large portrait hanging behind the piano, completely oblivious to Bettie's presence in the room.

"What?" Claire whispered, turning her head slightly in Bettie's direction.

"I need to talk to you," Bettie said with a furtive look.

"I know. You interrupted my tour three times to tell me that." Claire threw another look at the tourists across the room. "You're lucky we didn't have any sensitives with us tonight."

Bettie huffed, sending out another ripple of energy. "I could tell none of them had the gift, and this is important."

"I'm sure whatever it is, it can wait another ten minutes until these people have finished admiring your paintings."

Bettie straightened her posture and turned her attention to the far side of the room. "Yes, well, I suppose you are right. I will wait until they have finished."

Claire shook her head and smiled. Seeing the tourists admire her work was about the only thing that would have distracted Bettie from her current mission.

Everyone thought they know the truth about ghosts, but Claire's employer, The Bureau for Historical Preservation, had made sure very few people actually did. Ghosts aren't wayward spirits caught between this world and the next, though the Bureau wanted people to believe that. For centuries, Bureau-influenced story tellers have promoted this idea, steering the general population away from the more complicated and less romantic truth. With technology advancing at its current rate, Claire figured one day someone would stumble on to the true nature of ghosts, but until that day, the realities of the paranormal world were proprietary information of the Bureau.

The remaining tourists began making their way toward the exit. As they approached, a pre-teen boy held his cellphone out in Claire's direction.

"My ghost hunting app didn't pick up anything. Are you sure this place is haunted?"

Claire smiled at him, not at all surprised that a free cell phone app had missed Bettie's presence in the mansion. "Maybe next time."

The woman walking behind ghost app boy urged him forward with a scowl.

"Don't worry about him, sweetie," another woman from the group told Claire, patting her on the arm. "I'm certain I felt Bettie's presence with us during our tour."

Claire raised her eyebrows. "Really?"

The woman closed her eyes and smiled serenely. "Oh, yes. I believe she was very pleased to have us in her home."

Claire nodded, resisting the urge to laugh. Not even the lowest level sensitive would have described Bettie's mood that evening as being "pleased."

Claire urged the final few stragglers toward the exit. "I hope you all had a wonderful experience tonight," she said as she closed the door behind them. She turned the lock with a loud sigh, then spoke to the seemingly empty mansion. "Okay, Bettie. You've got my undivided attention."

Another ripple of energy coursed through the entryway and Bettie materialized on the staircase. "They seemed like lovely people. Wonderful taste in art."

Claire sighed again. "You said you had something important you need to talk to me about."

"Yes, that." Bettie floated to the bottom of the stairs and pointed a finger in Claire's direction. "You need to have a talk with those new historical society volunteers."

"What've they done now?"

"They keep moving the furniture." She gave Claire an accusing look. "Did you not tell them I abhor when people disturb the furniture arrangement?"

Claire leaned her head back against the door. "Of course, I did, Bettie, and I'm sure that's why they're doing it. They're new. They just want an encounter with the Ashton Villa ghost."

"Of all the impertinence…" The air shimmered around Bettie as she turned away. She paused with her hands on her hips then shot a look over her shoulder at Claire. "Well, you need to make them stop."

"No, Bettie, *you* need to make them stop."

Bettie huffed. "And how am I to do that? They are low-level sensitives at best. I am certain they lack the acumen."

Claire pushed away from the door and headed across the room. "I didn't mean you should have a conversation with them." She turned the lights off in the Gold Room and began her check of the other rooms in the house. She could sense Bettie following her. "Give them what they want. If they want to encounter the ghost of Ashton Villa, then give them an encounter." She started up the stairs to the second floor and tossed over her shoulder, "That *is* your job, after all."

Bettie was waiting at the top of the staircase when Claire arrived. "I already have," she insisted. "Every night, I move the furniture back, which is no small feat, as you well know. And then the next day they mess it all up again."

Claire gave her a look. "What are you, an amateur? I've seen you do more than that on an off night."

Now it was Bettie's turn to sigh. "Would it not be easier for you to talk to them about it?"

Claire resumed her check of the house. "Maybe, but it certainly wouldn't leave as much of an impression."

"Okay," Bettie finally conceded, floating along behind Claire. "I will give them an encounter, but do not blame me if they quit."

"Of course not. If they can't handle the haunting, they shouldn't poke the ghost."

Bettie's image shimmered and the temperature in the room dropped several degrees. "Claire Abelard," she scolded, "you keep using that word. You know I do not like it."

"I'm sorry," Claire said, genuinely apologetic. "It's hard to shift gears after a tour." She cleared her throat dramatically. "They shouldn't poke the *projection*."

Bettie smiled. "Thank you, dear. 'Ghost' is such a demeaning word." She hovered a few feet from the doorway, a thoughtful expression on her face. "I suppose you are right," she finally said. "Maybe I *should* give them a memorable encounter." She gave Claire a wink. "This could be fun."

"I'm glad you see things my way."

Claire finished her check of the house and retrieved her purse from the locked cabinet in the kitchen. When she returned to the Gold Room, Bettie was seated at the piano, her fingers hovering over the keys. Bettie's projection energy was strong, so she had the ability to interact with material objects, but since it required a great expenditure of energy Bettie usually saved those interactions for truly special occasions.

"Before you go," she said, her hands moving through the motions of playing the piano without actually affecting the keys. "Jean Lafitte needs to talk to you."

Claire sighed. "Bettie, you know that's out of my jurisdiction. Jean is a rogue. I could get into a lot of trouble for getting involved with whatever he's got going on."

Bettie's hands stopped moving. "I know that, dear, and we both know how much he enjoys being a rogue." She glanced over her shoulder. "After all, he is a pirate." With a chuckle, she turned her attention back to the piano. "I am sure he would not have asked for your help if it was not important."

Claire hesitated. If the Bureau found out she was interacting with, much less assisting, rogues again, she'd receive a serious reprimand or reassignment...or worse.

Bettie looked at her, a sad expression on her face. "He was very upset when I spoke to him. Will you at least go talk to him and see what is wrong?"

Claire nodded. Had there ever been a doubt that she would? "Fine. I'll seek him out as soon as I get a chance." She removed her keys from her purse. "But tell him to stay in Galveston this week. I'm not going to hang around the docks all night waiting for him to show up."

Bettie smiled broadly. "I will get word to him."

To most agents, energy projections were simply assets or resources to monitor and assist. Though many sensitives could feel a projection's emotions, for Claire it was different. As a Level-5 sensitive, she experienced their emotions as if they were her own. Sometimes that made her job a lot easier, but more often than not it simply complicated things.

Clare nodded again and opened the front door to leave. "Good night, Bettie."

"Good night, my dear." She blew a kiss in Claire's direction before fading from view.

Claire stepped out onto the porch and pulled her jacket tighter around her chest. A typical Texas cold front had blown through that evening, dropping the temperature by close to twenty degrees in a matter of hours. She knew the crisp autumn weather wouldn't last long on the Gulf Coast, but tonight the cooler temperatures reminded her of Boston, flooding her mind with bittersweet memories.

The wind whipped around the Victorian mansion, blowing Claire's shoulder length brown hair into her face. As she pulled her hair back into a ponytail, she looked up. A full autumn moon shown in the sky, illuminating the sidewalk in front of her. She wasn't a particularly superstitious person, but she couldn't shake the feeling it was some kind of omen. She already regretted agreeing to meet with Jean Lafitte, but it was too late to back out now. She had told Bettie she would help, and if she didn't follow through the projection would never let her hear the end of it. Even more than the living, projections could have long memories, and they loved to gossip. Claire would lose credibility with every projection on the island if she went back on her promise.

"Hey, Claire!" a voice that had become all too familiar called out.

Claire jumped in surprise. "Hey, Ann," she said, willing her heart rate to return to normal as the woman approached. "What are you doing still hanging around? The tour ended a half hour ago."

Ann Menefee was a retired school teacher who had come to the island a few months before to work on her retirement career as a writer. She had published one book about haunted locations in San Francisco and another on New Orleans, and now she was researching Galveston's ghosts for her third book. She had taken most of Claire's tours over the past few months. Some of them, like the Ashton Villa tour, she had taken several times. By this point, she should know the house and its haunted history almost as well as Claire did.

"I wanted to bring you this," Ann said, handing Claire a medium-sized mailing envelope. "I meant what I said the other day. I'd like to hear your thoughts on some of my theories. They aren't exactly mainstream."

Claire nodded and accepted the package. She didn't have to open it to know what was inside. "Thanks, Ann, but I really don't know when I'll be able to read this. Things are kind of busy for me right now."

"I understand," Ann assured her. With a conspiratorial smile, she added, "You could always send it up your chain of command. I think your superiors might be interested in my theories as well."

Claire slipped the package into her bag. "Honestly, Ann, I don't think Craig reads books. He's more of a movie guy."

"That wasn't who I was referring to."

Claire let out an exaggerated sigh. This wasn't the first time Ann had hinted at knowing something about the Bureau. Claire didn't know where her information might have come from, but she certainly wasn't going to be the agent to confirm anything.

"You've got to let go of these conspiracy theories," she told her. "I only wish my life was that interesting." She started walking toward the parking lot, hoping the tenacious writer would get the message. "I lead ghost tours. That's all."

She felt no guilt about lying. Maintaining Bureau secrecy was one of the primary directives drilled into every agent from the first day of training.

"If you say so," Ann conceded, though Claire could tell she wasn't convinced. "But I'd still like to hear your thoughts after you read the book. I should be getting my copies of the New Orleans book any day now. I'll bring one by as soon as they're delivered."

"Sure," Claire said, pressing the button to unlock her door. "That would be great." She held up the package. "I'll let you know when I've finished reading this."

Ann stood a few feet away from the car as Claire started the engine. Claire waved as she pulled out of the parking spot, resisting the urge to roll her eyes. Dodging Ann's conspiracy theories was the last thing she needed right now. She thought again about Jean Lafitte and his request for a meeting. Whatever he wanted to talk to her about, Claire was sure it wasn't going to make her life any easier.

Chapter 2

As she pulled into the driveway of her house, Claire smiled. She never took the beauty of the quaint, Victorian-era home for granted. The deed for the house officially belonged to the Bureau, but as the senior agent on the island, Claire was allowed to live there. Honestly, it was one of her favorite perks of her extremely challenging job.

As part of Claire's cover story, the house had supposedly been in her family for generations, which wasn't far from the truth. In the two years she had lived on Galveston Island, though, she'd never had to lie to anyone about it. *That's what happens when a person's job keeps them so busy they don't have time for a social life,* she thought as she climbed the front steps.

She opened the front door and was immediately greeted by a shimmering ripple of energy and a swirl of sparkling translucent sequins.

"Claire! I'm so glad you're home!"

"Hey, Thelma," Claire said with a tired smile.

The projection rippled with excitement as she moved closer. "Claire, please say, 'Yes!'"

Thelma Gates had been a Galveston society party girl in the 1920s before dying in a car crash after a wild night on the town. As with all energy projections, the remnants of her personality that lingered after her death were basically a purified and amplified version of who she'd been when she was alive. In Thelma's case, that meant she was a flighty, twenty-year-old flapper who unfortunately never had the opportunity to grow into a mature adult. Claire seriously doubted she was going to say "Yes" to anything Thelma had planned.

"Would you let the woman catch her breath, please." The air to Claire's left shifted as Sarah Meriwether materialized.

"Thank you, Sarah," Claire said, closing the door behind her.

Sarah had been the only daughter of John Meriwether, the man who built Claire's house in 1881, the year before Sarah was born. Not only was John a loving father and devoted husband, he was also one of the first Bureau agents to work on the island.

In 1900, a massive hurricane hit Galveston, killing thousands of people and wiping out a majority of the buildings on the island. The Meriwether house was one of the few structures that survived the storm with only water damage. Unfortunately, Sarah's family didn't fare as well. Sarah survived, but she lost both of her parents and a younger brother. In keeping with her father's wishes, upon Sarah's death in 1944 the house was bequeathed to the Bureau and Sarah's energy projection tethered itself there.

"You look absolutely exhausted," Sarah said in her usual motherly fashion. She reached out and touched Claire's arm, sending a pulse of energy shooting through her. For a split second, Claire's tired ache dissipated as Sarah shared some of her energy with her. "You need to eat something."

Claire smiled and set her purse on the table next to the door. "Actually, I just want to go to bed. I've got a shift at the candy store tomorrow."

Sarah furrowed her brow. "Are you sure that's such a good idea? You'll be absolutely spent."

On the weekends, Claire led ghost tours for Historical Ghost Encounters, a shadow company owned and operated by the Bureau. In keeping with the organization's mission, this branch of the Bureau operated tours of historically significant locations to keep their stories and the local history alive. With offices in every major city around the world, the tour company's reach was extensive, and all employees were Bureau agents.

During the day, though, Claire worked at a local candy store on the Strand, a street in Galveston that was popular with tourists because of its atmosphere and shops. The job was a lot of fun, and every day Claire had opportunities to promote the history of the island, particularly the haunted history, as she interacted with customers. Since leading tours kept her out late, and conducting Bureau business after that kept her out even later, she rarely worked a day shift on the weekends.

Claire smiled at Sarah, genuinely appreciative of her concern. "I'm covering for a coworker."

"Well, you still need to eat something before you go to bed. If nothing else, then a banana and some peanut butter. At your age, you can't afford to let your metabolism get any slower."

Claire sighed. One drawback to Sarah's motherly personality was that it was extremely motherly, even too motherly, at times. Ever since Claire's thirtieth birthday the year before, Sarah had made it a mission to remind her she wasn't getting any younger.

"That's it," Claire announced, shaking her head. "I'm not leaving the TV on during the day for you guys anymore. Those talk shows get you too worked up."

Thelma cleared her throat and the temperature in the room dropped a few degrees. "Could we please get back to me now?"

"Of course, Thelma. What did you want to ask me?"

The projection's eyes lit up and the sequins on her dress began to shimmer again. "Now, let me finish before you give me your answer."

"I've been telling her all night this is a bad idea."

Claire had been wondering when the third projection would make her appearance. April Parish was as introverted a personality as Thelma was extroverted. The lingering trauma surrounding her death often caused her to stay out of sight, only making appearances when she really deemed it necessary.

"Oh, would you stop being such a fire extinguisher!" Thelma exclaimed, dropping the temperature a few degrees more. She turned her attention back to Claire and put on a charming smile. "You're going to taint Claire's opinion before she's even heard my request."

Claire sat down on the couch with an exhausted huff. "Thelma, please spit it out. I need to get to bed."

"Alright." Thelma floated over and hovered on the couch next to Claire. "But remember, don't answer too quickly."

Claire sighed loudly, hoping she'd take the hint.

"Okay, okay, I found out today that some of the rogues on the island have been meeting at the Old City Cemetery, you know, to hang out and pass the time, and I really want to go, too." Claire opened her mouth to respond, but Thelma rushed on. "I know it's outside my tether zone, but I was hoping you could put in a request for me."

Claire stared at her for several seconds. "Are you serious?"

Thelma raised her eyebrows, confused that she would even ask. "Of course. It sounds kippy." She let out an overly dramatic sigh. "I'm so bored here, stuck in this neighborhood. Nothing exciting *ever* happens here."

Claire didn't have to look at April and Sarah to know what they were thinking. She could feel their amusement.

"Thelma, even if it wouldn't require me to wade through piles of paperwork to submit the request, you know there's no way anyone at the Bureau is going to agree to something like that. They aren't going to untether you so you can go to a party."

"I don't see what the big deal is," Thelma exclaimed, launching off the couch to hover in front of Claire. "I just want to go hang out with some friends." She looked at April and Sarah. "Well, with some friends who know how to have a good time."

"Isn't that what got you here in the first place?" April asked.

Thelma glared at her but didn't respond. She turned her attention back to Claire and leaned in close with pleading eyes. "Please, Claire, please. I really want to go to one of these shindigs. Please do this for me."

Claire stood up, even more ready to get into bed than when she had first arrived home. "You have to know that I can't." She sighed again. "In fact, honestly, now I have to decide if these meetings are something I need to report to the Bureau."

Thelma let out an indignant huff. "The rogues aren't doing anything wrong. No livings are in any danger, so I don't see why it's such a big deal." She reached out toward Claire but stopped short of touching her. "Please don't turn them in to the Bureau."

Claire gave her what she hoped was a reassuring smile. "I'm sure you're right. I'm sure the meetings are perfectly innocent."

Thelma's face brightened. "Then you'll submit the request for me?"

Claire shook her head. "I'm sorry, Thelma. The answer is no." Thelma's disappointment washed over her like a wave. "Even if I wanted to let you go," she tried to explain, "I know the Bureau would never approve the request."

Thelma's scowl returned, her disappointment quickly turning to anger. "I thought you were different from all the other agents, but you're just a slunge like the rest of them." She stuck her tongue out at Claire then blinked out of sight.

"Don't let her insults bother you. She's just upset," Sarah said.

"You made the right choice," April assured her. "Nothing good would come of Thelma hanging out with a bunch of rogues."

Claire offered them both a half-hearted smile as she turned and headed toward her bedroom. "I know, but that doesn't make it any easier."

Before she had taken three steps, April appeared in the hallway in front of her. She reached out and touched Claire's hand. Almost instantly, Claire's physical exhaustion and the lingering effects of Thelma's disappointment melted away. The reprieve wouldn't last long, but at least for a moment the exchange left Claire feeling peaceful and relaxed.

"Thank you, April," she said, genuinely appreciative of the gesture. "I needed that."

"You're welcome." Before fading from view, she added, "Now, get some sleep."

Claire happily obeyed, falling into bed still fully clothed. Her head had barely hit the pillow before she was sound asleep.

(Excerpt from A Concise Accounting of the Conservancy of Energy-based Metaphysical and Transcendental Entities: A History of the Bureau for Historical Preservation (1680-1973))

In the spring of 1680, while conducting research into the burgeoning scientific field of electricity, a group of French scientists and scholars discovered the surprising fact that the human body generates a significant amount of electrical current. The amount of current differed from person to person, but at least some degree of current existed in all their test subjects. The four men, Pierre Abelard, Guillaume Monterel, Geoffroi Grignon, and Charles Bricout, found this was true even among their own group, with Abelard giving off the strongest degree of electrical current.

In the course of their research, the four scientists also stumbled upon the realization that certain people leave behind a remnant of their electricity signature after death. The more electricity a person gave off when they were living, the more likely they were to leave behind an electricity projection. These remnants of energy were in fact the entities that were commonly referred to at the time as specters or spirits. In modern language, they would be known as ghosts.

The four scientists tried to share this information with the scientific community of their day, and with anyone else who would listen, but the rigidity of thought and deep-seated superstition of the time caused their findings to fall on deaf ears.

Undaunted, the men continued their research into these energy-based projections. With a certain amount of practice, they were able to make direct contact with, and eventually interact with, several projections. Each scientist *had a different communicative skill, but all four were able to interact with the energy projections to some degree.*

Through these interactions, the scientists learned that the projections had no idea why they existed or what they were supposed to do, a fact that often led them to despair and many times to engage in violent activities as a result of their frustration. The four men conferred and decided the best thing the projections could do was to help preserve history by keeping their own life stories and memories alive. The projections found this to be a reasonable, and even appealing, task and set out to do just that.

The four scientists realized that if the few projections they had encountered felt frustrated and confused about their continued existence, it stood to reason that others must feel the same way. They each spread out across Europe, seeking out individuals who were open to their research and sensitive to the energy projections to assist them in their task. They began calling their assistants "surveyors," and by the turn of the century there were more than a hundred men across the European continent actively involved in assisting energy projections.

As the number of surveyors grew and the group's reach began to extend beyond Europe, the four men realized the need for a more organized means of monitoring the surveyors' progress and activities. And so was born the Bureau for Historical Preservation.

Chapter 3

The next morning, Claire stood behind the counter of Keeling's Confectionary, struggling to keep her eyes open and stifling several yawns as she doled out sugary treats to the tourists. This part of her cover story provided opportunities to talk to people about the island's history and point them toward the most "haunted" locations, but in her current condition, she was making Galveston look like the most boring place on the planet.

As she handed a carefully weighed-out bag of chocolate truffles across the counter to a middle-aged woman wearing a fanny pack, Claire forced a smile and stifled another yawn before thanking the woman for her visit. She turned away from the counter to see one of her coworkers approaching with a steaming paper cup extended in her direction.

Claire sighed appreciatively as she took the cup. "You are my absolute favorite!"

"Who? Me, or the coffee?"

"It's a toss-up." Claire took a sip of hot liquid and moaned contentedly.

Monica smiled. "You looked like you could use another cup this morning." They had worked together for two years, so Monica was well-acquainted with Claire's coffee addiction.

"What do you mean 'another'? I was running late so I didn't get to stop at the coffee place."

"Well, that explains your zombie act."

"Oh, zombies are much worse than this," Claire said with a wink.

Monica shook her head and chuckled. "You need to stop watching so many horror movies. First, it's ghosts, now zombies." The bell above the door jingled and she nodded at Claire's coffee cup. "You better not let Chris see you drinking that in front of the customers."

Claire took one more glorious sip then set the cup behind the counter. When she looked back up, she spotted Philip Graham, one of their regular customers, making his way across the shop in her direction. She smiled and waved.

Philip had come to Galveston at the beginning of the summer, working on a government grant to study the impact of the petroleum industry on coastal wildlife. He had tried to explain his work to Claire once, but all the scientific jargon had gone over her head.

Claire knew from their first meeting that Philip was a mid-level sensitive, which explained why they had an instant connection. He was an older man, Claire guessed probably in his late-fifties or early-sixties, though she couldn't tell for sure. There was a youthfulness and energy about his demeanor that she envied, especially in her current near-comatose state.

Claire never asked Philip his age because she was sure he wouldn't willingly offer the truth about that topic any more than he was willing to fill her in on the source of his peculiar accent. For months she had tried to place it, but with no luck and no help from Philip. He claimed he liked to keep an air of mystery about his persona.

"Sweden," Claire said as Philip approached her workstation. She had given up making serious guesses weeks before.

"You're getting warmer," he told her with a smile. Of course, that's what he always said, no matter what country she guessed.

Growing up in a Bureau family with relatives in every echelon of the administrative hierarchy, Claire had met agents from all over the world, so she had encountered just about every accent imaginable. At some point she must have guessed Philip's. It was eastern European, she believed, though she'd probably never know for sure, and he wasn't about to let her off the hook.

As Philip drew nearer, Claire felt some of her exhaustion dissipate, leaving in its place the familiar hum of energy that always accompanied an encounter between two sensitives. For projections to share energy with a living person, they had to touch them, but it wasn't the same with sensitives. Proximity did the trick. Even as a mid-level sensitive, Philip carried enough energy with him to cause a reaction to take place.

"Do I even have to ask what your order will be today?"

Philip's smile broadened. "If you do, I'll be seriously disappointed."

Claire returned his smile as she reached into the vat of individually wrapped pieces of taffy. The store was famous for its hand-pulled taffy, with demonstrations and samples being given out at regular intervals throughout the day, even during the off-season.

She dropped the candies into a bag and weighed it on the scale. Every day, Philip's order was the same, a bit of nostalgia from his upbringing in whatever mysterious country he was from. Claire handed him the bag and he handed her his money, then immediately unwrapped one of the pieces and popped it into his mouth.

"Mmm," he sighed, "just like when I was a boy."

"In Morocco?"

"You're getting warmer."

"I'll figure it out one day," she assured him.

He winked at her. "Maybe you already have." He nodded in Monica's direction then turned to leave.

Claire chuckled as she watched him head out the door into the sunny autumn day. The effects of their encounter would only last a short while and then her exhaustion would return, but at least for the moment she felt energized.

"Isn't he a little old for you?" Monica asked as she moved closer. "I mean, sure, he's a charming man, but he's got to be at least what? Fifty? Sixty?"

Claire gave her a look. "His age doesn't matter. He's a customer. That's all."

"Well, the way you flirt with him, and the way you light up when he walks in the room, that tells a different story."

"I do not flirt," Claire said defensively. She couldn't argue about lighting up, though she also couldn't tell Monica the truth about it either. "He's a nice man who has a pleasant personality," she said instead. "I would think his coming in here every day would brighten anyone's mood."

"Not as much as it seems to brighten yours."

Her cell phone began to ring and she pulled it out of her pocket with a frown. "I do *not* flirt with him," she insisted again. "He's a nice man. That's all."

"Of course, my mistake. That must be all it is."

Claire looked at her phone's caller ID and her frown deepened. "I need to take this." She didn't wait for Monica's response as she made her way to the back of the store. "This is Claire," she said, raising the phone to her ear.

"We've got another one," a familiar voice replied.

There was no need for greetings or the exchanging of pleasantries. There would only be one reason Deputy Rick Martens was calling her.

Though Deputy Martens didn't work for the Bureau, he was a mid-level sensitive who possessed the Sensory Acumen, which meant he could sense when a projection was present. Martens's job in law enforcement put him in a prime position to be on the scene at or around the time of many deaths. As a result, he could sense when new projections had formed, though unfortunately, he lacked the acumen to interact with them. That was where Claire came in. Working in conjunction with the Bureau, Martens reported the new projections to Claire, and she handled it from there.

"Where?" Claire asked after only a second's pause.

"There was a wreck last night off Stewart Road and 83rd. A mother and her young child were hit by a drunk driver." He hesitated. "They were all killed."

Claire closed her eyes. This was the part of her job she hated. "Could you tell which one it was?"

"Sorry, no."

She nodded even though the deputy couldn't see her. "I'll go check it out tonight."

"Would you let me know how it goes?"

Claire smiled sadly. *An energy connection is always powerful, even for a low-level sensitive.* "Of course."

Claire disconnected the call but didn't immediately return to the front of the store. The energy boost she had received from Philip was completely gone and her exhaustion had returned full force. Given the situation Deputy Martens had described, it was going to be another long night. Whichever projection had formed, Claire was dreading introducing them to their new reality.

Chapter 4

After Claire returned to her station behind the counter, the rest of the morning passed with little incident. She pushed past the dread of the unpleasant task waiting for her that night, and with the help of the rest of her cup of coffee, felt practically human again, or at least less like a zombie.

Right before her shift ended that afternoon, she felt a massive pulse of energy slam into her, almost doubling her over and causing her breath to catch in her throat. She leaned against the counter for support, gripping the edge of the antique wood with white knuckles.

"Are you okay?"

Claire looked up to see the customer on the other side of the counter staring at her, concern and a hint of fear clearly written on her face. She took several deep breaths and nodded. "Yes, I'm fine." The energy pulse was still pressing against her, but her body had started to adjust to the sensation. She forced a smile and straightened her posture as best she could. "I'm so sorry. I think maybe my blood sugar is a little off today."

The woman clearly wasn't convinced, but at least she didn't push the issue. She picked her bag of sweets up off the counter then hurried out of the shop, obviously worried that whatever was wrong with Claire might be contagious.

Claire took a step back from the counter before any more customers could make eye contact with her. She needed to figure out where the pulse had come from, and she couldn't do that easily while dishing out candy. She crossed the room to where the taffy pulling machine stood unattended. The next demonstration wouldn't be for a few hours, so she could stay there unnoticed for a minute or two as she pretended to refill her stock of taffy.

She scanned the room as casually as she could, looking for any sign of what, or who, had caused the energy pulse. She hadn't felt anything so powerful in years. It could only mean another high-level sensitive was near, most likely another Level 5. She had encountered only a few of them in her life, even among Bureau leadership, so it was a strange and exciting sensation.

Her heart raced as she considered each possible candidate. She quickly ruled out the family of four sitting at the tables in the middle of the room enjoying their ice cream cones. They had been there for close to an hour without triggering any reactions. The young couple ordering shakes? Nope. Nothing there. The college kid with the backpack? Not him either.

When her eyes settled on a group of men checking out the chocolate bar, she knew she had found the source. The problem was, there were four of them there and she couldn't tell which one had caused the energy pulse. As strong as the reaction was for her, she had to imagine the sensitive in the group would be trying to locate her as well. Of course, if he had never learned to develop or harness his sensitive abilities, he might not be as in tune to them as a trained agent would be. He might just write off the experience as an intense bout of *déjà vu*.

Claire took several deep breaths and returned to her station, keeping an eye on the group of men without being too obvious about it. They all appeared to be in their late-twenties or thirties, and at the moment their attention was entirely focused on the chocolate. She moved a little closer as she replenished the taffy supply in the display cases.

She studied the men individually from a distance. The taller man in the group was talking to Monica, but their conversation was merely background noise as she concentrated on identifying the source of the pulse. She closed her eyes and took a deep breath, trying to connect to the energy around her.

"Oh, then you definitely want to talk to Claire."

Her eyes popped open at the mention of her name. She looked over to see Monica pointing at her. The tall man smiled and began moving in her direction. Claire could tell right away he wasn't the sensitive, but her heart began to beat faster all the same.

She forced a smile. "What about me?"

"These guys are looking for ghosts," Monica told her.

Well, no surprise there, Claire thought.

As the man approached, he stuck out his hand and Claire shook it. The rest of the group began moving in their direction as well.

"Spencer Lemus," the man said with a huge grin. "You know about ghosts here on the island?"

"I like to think so." Claire tried not to be too distracted as the energy pulse grew stronger. "I lead ghost tours every weekend, so I hope I know a little about the haunted history of the island."

Spencer beamed. He turned and slapped the man standing next to him on the shoulder. "See, I told you this was the right place."

"Actually," one of the other men said as he stepped toward the front of the group. "I think *I'm* the one who suggested we come in here."

Claire made eye contact with the man and forgot how to breathe. *And there he is,* she thought. His dark hair and brown eyes, paired with their strong energy connection, made it almost impossible for Claire not to stare at him with her mouth open. And she was pretty sure she lost her ability to put words into sentences for a few seconds. She forced her eyes to look somewhere else before she made a complete fool of herself.

Spencer brushed the dark-haired man's comment aside and focused his full attention on Claire. "Would you be willing to give us a tour?...or two?...or three?"

Claire tried to control her breathing, but the pressure from the energy connection she had just made was almost too much for her. Not only had she not met many Level-5 sensitives in her lifetime, the ones she had met had all been her father's age. The experience was drastically different when there was a physical attraction as well.

"Of course," Claire eventually said, forcing what she hoped was a casual smile. "Our tours are open to anybody."

Spencer laughed a little harder than Claire thought was necessary. "No, I mean a private tour." He leaned in close to her as if sharing a secret. "You see, we're a team of paranormal investigators. We've heard how many haunted places there are on this island, and we'd love to check them out."

Now it was Claire's turn to laugh. "It really doesn't work like that. Most of the places you're talking about are private property, so you can't go there whenever you feel like it."

"Okay, I'm going to be honest," Spencer said, again in that conspiratorial way. "We've got an internet show and we've come here to shoot some episodes. We're actually hoping it might land us a TV gig."

Claire raised her eyebrows. "That doesn't make trespassing any less illegal."

The Level 5 spoke up. "Maybe there's someone you could talk to who could give us permission to have a private tour."

Claire avoided making eye contact with him. "I could give you my boss's number, but I doubt he'll go for it."

Spencer slapped his friend on the shoulder again. "Awesome!"

Claire tore off a piece of receipt paper and wrote down the number for the Bureau's Houston office. "Ask for Craig Gardner," she said as she handed the paper to Spencer. "But don't get your hopes up. I seriously doubt he'll say 'yes'."

Spencer winked at her. "I can be very convincing." He turned and headed across the room, holding the piece of paper over his head as if it were some kind of prize.

As the group made their way toward the ice cream counter, Claire turned her attention back to the taffy bins in front of her. She could sense the Level 5 was still nearby but didn't dare look up to see exactly where he was.

"Thank you for helping us out."

And now she knew. He was standing right across the counter from her. She took a deep breath and let it out slowly. Hearing his voice this close had the same effect as their eye contact had.

"It's no big deal," she assured him, still focusing her attention on the taffy bins and hoping he wouldn't notice the slight tremor in her hands. Eventually she wiped them on her apron and glanced up at him. "Like I said, I doubt Craig will go for it."

"At least we can say we tried." He extended his hand in her direction. "I'm Drew, by the way."

Claire hesitated, uncertain what actual physical contact with him would be like. "Claire," she finally said, taking a deep breath before reaching out to shake his hand.

A spark of energy shot between them, travelling up her arm and through her entire body. Drew flinched at the contact as well and a slow smile crept across his lips.

"Wow, static electricity, huh?"

Claire nodded and pulled her hand away. "So, where are you guys from?" She hoped she sounded more casual than she felt.

"Beaumont."

"That's east of here, right?" Not a native Texan, she still didn't have the massive state's geography down, but since the Bureau's Houston office had jurisdiction in Beaumont as well, she was at least familiar with the city's location.

Drew nodded. "About two hours."

Claire stood awkwardly behind the counter for a several seconds. He didn't seem to be in a hurry to join the rest of his group, but she struggled with the idea of making small talk under the circumstances. "So, do you hunt ghosts full time?" she eventually asked.

He chuckled. "No, it's just a hobby. Something we do on the weekend." He glanced across the store to where Spencer was chatting with Monica again. "Spencer takes the show a little more seriously than the rest of us."

"You're just in it for the fun, then?"

He smiled. "Something like that."

"Drew," Spencer called from across the candy shop. "We're heading out. C'mon!"

"It was nice to meet you," Drew said, though he still didn't seem to be in a hurry to leave.

"You, too." Claire forced herself to make eye contact with him and smiled.

He nodded and looked over his shoulder to where the rest of his group was waiting for him. "I guess I better get going."

All Claire could do was nod. He gave her another smile that made her catch her breath, then turned and began making his way toward the door.

"You guys should probably check out the cemetery over on Broadway," she called after him. He stopped and turned back to look at her. She shrugged. "There's a section of the fence on Avenue L that fell in a few weeks ago, but you didn't hear about it from me."

"Thanks again." He tipped an imaginary hat in her direction. "I hope we'll see each other again soon."

Claire watched as he joined the rest of his group and they left the shop. She didn't realize she was still staring after them until Monica's voice snapped her back to reality.

"Wow, that was…weird."

Claire nodded and chuckled as she finished filling the taffy bins. "Yeah, I can't believe they'd come all the way to Galveston just to chase ghosts."

Monica laughed. "Actually, you of all people should get that. That's not what I was talking about." She elbowed Claire. "You talking to that guy. I felt like I was watching my twelve-year-old cousin at a junior high dance." She thought for a second. "Is the problem that he's too young for you? You seem perfectly comfortable talking to Philip."

Claire glared at her. "I didn't want to be too nice. I was trying not to get their hopes up about getting a private tour."

"If you say so." She gave Claire a wink then returned to her station to help a customer, leaving Claire to stew.

Claire tried to focus on her work, but she couldn't stop thinking about Drew. She was confident Craig would shoot down their request, but she hated to admit there was a part of her that prayed he wouldn't.

Chapter 5

That night after work Claire drove to the location Deputy Martens had given her over the phone. She felt sick to her stomach the entire way. This part of her job was absolutely necessary, but she hated it.

Bureau agents discovered long ago that when a projection forms, they rarely understand what has happened to them, especially if their death was traumatic. They still feel like the person they used to be, but they know something isn't right. Most projections never figure it out on their own, which is why it's essential for a Bureau agent to make contact with them as soon as possible. A confused and unguided projection will often deteriorate quickly into an angry or aggressive presence. After a point they become unreachable, even to a high-level sensitive.

As Claire pulled into a parking lot close to the intersection, she took a few deep breaths to calm her nerves. At that time of night there wouldn't be a lot of traffic, which should simplify her task of making contact with the new projection. She had no idea how the encounter would go, and the last thing she needed was a passer-by calling the cops because some crazy woman was talking to herself on the side of the road.

Claire exited her car and walked to the location where the accident had taken place. She could feel the strong energy signature of the newly formed projection, though she still couldn't identify which accident victim it was.

When she reached the scene, two white crosses, a large one and a heartbreakingly smaller one, had already been erected to mark the site. Though child projections weren't as likely to form as adults, they weren't entirely uncommon either, and they presented a particular challenge since children often struggle to fully grasp the concepts of life and death in the first place. Claire prayed she wouldn't have to take on that task again with this encounter.

She moved past the white crosses, following the energy projection's signature as it moved slowly through a nearby field. The gut-wrenching sorrow that threatened to engulf her removed any doubt of whose projection had formed.

"Hello," Claire called out gently. She waited a few seconds, then added, "My name is Claire. I'm here to help you."

She felt the air begin to ripple a few feet away from where she stood. She turned to see the faint image of a woman materializing slowly. She had a hard time judging the woman's age since her face was distorted from crying, but she appeared to be in her mid-twenties.

Claire fought back her own tears as she approached the young woman. The strong emotional connection she always experienced made it easier for the projections to trust her, but it tore her up inside every time.

"Hi," Claire said, swallowing past the lump in her throat. "Are you Stephanie?"

Deputy Martens had texted her the details of the accident victims earlier that afternoon. The more information she had about them, the stronger her connection would be.

The young woman didn't answer right away. She looked around the field and back at the road, then turned back to Claire with a look of complete desperation.

"I can't find my baby. I don't know where she is."

Claire's heart felt like it was in a vise. The young mother's grief shot through her like a knife, making it difficult to respond.

"Your baby isn't here," Claire eventually said, fighting past her own grief. "But she's in a good place."

The words provided little comfort.

"Can you take me to her?" Stephanie asked through her tears.

Claire nodded. "If that's what you really want."

She wasn't lying. New projections were always given the option to come under the jurisdiction of the Bureau and receive guidance and assistance, or simply to make do on their own. Claire always felt there would only be one logical choice, but a surprising number of projections didn't see it that way and chose to go it alone.

Stephanie looked down at her hands then back up at Claire. "What's happened to me?" she said through her tears. "I don't understand what's happening."

Claire took a step toward her and extended a hand. "That's why I'm here. I'll explain everything."

Stephanie reached out to take Claire's hand and passed right through instead. The air around them rippled as a wave of panic welled up inside the new projection.

"It's going to be okay," Claire assured her gently. "I'm here to help you."

The panic slowly began to subside, only to be replaced by confusion. "What's wrong with me?" Stephanie asked again. Her head popped up and she looked around frantically. "Where's my baby?"

The intense roller coaster of emotions confirmed Claire's worst fears. The woman hadn't died instantly in the wreck. These were the last thoughts and feelings she had experienced in the final moments of her life. Now they were all jumbled up inside of her, repeating on a torturous loop. If Claire couldn't get through to her, she would deteriorate quickly.

"It's going to be okay," Claire said again, taking another step toward the projection. "There was an accident last night, but I'm here to help you."

Stephanie locked eyes with her. Claire could feel the confusion slowly begin to melt away. "An accident?"

Claire nodded.

Stephanie looked back toward the intersection. "We were coming home from my parents' house."

Claire knew the young mother wasn't actually talking to her. She was working things out for herself, which was good. It was progress.

"I saw the other car's headlights, but there was nothing I could do to avoid it. It happened so fast."

Claire waited, reliving the woman's emotions as if she had been in the driver's seat with her. Stephanie turned to look at Claire again, tears glistening in her translucent eyes.

"My baby?"

All Claire could do was shake her head, but Stephanie understood. She closed her eyes and another energy wave shot through Claire. The grief was almost unbearable.

"And the person who hit us?" Stephanie asked.

Claire hesitated. "He was a drunk driver. He died as well."

A current of anger began building inside the projection, quickly eclipsing the grief. Claire needed to distract her and stem the tide of negative emotions or she would lose her.

"Try not to think about that," Claire said. "We need to take care of you right now."

Stephanie frowned and opened her eyes, examining Claire. "Can you bring my baby back to me?"

"Unfortunately, no, I can't do that."

"Then how can you help me?"

Claire took a deep breath and swallowed hard. "I work for an organization that helps people in your situation adjust to your new life."

Stephanie looked around the field, then down at her own translucent hands. "You call this a life?"

"It can be if that's what you want."

"What do you mean?"

"You have a few options." Claire cleared her throat, hating how clinical the explanation sounded. "First, you can choose to come under the jurisdiction of the organization I work for. Our job is to preserve history and the stories of people who have passed on. If you choose to join us, we'll provide you with whatever assistance you might need in the future."

Stephanie looked around the field again and frowned. "What history would I be preserving here?"

Claire was at a loss. Any comfort she tried to offer would be hollow consolation at best. "Maybe your story could prevent someone else from being killed by a drunk driver," she said lamely.

The look on Stephanie's face spoke volumes. "And if I don't want that? What will your organization do to me?"

Claire shook her head. "Nothing, actually, but they won't provide any assistance to you if you need it in the future." She took another step toward Stephanie. "If you choose to stay, I recommend working with the Bureau. It can be very lonely on your own, and many people in your position don't handle it very well."

"What does that mean?"

Claire hesitated again before answering. "It means you could lose touch with the things that made you who you were. Many people in your situation become angry and bitter and often end up hurting other people."

Stephanie thought for several seconds. "So, are those my only two options? A minute ago, you said 'if' I choose to stay."

Claire nodded again. "Yes, you don't have to stay. I can help you move on."

As a Bureau agent, this was supposed to be the last option she presented to a new projection. A voluntary dissolution wasn't ideal, but it was much more pleasant than a forced one.

"What does that mean?" Stephanie asked.

Claire wasn't sure how much to tell her. "You're a projection of the energy signature you carried when you were alive. If I help you move on, your energy gets re-absorbed into the world around us, back into nature."

"Does it hurt?"

Claire shook her head and smiled. "No. It's very peaceful."

Stephanie thought for a few seconds more. "Without my daughter and my husband here with me, I don't have any reason to want to stay here."

Claire nodded. "I can understand that."

"So, what do I need to do?"

"Close your eyes and take slow, deep breaths."

Stephanie followed Claire's instructions. The process of moving on wasn't complicated, but energy projections rarely figured it out without the assistance of a trained Bureau agent.

Claire waited several seconds as the projection hovered in the middle of the field, breathing slowly and evenly. If anyone else could have seen her, it simply would have looked like she was meditating.

Claire smiled again as she sensed Stephanie's emotions in that moment. It felt almost like they were both floating. "Can you see an orb of light?" she asked.

Bureau scientists speculated that the orb represented the projection's own piece of the universe's energy, though no one could say for sure.

Stephanie nodded. "It looks like a little sun, and it's warm like the sun."

Claire spoke very softly. "Stephanie, I want you to reach out for that little orb."

It was the projection's turn to smile as she extended her right arm out in front of her. "It's so warm." At that point, she didn't need Claire's help anymore. The process would continue on its natural course.

Claire watched as the projection's energy signature began to glow more and more intensely. Against the darkness of the night, the light became almost more than she could bear. She closed her eyes and turned her head away from it.

An intense wave of energy washed over her and she opened her eyes again, knowing the process was complete and Stephanie was gone. Claire felt the waves of residual energy rippling out into the night sky, as if someone had dropped a pebble into a pond.

When the night around her became still once more, Claire fell to her knees in the middle of the field and let the tears flow down her cheeks as if an emotional dam had burst.

(Excerpt from the Bureau for Historical Preservation's Agents Training Manual)

Section 4.1 – Classification of acumens

1. *Sensory Acumen – The most basic ability possessed by even the lowest level sensitive. It allows a sensitive to sense when a projection is nearby, though no interaction is possible with this acumen alone.*

2. *Affective Acumen – The sensitive can feel and experience the projections' emotions, but again there is no interactive ability. Often this acumen also provides insight into the reasons a projection might be experiencing his or her feelings, though that isn't always the case.*

3. *Visual Acumen – The sensitive can see projections, though the clarity of appearance is directly proportional to the sensitive's own sensitivity level. Low-level sensitives can only see projections in dark surroundings, while high-level sensitives can see them clearly even in daylight.*

4. *Auditory Acumen – The sensitive can hear projections. This acumen rarely exists on its own and almost always exists as part of Communicative Acumen. In the rare cases when this acumen exists in isolation, the individual describes they are "hearing voices" and are often believed to have a mental disorder.*

5. *Communicative Acumen – The sensitive can verbally communicate with projections. Not all sensitives possess Communicative Acumen, and therefore not all sensitives can interact with projections in a meaningful way. Communicative acumen is an absolute basic requirement for admission to the Bureau's agent training program.*

6. *Attractive Acumen – The sensitive possesses some quality (heretofore unidentified by research) that draws projections to them. Projections seem to instinctively know the sensitive can interact with them and respond accordingly. It is a fairly rare acumen, appearing in an estimated less than five percent of all sensitives.*

7. *Force Perceptive Acumen – The sensitive can see the energy given off by projections, and sometimes even the energy of living persons as well. It is the rarest acumen and is estimated to be present in less than one half of one percent of all sensitives.*

Chapter 6

The next morning Claire woke up early, still emotionally drained from her encounter the night before. It was her day off, and to help ease some of the emotional turmoil still rolling around inside of her, Claire had opted for a trip to the local hardware store. From the moment she moved to the island two years earlier, she had dreamed of having a vibrant patio garden, and that morning had seemed like the perfect time to start working on it.

Thelma materialized next to Claire when she returned home from the hardware store. "Another sacrifice to the goddess Flora?"

Claire set her new bromeliad on the kitchen counter and frowned. "What's that supposed to mean?"

Thelma laughed. "This will make how many plants you've killed in the past year?" With an overly dramatic pout, she pointed to what was left of an orchid stem sitting on the window ledge in the dining room.

Claire glared at her. "I'm not going to kill this one." She knew she didn't sound very convincing, but it was worth a try.

The air rippled and Sarah appeared on the opposite side of the kitchen island.

"I keep telling you you'd be better off planting a flowerbed outside. There would be less maintenance for you with your busy schedule."

Claire's frown deepened. She would love to have a flowerbed outside. She'd love for her entire yard to be covered in flowers, but it was an investment of time and energy she couldn't bring herself to make. The Bureau had moved her to three different cities in the past six years, so she had no reason to think her assignment in Galveston would be permanent either. As much as she had come to love the island and its projections, there was no way she could lay down any roots, literally or figuratively.

"Maybe I'll plant a flowerbed in the spring," she told Sarah, forcing a smile.

"Of course, dear."

They both smiled at each other, but Claire knew the projection didn't believe her any more than she believed herself. She sadly touched the leaves of the bromeliad, already regretting the fate that most likely awaited it.

Her cell phone rang and she pulled it out of her pocket, happy for the distraction. It was her dad. With a huge smile, she answered the call and put the phone to her ear.

"Hey, Dad."

"Hey, Pumpkin. I just wanted to call and see how things are going down there. We had our first cold snap up here, so it's almost time to break out the heavy coats. How about you?"

Claire laughed. "This part of Texas really only has two seasons – summer, and not as much summer. Even with the cold front we just had, I doubt we'll be needing heavy coats anytime soon."

"That's too bad. I know how much you love our New England autumns."

Claire fought back tears. As much as she enjoyed living in Galveston, there were many things she missed about Boston, her family being at the top of that list. They had all known when she joined the Bureau that unless she got a job at headquarters, she'd have to move wherever she was assigned. While there had been a time when it seemed like a position at headquarters might be in her future, that wasn't the case anymore. She was certain of that. And sometimes, particularly when her emotions were raw from an encounter like the one she'd had the night before, the prolonged separation from her family was almost unbearable.

Claire heard a commotion on the other end of the phone line, then her father whispered something before returning to their conversation.

"Emma Lynn wants me to tell you, 'Hi!' and ask when you're coming home for a visit. She really wants to see you."

Claire chuckled. Emma Lynn was her oldest and dearest friend, and she also happened to be an energy projection. Claire couldn't remember a time when Emma wasn't there to be her playmate. It wasn't until her seventh birthday that Claire realized Emma wasn't growing up like she was. They celebrated their birthdays together every year, but Emma remained four years old. Claire was heartbroken when her parents told her the truth. Emma had died during a smallpox epidemic in the late 1800s. She was tethered to their home but wasn't actually a member of their family.

"Tell her I'll do my best to get up there for Christmas this year," Claire said. "It all depends on work, you know."

Claire could hear her dad relaying the message, but she couldn't hear Emma Lynn's response. It required a great deal of effort for energy projections to communicate over cell phone networks.

"And tell her I'll bring her something special the next time I come home," Claire added with an amused smile. When you grow up in a house full of sensitives with a family heritage deeply rooted in the Bureau for Historical Preservation, nothing about your childhood or the trajectory of your life is normal. After all, what normal person has to think about buying Christmas presents for a ghost?

"Please not another one of those talking dolls," her dad whispered. "She drains those batteries so quickly when she's playing with it. It's costing your mom and me a small fortune to replace them all the time."

"Got it," Claire said. "No electronic toys this time." She thought for a second, at a loss for what else to bring her. "Ask Emma what she'd like."

There was a muffled conversation on the other end of the line, then her dad returned. "She says a pony."

Claire laughed. "Tell her I'll see what I can do."

Again in a whispered voice, he asked, "You're not *really* going to get her a pony, are you?"

"Not a real one, no."

"And nothing electronic. Don't forget."

"I won't."

Claire heard more muffled conversation, then her dad said with a chuckle. "Well, that did the trick. She went skipping off down the hallway, just as happy as a clam."

Claire could picture it in her mind – Emma's small, translucent form bopping down the hallway, completely oblivious to the truth about her situation. Claire missed the simplicity of their childhood together and envied the fact that Emma would never have to deal with all the problems and complications that go along with growing up.

It was a widely accepted fact in Bureau circles that people who die a premature or tragic death will leave behind a projection of themselves at the age they were when their death occurred. To Claire that was obvious and fairly self-explanatory. But Bureau researchers hadn't yet been able to explain what determined the age of those who died of natural causes or of old age. It seemed to be a question of what age was particularly significant for the person, or what age they most identified themselves with, but honestly, it was all still speculation.

"How's everything with you guys?" Claire asked her dad, changing the topic before her stroll down memory lane turned into melancholy. "Are you and Mom keeping yourselves busy?"

For as long as Claire could remember, her dad had served in various upper-level positions at the Bureau. As Claire's brother, Zach, began to climb the ranks, Noah Abelard had decided it was time to step aside and let his son have a turn to shine, though he hadn't completely disconnected from the Bureau. Headquarters' brass wouldn't have allowed that, so now he mostly served as a consultant on particularly tricky or complicated issues.

Noah sighed. "Honestly, I'm still trying to find myself a hobby. Your mom's got her crafting classes and her Jazzercise, but I haven't found anything that works for me yet."

"Weren't you going to sign up for some woodworking classes?"

"I thought about it, but I'm not sure that would be a good fit."

"You won't know if you don't try."

"Who's the parent here?" Claire could hear the affection in his voice. After a pause, he added, "I'll look into it this afternoon."

"Good for you. I think you'll enjoy it."

"Maybe you're right." She heard another commotion on the other end of the line and then a quiet, "I'm getting to it." She knew he had to be talking to her mom this time. When Noah returned to the line, he said, "So, your cousin Andrea had her baby this morning. A healthy young lad named Christopher."

Claire smiled, genuinely pleased to hear the news. "That's wonderful. I can't wait to see pictures."

"Oh, you can be sure there will be plenty. Your aunt's already posted dozens of them all over social media."

"I'll go check them out." There was silence on the phone line for a few seconds. "Is everything okay, Dad?"

"Oh yeah, everything's fine." Noah didn't sound very enthusiastic, and the sigh that followed didn't help either. "Your mom and I were just discussing how nice it would be if we had some grandchildren of our own to post pictures and brag about."

Claire roller her eyes. "Shouldn't you be harassing Zach about this?" she asked. "He's older than me and he's the one who's been married for six years."

"Believe me, we've spoken to him about it, too. He's so focused on his career right now, they aren't thinking about kids." Noah paused. "It's not just the grandchildren thing that has your mother and me worrying about you, you know."

Here it comes, Claire thought, dreading the direction the conversation was about to take.

"We would really love to see you happily married, too."

Claire let out a sigh that was much louder than she had intended. "And exactly when and how am I supposed to accomplish that for you? It's not like I can date just any guy I meet, you know."

"We know," he assured her. "We worry about you. That's all."

"Well, don't. I'm fine."

Marriage was something Claire had always figured would be in her future one day, though she had never chased after it. And her job, and her sensitive abilities in general, had seriously narrowed her options in that department.

"What we do is very important. You know I believe that," Noah said. "I just don't want to see it take too much from you." When Claire didn't respond, he added, "Promise me you won't let this job become your whole life."

"I promise, Dad." She didn't have the heart to tell him it was too late. She looked sadly out the kitchen window at her unremarkable front yard.

They talked for a few more minutes before saying goodbye. Almost as soon as she ended her call with her dad, her phone rang again. This time it was her supervisor from the Bureau's Houston office. She figured he was probably calling to laugh with her about the ghost hunters and their request for a private tour.

"Hey, Craig, what's up?"

"Hey, Claire. I hope I didn't wake you."

She laughed. "It's after noon."

"Well, I didn't know how you'd be feeling after your acclimatization assessment last night. I heard it was a rough one."

"Yeah, well," she said unenthusiastically, "that's the job, isn't it?" She had filed her report on the assessment as soon she got home the night before. The sooner the paperwork on the encounter was submitted, the sooner she could push past the emotions.

"Part of it anyway," Craig said. "And the other part is why I'm calling."

"Did those ghost hunters get in touch with you?" she asked, looking forward to a lighter turn in the conversation. She tucked the phone between her shoulder and cheek and picked up the bromeliad to carry it into the dining room where it could get better light. "I told them you wouldn't be on board with letting them have a private tour."

He didn't respond and for a second she feared the call had dropped. "Yeah, about that..." he eventually said.

She stopped in her tracks. "Oh God, please, don't tell me you agreed to let them have a private tour?"

"Not exactly."

She breathed a sigh of relief.

"You're going to give them four private tours."

Claire set the plant on the dining room table. "You can't be serious. We don't give private tours."

"It looks like in this case we do."

She couldn't believe what she was hearing. "But, Craig, they're ghost hunters…ghost hunters! And with a TV show."

"Actually, it's an internet series."

"Oh, that's so much better." Sarcasm dripped from her words. "Thanks."

Craig laughed. "Apparently the P.I.D. office checked them out and they're one of the more legit groups out there, not as much hype and sensationalism as some of the others."

The Paranormal Investigation and Dissolution division of the Bureau was an elite team of sensitives who were dispatched to investigate reports of "paranormal" activity. The division's name was a bit of a misnomer, since most of what the Bureau dealt with had more to do with the science of energy than with the paranormal. Even so, it was the name they were given when the division was first formed, and no one had seen fit to change it over the years. For those rare cases when there was something paranormal happening, though, the P.I.D. agents were the ones best equipped to handle it.

"Actually," Craig continued, "there's a lot of solid science in this team's research. I don't think it'll be as bad as you're making it out to be."

She laughed humorlessly. "Not for you, no."

"Look, I wasn't on board with it at first either, but the higher-ups at HQ think it will be a good step forward in promoting the history of the island." He paused. "And that *is* our job after all."

Claire looked out the window for several seconds. "Fine," she finally conceded. "You're right, and I think Isabel will do a great job leading the tours." Thank God she wasn't the only agent on the island.

"I'm sure Isabel *would* do a great job," Craig agreed, "but the hunters asked for you specifically, and HQ agreed that you're the best one for the assignment."

She scowled. "Oh, 'HQ' decided that, did they? Okay, I see what's really going on here. This is Zach's doing, isn't it?"

"I don't know who all was in on the meeting, but I seriously doubt it's personal."

"Oh yeah, sure," she mumbled. "He's probably still mad at me for outing him as a bed wetter in second grade and this is his revenge."

Craig burst out laughing. "Well, thanks for that bit of leverage on your brother, but it doesn't change the fact that you'll be leading some private tours over the next week or so. HQ wants this to go forward, and they told me the assignment is yours. I'll get someone to cover your usual tours this weekend."

"You're too kind." Claire took a deep breath and let it out slowly. She still wasn't happy about the situation, but there was no point taking it out on Craig. It wasn't his fault. He was only handing down the orders. "Where will I be taking them?"

"Ashton Villa, the Galvez, Bishop's Palace, and the Strand."

She raised her eyebrows. "Ashton Villa? Are you sure it's a good idea to let a film crew loose around Bettie? God only knows what she'll say or do."

Craig chuckled. "It should definitely make for some good TV."

"When do I start this torture?"

"Tomorrow night. Ashton Villa first."

"Awesome." She hoped her displeasure was clear in her tone.

Craig chuckled again, clearly enjoying her irritation. "Have fun, Claire."

"Bite me, Craig."

Chapter 7

Later that afternoon, Claire still wasn't ready to admit defeat. She had contemplated calling Zach and letting him know exactly what she thought about her latest assignment, but that would only make things worse. Instead, she decided to take matters into her own hands. She had always heard it was better to ask for forgiveness than permission, and she was about to find out if that was true.

She had called Isabel Mercado, one of the other agents on the island, but Isabel couldn't take the ghost hunters off her hands. Her second job as the concierge at the Hotel Galvez didn't allow her time to take on extra tours.

Thankfully, Claire had one more sliver of hope to cling to – Aaron Rainer, the third Bureau agent assigned to Galveston. Aaron had only been on the team for less than a year, so his knowledge of the island's history wasn't as extensive yet as Claire would have liked, but it was adequate enough that she only felt only slightly guilty for trying to pawn the assignment off on him.

Most cities only had one Bureau agent, if that, monitoring projection activity, and often a single agent was responsible for multiple cities in a region. But Galveston, with its rich history of Civil War battles and hurricane disasters, warranted a larger team. The 1900 hurricane alone took thousands of lives and resulted in hundreds of energy projections.

Aaron's cover job was as a waiter in one of the popular restaurants on the Seawall, not far from an amusement park called Pleasure Pier. When Claire entered the restaurant, she spotted Aaron near the bar, entering payments into the computer. When he saw her, he acknowledged her with a simple nod. Claire wasn't surprised by his less-than-warm greeting. When he wasn't leading tours or chatting up tourists at their tables, Aaron wasn't exactly personable, almost like Jekyll and Hyde.

Claire made her way to the bar and ordered a soda. They were between the lunch and dinner rushes, so the restaurant wasn't very crowded. She didn't have to wait long before Aaron joined her.

"I've only got a few minutes," he said without any greeting. "What's up?"

"Are you working tomorrow night?"

He raised his eyebrows, an amused smile on his lips. "Why? Are you asking me on a date?"

She gave him a look that let him know she didn't think he was funny. "Hardly."

Her job didn't afford her much of a social life, but she wasn't that desperate yet. She had tried dating fellow agents in the past, but it never worked out, and she wasn't in any hurry to make that kind of mistake again, and especially not with Aaron.

She turned on the barstool to look at him. "So, are you working or not?"

"Not."

"Good, how would you feel about leading a couple of private tours?"

His eyebrows went up again. "Private tours? Are you starting a side business?"

"I wish." She considered how much to tell him. "Headquarters wants someone to take a paranormal investigation team out to some of the more active places on the island. I thought you might want the assignment."

He frowned. "A P.I.D. team? From headquarters? That's weird."

She used her straw to stir the ice in her drink. "Well, the team isn't from headquarters, just the assignment. It's actually a group of independent paranormal investigators who'll be taking the tours." She tried to look excited. "You'll probably even get to be on TV."

Aaron shook his head several times and took a step back. "Oh, no, no, no, no, no. I've got my P.I.D. test in a few weeks. There's no way I'm going to jeopardize my chances by being seen with a bunch of wannabe ghost hunters, and especially not on TV!"

It was no secret Aaron had grander aspirations than simply being a field agent the rest of his life. And considering the rigorous admittance process for becoming a P.I.D. agent, Claire couldn't blame him for balking at the request. That didn't mean she wasn't irritated, though.

"Oh, come on, Aaron," she said, trying to sound upbeat. "It won't be that bad."

"Then you shouldn't have any problem doing it yourself." He studied her for a few seconds. "Hold on. As senior agent on the island, why are you *asking* me to do this instead of just giving me the assignment?" When she didn't respond, he began to nod slowly, a knowing smile spreading across his lips. "You *can't* order me to do it, can you? They gave the assignment to you, and you're trying to push it off on me."

She let out a frustrated grunt. "Come on, Aaron. I'll cover your tours for the next month if you'll do this for me."

"Sorry, but no way." He pushed away from the bar. "The only thing I hate more than rogue projections is amateur ghost hunters."

Claire frowned as she watched him walk away. As if on cue, her phone began to ring. She didn't recognize the number, but she had a good idea who would be on the other end of the line.

"Hey Claire, this is Spencer. I got your number from your boss, Craig. We're super stoked that you're going to be leading these tours for us. How soon can we get started?"

"Does tomorrow night work for you?" she asked with a heavy sigh. Her fate had been sealed. She might as well embrace it.

In the summer of 1939, a brilliant, young physicist named Werner Vogel came to work in the Bureau's research division. His achievements in the field of bioelectrical mechanics had already garnered him a great deal of praise among the international scientific community, so Bureau leadership was eager to see what contributions he might make to the furtherment of energy projection research.

Vogel quickly built upon preceding research, then progressed the research division forward at an astounding pace, deepening the Bureau's understanding of the nature of energy projections and better equipping agents to assist and monitor sanctioned projections.

In addition, Vogel developed several tools to assist agents in their interactions with projections. Most notably among these tools are energy dampening cuffs, residual energy detectors, and projection dispatchment devices.

With the introduction of Werner Vogel's inventions, a new department of the Bureau's Paranormal Assistance and Monitoring Division was formed. The Paranormal Dispatchment and Dissolution Division was created in the mid-1940s to address the issue of rogue projections.

Until that time, little could be done to prevent energy projections from injuring or terrorizing the living. Sanctioned projections caught engaging in such behaviors were quickly deprived of any further Bureau assistance, but there were no such consequences for rogue projections. With the development of energy dampening cuffs and dissolution tools, agents could more effectively deal with dangerous projections. With the new option of permanently dispatching projections, there was also a need for clear guidelines and a great deal of accountability. As a result, the P.I.D. Division was born.

Today, entrance into the P.I.D. Division is a high honor reserved for only elite agents who possess extraordinary skills and discernment when interacting with energy projections. No forced dissolution is ever to be conducted simply on an agent's whim. Bureau policy dictates that a series of strict protocols must be followed to ensure fairness for all projections.

Chapter 8

After her disappointing meeting with Aaron, Claire returned home with hopes of salvaging the rest of her day off. She plopped in front of the TV with plans to spend the afternoon binge-watching some of her favorite shows, but nothing held her interest.

She spotted her laptop sitting judgmentally on her desk, taunting her with the abundance of Bureau-related emails she knew were probably clogging her inbox. Since her day off had turned out to be a bust, she might as well get some work done.

With a disgusted sigh, she crossed the room and booted up the computer, then clicked her way through email after email, unrealistically hoping to find one from Craig saying headquarters had changed their minds about the private tours. Of course, there was no such email, but she did have one from her brother.

Claire,

I need some clarification on your evaluation of Aaron Rainer. As you know, he's applying for a position with P.I.D., so your input as his supervisor plays an important part in our decision-making process.

Thanks,

Z

Claire leaned back in her seat and sighed again. Of course, she knew her input was important. She had purposely been vague on Aaron's evaluation *because* she knew her input was important. She didn't want to be the reason he wasn't accepted into the P.I.D. division, but she couldn't give him a glowing endorsement either. His extreme anti-rogue attitude gave her good reason to hesitate about entrusting him with a tool that could dispatch projections. She had no actual evidence that he would abuse the power, but still, she couldn't recommend him with a clear conscience. But how could she explain that in an official document without doing serious damage to his career at the Bureau?

She pulled up the evaluation document and began re-reading her previous comments.

"I don't think 'unpersonable' is a word," April's voice said from over her shoulder. "A better choice would probably be 'unsociable'."

April had been a high school English teacher when she was alive, so these types of impromptu language lessons were fairly common. Claire wasn't in the mood for it that afternoon, so she pretended not to hear her.

Of all the projections Claire had met, April's story was one of the most tragic. Living in the 1950s, at a time when husbands were considered the ultimate authority over their wives and spousal abuse was not exactly a societal taboo, April's situation unfortunately had not been an uncommon one. One night, when her husband was in a drunken rage, he took the abuse even farther than usual, and that time the tumble she took down the stairs was fatal.

Per Bureau policy, when an agent learns that a projection's death was not an accident, the agent is allowed to covertly assist police investigations, though not to any degree that would risk exposing the Bureau. When April's supervisory agent provided the authorities with information proving her death was a result of her husband's abuse, they turned a blind eye and never pursued the case. When such an injustice takes place, the projection involved will often deteriorate into a dangerous entity. Thankfully in April's case, for some reason that didn't happen.

Less than a month after April's death, the house she had shared with her husband burned to the ground with her husband in it. The fire apparently started in the breaker box and was ruled accidental, but the timing was too coincidental for the Bureau to completely rule out poltergeist activity on April's part. Since no clear evidence was found to convict her, no action was taken, and April was offered a new tether location. The Meriwether home was a few doors down from her own, so April had chosen to be tethered there.

Determined to finish Aaron's evaluation, Claire smiled up at April and nodded, then focused her attention back on the computer screen. She sat for several seconds with her hands poised over the keys, uncertain what to type. She didn't have to think about it for too long, though, as a knock on the door provided an uninvited but welcome reprieve.

Claire was halfway across the room to answer the door when she realized April was still hovering next to the desk, reading the report. Claire could tell the visitor wasn't a sensitive, but still it was better to be safe than sorry. "April," she said in a hushed but insistent voice.

April looked up, her forehead wrinkled in confusion. Claire motioned toward the door and waited. It didn't take long for April to get the hint. With a nod, she disappeared. Claire waited until she was certain her energy was completely out of the room before turning back to the door.

Peeking through the peephole, Claire rolled her eyes, pausing longer than she probably needed to before releasing the deadbolt. "Hey, Ann," she said as she pulled the door open.

"Hi, Claire," the older woman said with a warm smile. "I hate to bug you on your day off, but my books were delivered this morning, and I wanted to bring you a copy like I promised." She handed Claire a paperback book with a ghostly image on the front. "I even signed it for you."

Claire returned her smile. The woman was nothing if not persistent. "Thanks so much. I look forward to reading them both as soon as I get a chance." She hated to lie to her, but she hated the idea of being rude even more.

Ann's smile widened. "I really would love to hear your thoughts," she told Claire again. "Like I said, some of my theories aren't exactly mainstream."

"The interesting ones usually aren't."

The two women stood in awkward silence for a few seconds, then Ann said, "Well, I'll let you get back to enjoying your day off."

"Thanks." Claire held up the book. "And thanks for this, too."

Ann nodded and waved as she retreated down the porch steps. Claire felt a shimmer of energy behind her but didn't have to turn around to know April was once again standing next to the desk.

"Or, if you want to use a strong word," the projection continued as if they had never been interrupted, "you could try 'taciturn'."

Claire closed the door, resisting the urge to sigh again. "I was trying to be diplomatic," she told April. "'Taciturn' would definitely be more accurate in describing Aaron, but that's the problem."

She set the book on the desk with the other package Ann had given her then sat back down in front of her computer. As she tried to re-read the first paragraph of her evaluation for the fourth time, she could sense April still hovering, reading the document over her shoulder.

She was about to ask April to leave and let her work in peace when Thelma burst into the living room, Sarah following close on her heels. The temperature in the room dropped several degrees, though Claire couldn't tell which projection's emotions had caused it.

"Claire," Thelma declared, coming to a stop so her translucent form blurred Claire's view of the laptop screen. "Would you please remind Ms. Rock-of-Ages that she isn't my mother, or my grandmother, or anyone else with any authority over me? She doesn't have any right to tell me what to do."

"I wasn't trying to tell you what to do," Sarah insisted, folding her arms across her chest. "I was simply stating my opinion that it would be improper for you to spend time with that young man without a chaperone."

Thelma whirled around to face her. "We're dead! Nobody cares about what's proper or improper anymore!"

"Dead or not, you should still consider your reputation."

"That's it!" Claire slammed the lid of her laptop closed and stood up. All three projections stared at her as she shoved the computer into a bag then pulled the bag's strap over her shoulder and headed for the door. "I can't work like this. I'm going to the café."

"But it's your day off," Thelma said, sounding genuinely dejected, "and you've spent hardly any of it with us already."

Claire turned back around to face the three projections, her expression softer than it had been before. "We can watch a movie together tonight, but right now I need to get this evaluation finished."

"We can help you," April suggested.

Claire forced a smile. "I appreciate the offer, but I need to work on this myself. I'll be back in a few hours." She hurried out the door and closed it behind her before they could say anything else.

The café was only a few blocks from Claire's house, so she was able to drive there in a matter of minutes. It wasn't far from the Strand, and it was on her route to work at the candy store, so not surprisingly over the past two years she had become a regular there.

There were several reasons why this was Claire's go-to place to work outside the house. First, they had amazing artisan coffee, which only fed her already unhealthy addiction to the stuff. More importantly, though, the shop was housed in a newly constructed, free-standing building. Not only was the shop too new to have a history of projections tethered to it, it was also at least fifty feet from the nearest structure, the perfect distance to keep projections in other buildings from being able to interact with her. And sometimes, like that afternoon, she really needed the peace and quiet.

She ordered her usual specialty coffee and settled into a table near the back of the shop. If she was going to find a way to word Aaron's evaluation in an honest yet diplomatic way, she needed to focus.

She had just finished re-reading the evaluation for a second time when she felt an exhilarating yet unsettling sensation. She didn't need to look up to know who had entered the coffee shop, but she did anyway.

There he was. Drew.

He was with one of the other ghost hunters, and thankfully, it didn't seem like they had noticed her. She cursed softly and slunk down in her seat, praying the muted lighting in the back of the café would keep her hidden. Since it was her day off, she was dressed casually, very casually, with her hair in a ponytail and not an ounce of makeup on. Drew was the last person she wanted to see right then.

She pretended to focus on the computer screen in front of her while keeping a close eye on the two ghost hunters. They both studied the menu for a few seconds, then Drew began scanning the patrons in the café. Claire cursed again. Considering his high sensitivity level and the fact that they had already interacted with each other once, he had to be sensing her energy signature somewhere in the café.

Claire leaned down, but her computer screen wasn't tall enough to hide her, so it didn't take Drew any time at all to spot her. He tapped the other ghost hunter on the arm and nodded in her direction.

To Claire's dismay, they both began making their way across the café. She pretended to be deeply engrossed in what was on her screen as they approached.

"Claire?" Drew said when they had reached her table.

She looked up, feigning surprise. "Oh, hi." She had no idea what to say next.

"Fancy meeting you here," he filled in the gap for her.

From anyone else, Claire would have thought the line sounded cheesy. From him, it was charming.

She closed the lid of her laptop. "Yeah, of all the coffee shops in all the world, you walk into mine."

He chuckled. "*Casablanca.* Nice."

She stifled a foolish grin, pleased he had caught the reference. *Casablanca* was her favorite movie.

The ghost hunter with Drew extended his hand in Claire's direction. "I'm Keith," he said. "I didn't get a chance to meet you yesterday at the candy store. Spencer was on a bit of a mission."

Claire shook his hand. "It's nice to meet you." She folded her arms on the table in front of her and leaned forward. "Is Spencer always that laser-focused?"

"Pretty much," Keith said.

"We wanted to thank you for agreeing to take us on these tours," Drew told her. "We're all really looking forward to them."

"It's no trouble at all," Claire lied. She looked across the café to avoid making eye contact with him. "So, what brings you guys in here this afternoon?"

"We've been at the library all morning doing research while the rest of the team interviewed locals about paranormal encounters they've had," Keith answered. "We're on our way back to the hotel to regroup and sort through our findings from the day. It looks like it could be a long night, so we need something to keep us awake."

"What hotel are you guys staying at?" Claire asked, then immediately reprimanded herself for doing so. How creepy did *that* sound? They didn't seem bothered by her question, though.

"We're over at the Harbor House, on the wharf," Drew told her, motioning in the hotel's direction. "It's really nice."

Claire nodded. "Yeah, that's a good one. Not as haunted as some of the hotels on the island, but you might get lucky."

"We can hope," Keith said with a grin. He looked back at the café's counter. "So, what's good here? Any recommendations?"

"My favorite this time of year is the peppermint latte." She picked up her cup and took a sip. "But honestly, you can't go wrong here."

"Good to know." Drew elbowed Keith and nodded to Claire's laptop. "Well, I guess we better get our coffees and let you get back to what you were doing."

Claire smiled and opened her computer lid, though she didn't immediately get back to work. She tried to stop herself but couldn't help watching them walk back across the café to the counter. It was just a pair of jeans, but Drew wore them well. Giving herself another silent reprimand, she turned her attention back to Aaron's evaluation.

A few minutes later, Drew came back to her table. She looked up as he set a cup of coffee down next to her laptop.

"See you tomorrow night," he said with a wink before turning and heading toward the door where Keith was waiting for him, a goofy grin on his face.

Claire picked up the cup, sniffed it, and felt her insides do a flip. Drew had bought her a peppermint latte. She let out a heavy sigh. There was no doubt about it. She was a goner.

Chapter 9

That night around midnight, Claire drove to the northern side of the island near the cruise ship terminal. She prayed Bettie had gotten word to Jean Lafitte about their meeting. Considering Jean had been a notorious pirate when he was alive, it was no surprise his energy projection could be unpredictable and unreliable.

In life, Jean had conducted a good portion of his pirating activity in both Galveston and New Orleans, so his ship still travelled from one city to the other, completely at the whim of its captain. If whatever Jean wanted to talk to Claire about was as serious as Bettie made it out to be, though, maybe that night he would actually show up when and where he was supposed to.

Claire parked in the lot next to the Harbor House Hotel and made her way toward Pier 21. She was keenly aware of the fact that Drew and his team were somewhere inside the building. She could faintly sense his energy and wondered if he sensed hers, too. With a firm shake of her head, she forced her thoughts back to the task at hand.

She took another look around the pier. There were a few people milling around the dock, but this would have to do. Given the fact that Jean would be arriving on a large ghost ship, there would never be an ideal time or place to meet him, but the less tourist traffic there was the better.

She was a few minutes early, which gave her plenty of time to find a place for the meeting. It needed to be somewhere dark and secluded, where she would be less likely to be noticed or interrupted. Eventually, she found a spot not far from the Harbor House, just beyond the glow of the lampposts on the dock.

It wasn't the safest place to wait, but Claire wasn't too worried. Given the nature of Bureau work, and specifically the time of night that the work tended to be carried out, self-defense instruction was a key component of the Bureau's agent training program. She was no Jackie Chan, but she could take care of herself in a pinch.

A drunk tourist staggered past her hiding spot and she glanced down at her watch. She had been waiting in the shadows for at least fifteen minutes, ten minutes past her scheduled meeting time with Jean Lafitte. She frowned, even though she had expected he wouldn't be on time. Jean liked to make an entrance. After all, as Bettie had reminded her the other night, he *was* a pirate.

Ten minutes later, Claire was about to return to her car when she felt a massive ripple of energy coming toward her from the water, accompanied by the sound of cannon fire. Jean had probably been waiting, gauging her irritation and frustration until he knew his appearance would have an optimal effect.

She stepped out of the shadows as the shimmering form of Jean's ship, *The Pride*, materialized in front of her. The ship was resplendent as it glimmered in the moonlight, nothing like the dilapidated, seaweed-covered images Hollywood liked to portray.

Claire looked around, checking that the area was clear of foot traffic, then approached the edge of the dock.

"Ahoy, Miss Abelard!" Jean called out from the deck above. He leaned over the side of the ship and waved down at her, sword in hand. "It's a fine evenin' for a parlay, don't ye agree?"

She stifled a chuckle. Jean liked to play up his pirate image, but Claire knew it was just for show.

"Hey, Jean," she said quietly, giving a quick wave back. Though she hadn't seen anyone on the dock recently, she didn't want to risk being seen or heard talking to the empty ocean air. "Bettie said you needed to talk to me."

"Ah, right down to business she goes," Jean replied. "No need to waste words. I like that in a lass." He sheathed his sword and put both hands on the edge of the ship's railing. "Indeed, I do have a most pressing matter to discuss with ye. Very distressful and disturbing."

Claire sighed loudly. "Would you please come down here and talk to me about it? It'll be easier to look inconspicuous if I don't have to yell up at you."

She felt the air ripple next to her and Jean materialized. "A fine point indeed," he said. "You want to preserve the history, not frighten the tourists."

"I'm okay with frightening the tourists if it helps promote the history." Claire took a step back so she was hidden in the shadows once again. "But I don't want to look like a crazy woman talking to someone that only I can see."

"Now, we cannot have that, can we?" Jean's face softened and he offered Claire a genuine smile. "*Ma chère*, Claire," he said, kissing her on both cheeks. The direct contact sent a chill through her entire body. "*Merci d'avoir venue.*"

The exaggerated pirate accent was gone, replaced by the language and manners of a charming French gentleman. Now she was talking to the real Jean Lafitte.

"*Tu m'as douté?*" Claire asked, returning his smile. "You knew I'd come, even if it gets me in trouble with the Bureau."

"That is why we come to you. You are the only one we know will help us."

"I'm not sure what I'll be able to do for you," she admitted, "but I'll do what I can. What's the problem?"

He frowned and the energy around them shifted, a reflection of his genuine concern. "Two of my crew are missing."

"Missing?" she repeated. "What do you mean?"

"They were with us the last time we arrived in Galveston, but then when we returned to the Crescent City, they were nowhere to be found."

Claire sighed. This was one problem with rogues. Most weren't tethered to specific locations, and without those tethers and the Bureau accountability that went with them, it was often difficult to keep track of their movements.

"Are you sure they were with you when you left the island?"

Jean looked a little sheepish. "We cannot say for certain. We do not conduct role call before setting out. But we have scoured both New Orleans and Galveston. There is no sign of them anywhere."

Now it was Claire's turn to frown. "They couldn't have just disappeared. Did you check the Grove?"

"And what do you expect they would be doing there?" he asked with a sarcastic smirk. "Playing a few rounds of golf?"

Lafitte's Grove was a spot on the far western part of Galveston Island where Jean had once established a home base for his pirating activities back in 1817. He called the settlement Campeche, and eventually it had been home to close to two thousand people. From there, Jean and his pirate crew would prey on ships in the Gulf of Mexico. Or at least they did until 1821, when Jean burned the settlement and fled the island rather than surrender it and himself to the US Navy.

In recent years, a housing development with a country club and golf course had been built on the site. Now, all that was left of Campeche was a single historical marker telling a portion of his story. Hardly a fitting monument to such a sensational bit of history.

"Did the men say anything about being unhappy?" Claire asked. "Is it possible they found someone to help them move on?"

Jean stood up taller and puffed out his chest. "They've been a part of me crew for nigh unto two hundred years." The pirate persona was back. "Every hand on *The Pride* is as loyal as the day is long."

"I wasn't suggesting anything less," Claire assured him. "There just aren't a lot of options for where they could be or what we can do to find them."

"How can that be true?" He extended a hand in her direction. "Surely your all-mighty Bureau has the resources to make short work of this mystery."

She couldn't bring herself to look at him. "Yes, they probably could, but you know they won't." He opened his mouth to speak but she stopped him. "You made that choice when you opted to be a rogue instead of coming under the Bureau's jurisdiction."

His expression fell and a wave of deep sadness washed over her.

"Please, Claire," he said, "will you at least ask them to help?" He looked back over his shoulder at the deck of his ship where a half-dozen translucent figures stood watching them. "I know something has happened to them. You said it yourself, they could not have just disappeared."

Claire's heart ached, and not only because she could feel Jean's emotions. She truly wanted to help him, but after what had happened in San Francisco five years before, there was no way she could ask the Bureau to get involved. Things were already strained between her and Zach. The last thing she wanted was to add another log to that fire. Even so, she couldn't walk away from a projection who needed her help.

She took a deep breath and let it out slowly. "Okay," she finally said. "I'll see what I can do, but don't get your hopes up. You know the Bureau's rogue policies as well as I do."

"Thank you, Claire." He leaned forward and planted a kiss on her forehead, sending another chill down her spine.

"You're welcome, Jean." Claire stepped out of the shadows as Jean disappeared from next to her and reappeared a split second later back on the deck of his ship.

"It's a fine thing yer doin', Miss Abelard. We'll drink a toast to ye when we get back to the Blacksmith's Shop!"

Claire chuckled and waved as *The Pride* faded into the night. She would do what she could to help Jean find his crewmen, but there was no way she was getting Bureau resources involved, at least not until she had a better idea of what was going on. She couldn't afford another misstep.

In the fall of 1740, Pierre Abelard's son, Christophe, and a group of a dozen surveyors landed in Boston Harbor, eager to make contact with New World projections. They quickly recruited close to a dozen more surveyors among the colonists. Four of the original European surveyors went to Canada/New France and four went toward Mexico, eventually spreading through South America. The title "American Branch" refers to all of the Americas, not only the U.S., so Canadian and Latin American agents also fall under this branch's jurisdiction.

Today, the Bureau for Historical Preservation is an international non-profit organization whose mission is clearly stated in its title – they endeavor to preserve the history of significant locations around the world. The organization's international headquarters is in Paris, with its American branch headquartered in Boston, and additional branch headquarters in Tokyo, Japan and Cairo, Egypt.

Through aggressive public fund-raising efforts, each year the Bureau contributes millions of dollars to various projects and organizations that further the mission of preserving historically significant locations. These projects include:

- *The renovation and restoration of historic homes and buildings,*
- *Educational programs sponsored by public broadcasting, museums, and other entities,*

- *The creation of documentary film projects focused on historic events and people,*
- *Financial and manpower assistance for archeological digs and excavations.*

The Paranormal Assistance and Monitoring Division handles the Bureau's clandestine operations, functioning completely independently of the organization's public face. This department focuses on monitoring and assisting energy projections. Like every other aspect of the Bureau, this division also pursues the mission of preserving the history of historically significant locations.

Chapter 10

The day after meeting with Jean Lafitte, Claire was back at the candy store doling out treats to tourists and trying not to think about what the evening had in store for her. Unfortunately for her easily distracted thoughts, it was a particularly slow day at the store, so there wasn't much to keep her mind occupied.

During the numerous lulls, she found herself drawn toward watching episodes of the ghost hunters' web show, *Lone Star Haunts.* Under any other circumstance, she wouldn't be caught dead watching such a show, but she convinced herself it was necessary research for the tour that night. She needed to know what to expect, and this was the easiest way to get that information.

"Are those the ghost hunters who were in here the other day?" Monica asked, peering over Claire's shoulder.

"Um, yeah," Claire said, quickly tossing her phone beneath the counter.

Monica smiled. "You don't have to hide it." She motioned around the empty store. "It's not like we're swamped right now."

"It's research," Claire said lamely as she retrieved the phone and set it on the counter between them.

"If you say so." They watched a few minutes of the show in silence before Monica asked, "Do you think they're legit?"

Claire frowned. "For the most part." She couldn't tell her friend what she really thought about it. "Spencer is a little overly dramatic sometimes, but other than that they're sincere about what they're doing."

Monica winked at her. "He may be over the top, but he's also hot, so that kind of makes up for it, right?"

Claire made a face. "If you say so." As if on cue, her phone's text notification sounded. She glanced at the message and rolled her eyes. "Speak of the devil."

Monica leaned over her shoulder again. "Is that him? Is he professing his love for you?"

Claire laughed. "Hardly. This is about the fifth time he's texted me today wanting to confirm details about tonight's tour." She turned to look at her friend. "Oh, and by the way, thanks for pointing them in my direction the other day. You're a real pal."

Monica put her hands up in a defensive gesture. "Don't blame me. Your boss at the tour company is the one you should really be mad at."

"Oh, don't worry, he's on my list, too." She responded to Spencer's text message as politely as she could and debated watching another episode of *Lone Star Haunts*.

Monica patted her on the shoulder. "Well, I guess I'll leave you to your boyfriend and your research. Someone's got to keep this place running smoothly."

"He's definitely not my boyfriend," Claire insisted as Monica walked away, "and it really is research!"

She didn't want to admit to Monica, or to herself, that Spencer wasn't the ghost hunter she was actually focused on. From everything she had seen, it was clear Drew was a gifted sensitive. Since the shows were recorded and broadcast later, there was no way Claire could confirm the presence of any projections during their investigations. However, there seemed to be plenty of supporting evidence that very often the hunters' equipment had accurately identified them. In each case, Drew had recognized the presence of the projection before the equipment registered or confirmed it. Claire tried to convince herself it was professional curiosity, but she couldn't deny she was looking forward to learning which acumens Drew possessed.

As the credits began to roll on the episode she'd been watching, Claire sighed and turned off her phone before setting it back underneath the counter. Whatever Drew's acumens might be, he was clearly untrained, and his abilities had never been developed. She would eventually have to turn his name in to the Bureau for potential recruitment, which was the expected course of action in a case like this. She had already put it off this long, though, so she figured it could wait until after the tour that night. No one could fault her for wanting more information about him first, right?

Claire pushed all thoughts of the ghost hunters aside when she spotted Philip holding the door open so a young mother and her little girl could exit the candy shop. They made eye contact and he gave a little wave before heading her way. She didn't even wait for him to approach the counter before she began scooping taffy into a bag.

"Such efficient service," he said with a smile as Claire weighed the bag of candy.

"Anything for our best customer."

"You flatter me." He set his payment on the counter, then pulled a piece of taffy out of the bag and began to unwrap it.

Claire spotted Monica on the other side of the room, smiling impishly, as if she had figured out some great secret. She gave Claire a wink, but Claire didn't acknowledge her. What was the point? Any reaction on her part would only add fuel to the fire of Monica's speculations.

Looking for any kind of distraction, Claire turned her attention back to Philip. "That's a beautiful ring," she said, pointing to the piece of jewelry on the man's index finger. "I noticed it the other day and meant to say something."

Philip looked down at his hand. "I'm glad you like it."

"My father has one similar to it that he got from my grandfather," Claire told him. "Is yours a family heirloom, too?"

"Yes," he said with a nostalgic smile, "it's been in my family for decades."

Claire put the money in the register and closed the drawer. "Well, it reminds me that I need to call my dad more often."

"Then my work here is done," Philip said with an overly dramatic bow.

Claire chuckled. She was about to say something else but stopped short when she spotted Aaron making his way across the store in her direction. As far as she knew, in the entire time he'd been on the island he'd never visited the candy shop before, and she couldn't imagine what he was doing there now.

Philip snapped his fingers in front of Claire's face. "Earth to Claire." He studied her with a concerned look. "Are you alright?"

She shook off her surprise and smiled at him. "Sorry." She nodded in Aaron's direction. "I just saw someone I wasn't expecting to see."

As Philip turned to look, Aaron reached Claire's station. The two men stared at each other for a few seconds. Claire thought she spotted a look of surprise on Philip's face as well, but it quickly passed. He gave Aaron a short nod then turned his attention back to Claire.

"Do you two know each other?" she asked.

Both men shook their heads. Philip extended his hand in Aaron's direction and introduced himself. Aaron shook the offered hand and introduced himself as well.

"Well, I better get going," Philip said abruptly. "Have a good day, Claire." He nodded to Aaron. "Nice to meet you."

"Likewise."

Claire frowned as she watched Philip hurry out the door. "Well, that was weird." She looked at Aaron. "Are you sure you two don't know each other?"

Aaron examined the items in the display case. "Of course not. I've never seen that man before in my life."

Claire decided to let the matter drop. "Okay, whatever." She folded her arms across her chest. "What are you doing here, Aaron?"

"I wanted to apologize for yesterday." He looked up from the display case with a sheepish smile. "I acted like a jerk."

"Does that mean you've changed your mind and you'll do the tours for me?" Claire suspected his visit had more to do with his application to P.I.D. than being a friendly gesture, so she didn't get her hopes up.

Aaron smiled apologetically. "Unfortunately, no. I can't do that. I just didn't want you to be angry with me."

"Don't worry about it," she told him with a noncommittal shrug. "Like everyone keeps telling me, it's only a few tours."

"And maybe it won't be as bad as you think."

"A girl can hope." A few customers had trickled into the store, giving Claire an excuse to end the conversation. "I better get back to work."

Aaron looked around and nodded. "Okay, I just wanted to make sure we're good."

"We're good," she assured him.

He nodded again but made no move to leave. It seemed like he had something else he wanted to say but Claire wasn't sure she wanted to hear it.

After a few awkward seconds, he cleared his throat. "Actually, I was wondering if I could come back by after you get off work." Claire couldn't hide her surprise and he noticed it. "Don't worry, I'm not hitting on you or anything. I want to explain a few things about why I reacted the way I did yesterday. There are some things about my past that I feel like I should tell you."

She nodded, unsure what else to do. "Okay, but it would be better for me if we got together tomorrow instead. I have to give the ghost hunters their first tour tonight."

"Tomorrow works for me. I don't have to be at the restaurant until eleven."

"I could meet you for breakfast somewhere around nine."

"That sounds great." He flashed her a genuine smile.

They settled on the restaurant then said their good-byes. She watched him leave the store, uncertain what to make of it all.

When the rush of customers died down a few minutes later, Monica came to Claire's station. "So, who was that? Another boyfriend?"

"Seriously?" Claire asked. "Why do you keep assuming every guy I speak to is my boyfriend?"

Monica shrugged. "I don't know. Maybe I just want to see you happy. You don't have much of a social life after all."

She couldn't argue with her about that, no matter how much she wanted to. "Well, Aaron is a coworker at the tour company. There's definitely nothing romantic there."

"I don't know," Monica said, clearly not ready to let it drop. "It sure seemed like there was some tension between him and Philip. I think it could be the whole Alpha-male, that's-my-woman syndrome."

Claire laughed despite her irritation. "Is that a syndrome?"

"If it's not, it should be."

Claire didn't want to tell her friend that she had also sensed some tension between them, especially since she had no idea why there would be any. She certainly didn't share Monica's thoughts about either man's romantic interest in her, but she also didn't have an alternative explanation.

Before she could ponder it any further, her phone's text notification sounded again. At that moment, her greatest concern was surviving the Ashton Villa tour that night without making Spencer a part of it.

(Excerpt from A Concise Accounting of the Conservancy of Energy-based Metaphysical and Transcendental Entities: The History of the Bureau for Historical Preservation (1680-1973))

In the years following World War 2, Bureau researchers began to consider possible applications for the energy produced by projections, specifically the energy that had been drained from dispatched rogue projections. Since this energy is in a concentrated form, it is more powerful than energy generated from manmade sources. Unfortunately, it is also harder to harness and control.

As the world moved into the nuclear age, many within the Bureau believed the projection energy should be used in an effort to ensure world peace. Research indicated the energy represented a resource that could potentially save thousands of lives with the development of an energy expulsion device. While many viewed this as a possible deterrent to future aggression, others viewed it as a potential weapon.

The implications of using the projection energy in this way concerned many in Bureau leadership at the time, and ultimately all research in this area was halted. The possibility of weaponizing projection energy was never pursued.

However, not everyone connected to the Bureau agreed with this decision. The topic was hotly debated in multiple committees before being brought to a vote in an emergency session of surveyor representatives. Finally, in May of 1955, a mandate was issued by Bureau high-command that the Bureau would in no way move to weaponize projection energy. Furthermore, any agent who disagreed with the decision would need to fall in line with the official Bureau policy or else be expelled from the Bureau permanently. The result of this mandate was the expulsion of dozens of surveyors and several high-ranking Bureau officials.

This mass expulsion, known as The Schism of 1955, marks a dark time in Bureau history.

Chapter 11

Later that night, Claire met the ghost hunters in the parking lot behind Ashton Villa. She watched with an amused expression as the team piled out of their vehicles. There weren't any creepy panel vans like she had been expecting, just two very normal-looking pick-up trucks.

Now that she was tuned in to their energy connection, Claire could sense Drew's presence before he even stepped out from behind the wheel of his truck.

"Hey," he said, flashing her a knee-buckling grin as he approached.

She gripped her coffee cup more tightly. "Hey," she answered, pleased by how casual it sounded.

A man who appeared to be a slightly taller version of Drew walked up to them.

"This is my little brother, Luke," Drew told her.

"Younger brother," Luke corrected. He stuck out his hand. "Thanks so much for doing this for us."

Though he shared his older brother's looks, Luke didn't share Drew's energy output level. Claire figured he was a Level-2 sensitive at best.

She shook Luke's extended hand and smiled. "No problem." Her smile was genuine. Somehow, she knew instantly she was going to like him.

Drew put his arm around his brother's shoulders and gave him a manly squeeze. "My little brother is the brains behind a lot of the technology we use in our investigations."

"*Younger* brother," Luke repeated, clearly embarrassed by the praise. If it hadn't been so dark, Claire was sure she would have seen him blushing.

"Hey, lazy asses," Spencer called out from one of the trucks. "Get over here and help us unload."

Drew rolled his eyes. "Duty calls."

Claire stayed back and watched them take their equipment out of the trucks. Clearly they took their investigations seriously. After several items had been unloaded and the truck doors closed again, Spencer made his way over to Claire while the others stayed behind.

"We're super stoked about this investigation tonight," he told her for about the hundredth time.

Claire nodded, though she was distracted by the rest of the team's activity in the parking lot. Drew, Keith, and Luke were huddled up next to one of the trucks, their arms around each other's shoulders as if they were planning the next snap in a football game.

Spencer noticed he didn't have Claire's full attention and looked over his shoulder. "Yeah, they do that before every investigation." He winked at her conspiratorially. "I don't really think it's necessary, but it seems to make them feel better."

Claire nodded again but didn't offer a response. When the rest of the team had joined them, she motioned for them to make their way around to the front of the house. On the way, she fell in step next to Drew, who looked at her and smiled.

"Were you guys praying back there?" she asked, forcing herself to ignore the flutter in her stomach.

"Um, yeah." He shrugged. "Spencer thinks it's stupid, but I'd rather be safe than sorry. We never know what we're up against when we go into one of these places."

"I think that's not a bad idea at all," she told him honestly.

Though the projections monitored by the Bureau were for the most part harmless accumulations of energy, that didn't mean there weren't more sinister things in the world. Claire had encountered enough evil and demonic presences in the course of her job to know that a little divine protection was a good thing to have on your side.

Drew smiled at Claire again and another jolt of energy pulsed through her entire body. How could he not know the effect he had on her? She was dying to know if it was the same for him.

As they approached the front door of the Victorian-era mansion, Claire moved to the head of the group. "I've already turned off the alarm," she told them as she turned the key in the lock, "but I didn't want to leave the door unlocked and unattended."

She pushed the door open and the ghost hunters followed her inside. They set their equipment down and began looking around the entryway and into the two adjoining rooms. Since they'd be spending most of their time investigating in the dark, she let them have a few minutes to appreciate the beauty of the historic home.

The energy in the entryway rippled as Bettie joined them, though she stopped short of actually materializing. Claire had warned her that the ghost hunters were coming, but she had neglected to mention Drew's high sensitivity level. The less time Bettie had to prepare and plan for an encounter with him, the better. Claire prayed she would behave herself.

"So," Spencer finally said after they had looked around for a few minutes. "Tell us a little bit about the house."

Keith held a medium-sized camera up to his eye and pointed it in Claire's direction.

She took a step back. "I don't have to be on camera, do I?"

Spencer stared at her, as if that was the strangest question he'd ever heard. "Of course. You're our tour guide"

Keith moved the camera to the side slightly and smiled at her. "I'm sure our viewers would rather look at you than at our ugly mugs the whole time."

Claire smiled back at him and thanked him for the compliment, but it didn't change her mind. "Maybe you could film the house and then my voice could be in the background?" she suggested.

"I think that should be fine," Drew said, giving Spencer a serious look. He put a hand on Claire's shoulder and smiled again. "If the camera makes you uncomfortable, we'll work around it."

Claire swallowed hard and resisted the urge to pull away from him. The unexpected contact had caught her off guard, and the energy coursing through her body made it hard to breathe. "Thanks," was all she could manage to say.

"Alright," Spencer begrudgingly conceded, "but it'll look weird if they can't see who's talking."

"It'll be fine," Drew assured him, taking his hand off Claire's shoulder and picking up one of the bags of equipment.

The energy pulse subsided quickly once he broke contact. Claire was relieved for the chance to regain control of herself, but she was even more relieved that she wouldn't have to be on camera.

"Okay," Keith said, "now that that's all settled, back to the house."

"Well," Claire began as her breathing slowly returned to normal, "the house was built in 1859 by James M. Brown. It was the first private brick structure built on the island and the first house built on Broadway Avenue, which would eventually become the island's main thoroughfare." She began moving toward the staircase and the ghost hunters followed. "It was one of the few structures on the island that survived the 1900 hurricane with only water damage, at least partially because the family opened the front and back doors and let the flood waters flow freely through the ground floor. That way there was less pressure on the building itself and less structural damage as a result."

"It seems like the 1900 storm is a big part of Galveston's history," Drew said. "We keep hearing and reading about it everywhere we go."

Claire nodded. "Before the hurricane, Galveston was one of the wealthiest cities in America and it was the primary seaport on the Gulf of Mexico. More than seventy percent of the country's cotton crops shipped out of Galveston and people came from all over the country to vacation here." She stopped at the foot of the stairs. "In the years after the storm, as the island recovered, much of that activity and commerce shifted to New Orleans."

"So, exactly how bad was the storm?" Keith asked.

Claire pointed at the stairs. "The Brown's youngest daughter, Mathilda, sat here on the staircase as the flood waters rose. She reported the water reached as high as the tenth step."

"Wow," Luke said with a low whistle. "That's pretty intense."

Claire nodded. "The family and some close friends rode out the storm on the second floor." She led the group toward the Gold Room. "After the storm, when the entire island was raised, Bettie and Mathilda opted to have the aboveground basement filled in rather than raising the house. You can still see a portion of the basement windows peeking out from behind the flowerbeds in front."

"Tell us more about Bettie," Spencer said as Keith panned the camera around the Gold Room. "She's the real star of the show here."

Claire sighed. This was a frequent problem when a projection's personality was as big as Bettie's. Sometimes the ghost stories overshadowed the history.

"Well, this is a perfect room to talk about her in since she painted most of the paintings in here." Claire waited as the ghost hunters looked around the room. "She was an incredibly unusual woman for her time. She was fiercely independent and she never married. She loved to paint, and she very much wanted to be taken seriously as an artist."

"Why didn't she marry?" Luke asked.

Claire smiled. "Well, we aren't sure exactly why she never married, but the fact that Bettie was often described as being a 'Texas princess' might give us a hint. There's a story that whenever a man would come to ask for Bettie's hand in marriage, her father would show them the accounting records of how much it cost to maintain her in the manner she expected. Apparently, none of the suitors stuck around after that."

The ghost hunters laughed, and the temperature in the room dropped several degrees right before the piece of ghost hunting equipment in Luke's hand began to emit a beeping sound.

"The K2 meter just got a hit," Luke announced. He looked at Claire and grinned. "I don't think Bettie liked you telling that story."

Claire nodded. "Yeah, I'm pretty sure she didn't."

"What else can you tell us about her?" Drew asked.

"Well, she loved to travel." Claire led the way out of the Gold Room and back to the stairs. "In fact, there's a travel trunk in her room that's known to lock and unlock itself, even though the key has been lost for decades." She began climbing the stairs and the ghost hunters followed.

"Where is she seen the most?" Spencer wanted to know.

"She pretty much has free rein over the whole house," Claire explained. "She's been seen everywhere – in the Gold Room, on this staircase, in her bedroom, in the day room." She stopped and turned to look at them. "The day room was one of her favorite places because she could spend time there without having to wear her stays."

"Stays?" Luke repeated, clearly confused.

"That's what they called their undergarments," Claire told him.

His face turned red. "Oh, sorry."

Claire laughed. "It's okay. I'd be a little concerned about you if you had known that."

They continued with the rest of the tour and about an hour later finished back in the hallway. Claire was pleased by how interested they were in the history, both of the mansion and the island as a whole. Maybe the rest of the evening wouldn't be as unbearable as she had feared.

Chapter 12

Claire stood off to the side as the team pulled more equipment out of their bags in preparation for their formal investigation. After a few minutes, Luke approached and handed her a tablet.

"We've installed a night vision camera on this," he explained. "If you want, you can use it to help find your way in the dark and keep track of where everyone else is once the lights go off."

She gave him an appreciative smile and accepted the device. She had repeatedly encouraged them to do their investigation with the lights on so their viewers could appreciate the mansion, but Spencer insisted the paranormal activity would be greater in the dark. Honestly, it didn't make any difference. A projection's energy signature was easier for a sensitive with Visual Acumen to see in darker lighting because of the contrast, but they could manifest under any conditions. There was no point trying to explain that to Spencer, though, so Claire let the issue drop.

"What's that?" Claire asked innocently as Drew pulled a handheld device out of his bag.

"It's a spirit box." He held it so the display was facing her. "It sweeps radio frequencies and creates white noise to help us pick up on any communication when the paranormal entities reach out."

"Does it really work?" she asked, continuing to feign ignorance.

"It sure does," Drew said with a confident grin. "We've recorded hundreds of encounters with these things."

"Have you had any other kinds of encounters?" Claire asked, taking the opportunity to dig for information about which acumens he might possess.

Drew nodded. "Yeah, lots."

"Since becoming a ghost hunter or before that?"

He studied her. "Both, actually. It's why I got into ghost hunting in the first place."

"Was it anything serious?" she asked. "Or scary?"

"Nothing too interesting, but I don't like to talk about it too much." He turned his attention back to the equipment in his bag. "How about you? In your line of work, you've probably had all kinds of experiences."

"More than I'd care to think about," she said honestly.

"I bet." He looked down at the device in his hand. "Hopefully we'll get to talk to Bettie tonight with this thing."

Claire forced a smile despite her nerves. Firing up a spirit box in the presence of a projection as mischievous as Bettie was like handing a microphone to a toddler at a wedding reception.

"Alright," Spencer said enthusiastically, looking straight into the camera that was perched on Keith's shoulder. "It's time to go dark." Without pulling his eyes away from the camera, he pointed in Claire's direction. "Let's turn off those lights and get this party started."

Claire resisted the urge to roll her eyes as she crossed the room to the light switch. It was going to be a long night. She flipped the switch, plunging the whole house into darkness. Looking down at the tablet, she silently thanked Luke for the night vision camera as she made her way back to where the others were waiting.

Drew switched on the spirit box and began moving slowly up the stairs. "I think we'll start in the day room since that's where you said Miss Bettie spent so much of her time."

Claire didn't respond. They wouldn't need any help from her. She doubted they'd have any trouble making contact with Bettie. There was no way she'd pass up a chance like this.

When they reached the day room, Spencer shined the flashlight on the walls. "You said Miss Bettie painted most of the artwork in this house, right?" He didn't wait for Claire's response. "That must be why she's still attached to this place. She has an emotional connection to her artwork."

Claire didn't bother correcting him. It wouldn't do any good anyway.

"Bettie, are you here with us?" Drew asked.

He held up the spirit box and they all waited for a reply. Claire held her breath. It was all the invitation Bettie would need to put on a show.

"We don't want to hurt you," Spencer continued. He paused for a few seconds. The staticky white noise from the spirit box filled the room. "Will you come speak to us?"

The spirit box crackled then a woman's faint voice replied, "Yes."

"Did you hear that?" Spencer said, turning to look at the camera. "She said, 'Yes'!"

"Awesome!" Drew enthusiastically slapped Luke on the back.

Claire stifled a laugh. They had no idea what they were in for.

"Are you okay with us being here?" Drew asked.

The spirit box crackled again. "Necessary," came the faint reply.

Spencer looked at Drew then they both looked at Claire. She shrugged, genuinely confused. She had no idea what Bettie was trying to tell them.

"It's necessary for us to be here?" Drew asked, turning his attention back to the spirit box. "Why is it necessary?"

"Help," the voice replied.

A look of genuine concern came over Drew's face. "Someone needs help?" he asked. "How can we help them?" He paused, waiting for a response. Taking a step further into the room, he asked, "What can I do to help them?"

The spirit box crackled again but it was several seconds before the reply came, clear as day.

"Marry...Claire."

Claire sucked in a breath and immediately felt her face flush. Thank God, she hadn't pushed the issue of conducting the tour with the lights on. The last thing she wanted at that moment was to make eye contact with Drew.

She turned to hurry out of the room but bumped into Keith who was standing behind her in the doorway. He put a hand on her shoulder to steady her, but his attention remained on the scene unfolding through his camera lens.

When Claire turned back around, Drew and Spencer were both looking at her.

"Who's Mary Claire?" Spencer asked, his voice barely above a whisper.

Claire breathed a sigh of relief. They had completely misunderstood Bettie. She shook her head vigorously and shrugged her shoulders. "I've never heard that name before."

"Miss Bettie," Drew said, pulling his eyes away from Claire and looking around the room, "who's Mary Claire? We don't know who that is."

A faint tinkle of laughter echoed through the spirit box.

"That sounds like a child laughing," Spencer declared triumphantly. He turned to Claire. "Was there ever a child that lived here named Mary Claire?"

She didn't answer right away, debating if she should tell the truth or flat out lie to keep them off Bettie's intended track. Finally, she shook her head again, probably more vigorously than she needed to, and said, "Nope, no child by that name has ever lived here."

Spencer took a step in her direction and she took a step back, bumping into Keith again. It took a few seconds for her to realize that she wasn't actually the focus of his attention this time. He stared directly into the camera, which was now positioned over Claire's left shoulder, and addressed his viewing audience.

"We're going to get to the bottom of this Mary Claire mystery," he stated emphatically. "If there's a child out there in the spirit world that needs our help, we won't rest until we've helped her."

Another tinkle of laughter floated out of the spirit box.

Claire glared around the seemingly empty room, knowing Bettie's vision wasn't limited by the darkness. She was definitely going to have a serious conversation with the projection once the ghost hunters were out of the building.

Spencer led the way out of the day room and across the hall to Bettie's bedroom. As soon as Claire entered the room, she knew Bettie was there waiting for them. Though she hadn't manifested into a visible form, Claire could tell she was sitting on the bed.

Drew paused in the doorway next to her. "There's definitely a presence here," he said quietly.

She held up the tablet and studied his expression through the night vision camera. There was nothing flashy or theatrical about his statement. He was simply stating a fact.

Luke nodded enthusiastically. "He's right again. I've got a reading. The temperature is much lower in here."

"Is the presence green or red, Drew?" Keith asked.

Drew chuckled. "Green. Bright green"

Claire frowned. What on earth were they talking about? She was about to ask Drew what he meant when Spencer pointed to the travel trunk in front of the fireplace.

"There's the famous trunk," he said, motioning for Keith to keep the camera on him as he crossed the room and knelt down next to it. "This is Miss Bettie's personal travel trunk that she used when she would travel the world," Spencer explained to his audience. "It's been known to mysteriously lock and unlock itself, even though the key was lost decades ago. Earlier this evening when we did our walkthrough, the chest was locked." He looked straight into the camera. "But what about now?"

He paused dramatically for effect then lifted the lid.

"No way!" Luke exclaimed.

"It was totally locked before," Keith confirmed.

Claire grinned. She had to admit their enthusiasm was contagious.

"Whoa," Drew said, interrupting the celebration. All eyes in the room turned to him. "This may sound crazy, but I feel like Bettie's right here next to me."

He was only standing a few feet from Claire, so she had no trouble confirming it. She hadn't noticed Bettie move from her spot on the bed. Like everyone else in the room, her attention had been on Spencer and the travel trunk. Claire held her breath as she waited to see what Bettie would do next.

"The battery just died on my tablet," Luke informed the group, shaking the device several times.

Claire groaned inwardly. She knew what that meant. Since projections were made of pure energy, they required massive amounts of energy when they interacted with material objects. Bettie had drained the battery on Luke's tablet because she had something big planned.

Spencer moved slowly in Drew's direction. "Is she still with you?"

Drew nodded. He looked down at his left hand and smiled. "Actually, it feels like she's holding my hand."

"Spirit!" Spencer declared dramatically, raising his right hand. "You have no right to attach yourself to my friend, or to anyone else in this room!"

Claire put her hand over her mouth to hide her smile. That was exactly the kind of challenge Bettie wouldn't be able to resist.

They waited in silence for several seconds, then a strange look came over Drew's face. He turned his head slightly in Claire's direction, his brow wrinkled in confusion.

"What's wrong?" Spencer whispered.

"I think she just pinched my butt."

Claire couldn't hold in her laughter any longer. Thankfully, the rest of the group joined in.

Drew shook his head and chuckled. "Well, you said she could be mischievous."

The rest of the night passed without further incident. It was after two in the morning when Spencer decided to bring their investigation to a close.

"Overall, I think it was a good outing," he said as the others packed up the equipment. "We got some interesting readings and a new mystery to pursue." He looked at Claire and smiled. "There's definitely a presence here."

"Oh, definitely," she agreed.

He gave her a fatherly pat on the shoulder, as if his validation was all she had needed to make her life complete. With a soft chuckle, she followed the team as they filed out the door.

Drew hesitated on the porch while the others made their way to the trucks. "We're going to go grab a bite to eat if you want to join us."

Claire smiled, genuinely pleased by the invitation. "I'd love to."

"You could ride with me and Luke, if you want."

Of course, she wanted to, but she had other matters to attend. "How about I meet you guys there?" she suggested. She glanced over her shoulder and raised her voice slightly. "I've got a few things I need to take care of here before I leave."

Drew looked toward the street where Luke had pulled up in his truck. "I don't mind waiting for you."

She resisted the urge to accept his offer. "That's sweet, but this might take a while."

He nodded. "Okay, I'll text you the location when we figure out where we're going."

"Sounds good."

With a wave, he turned and headed toward the street. Luke waved at her as well as he shifted from the driver's seat to the passenger's seat of Drew's truck. Claire smiled and waved at them both before heading back into the house.

She shut the door then waited a few seconds to make sure no one was within earshot of the building. "Bettie!" she hollered. "Get out here!"

Bettie slowly materialized at the top of the staircase. She was wearing her traditional turquoise gown, an angelic smile on her face. As she descended the stairs, she batted her eyes at Claire innocently.

"Yes, my dear? What can I do for you?"

Claire crossed the foyer, pointing a finger at her sternly. "You, young lady, are dangerously close to an official reprimand."

Bettie stopped in the middle of the staircase and brought one translucent hand to her chest, feigning shock. "I have no idea what you mean."

"You know *exactly* what I mean." Claire stopped at the bottom of the staircase and glared up at her.

"I did not break any rules," she said as she resumed her journey to the bottom of the stairs. "All I did was put on a little show."

"Yes, an embarrassing show called *Paranormal Matchmaker*."

"I thought it would help." She floated past Claire and brushed a hand across her cheek. "After all, you need a little romance in your life."

Claire shivered involuntarily from the contact but maintained her irritated glare. "Says the woman who never married."

Bettie smiled coyly as she floated toward the Gold Room. "That does not mean I lacked my share of beaus." She paused in the middle of the room and raised a hand to her chin as if deep in thought. "You need to get married so you can start working on the next generation of Bureau agents. I cannot be expected to do all the work around here. After all, we *must* promote the history of this house!"

"Don't throw that line back at me," Claire told her. "What you did wasn't just putting on a show for some ghost-hungry tourists. You pinched his behind!"

Bettie giggled. "I did not pinch him. I only gave him a little pat." She moved her hand to the side, demonstrating the motion.

"That doesn't make it okay. You were *flirting* with him!"

Bettie whirled around to face Claire, her translucent dress spinning with the motion. "I knew it!" She snapped her fingers and pointed at her with a triumphant grin. "You like him."

Claire scoffed at the suggestion. "Bettie, he's a ghost hunter."

"A paranormal investigator," the projection corrected, "and a high-level sensitive. No wonder you are attracted to him." She thought for a second then raised her perfectly manicured eyebrows. "You did not deny it."

"Because it doesn't matter whether I like him or not. It doesn't change the facts."

Bettie acted as if Claire hadn't even spoken. "He likes you, too." With a wink, she added, "Which is why I like him."

Claire didn't have the energy to deny anything, but she also had to be realistic. "Bettie, listen to me. It doesn't matter if we like each other. What kind of a future could I possibly have with a ghost hunter? I could never tell him the truth, and I couldn't live with all the lies."

"That is ridiculous." Bettie floated across the room and sat down on the piano bench. "He is clearly a Level-5 sensitive. The Bureau will snatch him up as soon as they know about him." She studied Claire from across the room. "And that is exactly what you are worried about, is it not?"

Claire joined her next to the piano. "There are already three agents on this island. The Bureau's not going to assign a fourth."

Bettie frowned. "With his sensitivity level, you might have to tell him the truth before a rogue gets to him."

Claire frowned. "I think that may be one of the reasons he's became a ghost hunter."

Bettie tinkled a few notes on the piano and her form shimmered briefly. She paused then turned to look at Claire, genuine concern on her face. "How serious was it?"

Claire shook her head. "He didn't say much about it, but I'm sure it couldn't have been that bad if he decided to start hunting ghosts. It was probably standard stuff. You know, messing with the hairs on the back of his neck or something."

Bettie's smile returned as her fingers moved gracefully above the keys, playing a silent melody. "Honestly, though, I do not blame them."

"Who?"

"The rogues."

"What do you mean? Blame them for what?"

She gave Claire a wink. "Messing with him a little. I mean, I know I would enjoy playing with the hairs on the back of that man's neck."

Before Claire could respond, Bettie faded into the shadows with a tinkle of laughter.

Chapter 13

When Claire finally caught up with the ghost hunters at a local diner, they had almost finished their late night snacks. She didn't mind. Her body was used to keeping strange hours, and she rarely ate after leading a tour.

Drew spotted her as soon as she entered the diner and waved her over. As she crossed the room to their table, the guys scooted around to make room for her.

"Did you get everything taken care of?" Drew asked as Claire settled in.

She nodded.

"Do you want to order something?" Luke asked, passing her a menu.

"No thanks. I never eat this late. It gives me weird dreams."

"Thanks again for the tour," Keith said. "I think we've got some great evidence. I can't wait to get back to the hotel and start sorting through it."

"I'd be interested in checking out the data you collected," Claire said casually, though her interest wasn't just idle curiosity. They had all heard the messages Bettie had given through the spirit box, but they wouldn't know about any electronic voice phenomena until the recordings were reviewed later. Claire prayed the projection hadn't left any other embarrassing hidden messages in the white noise. "Bettie was really active for you guys tonight."

"So, she's not always like that?" Luke asked.

Claire shook her head. "You never know what you're going to get with her. It depends on her mood, honestly."

Drew studied Claire for a few seconds. "You talk about Bettie like she's a real person."

Claire shrugged, trying to seem nonchalant but choosing her words carefully. "I've been giving tours of Ashton Villa for about two years now. Bettie's almost like a flighty, unpredictable coworker to me by this point."

"But a coworker that you need to be careful with," Spencer pointed out. "Even the most seemingly innocuous spirit can turn dangerous in an instant with the right provocation."

Claire wanted to tell him how much he didn't know what he was talking about, but instead she took a sip from the water glass the waitress had just set on the table in front of her. She decided to change the direction of the conversation.

"So, how did you all get started with ghost hunting?"

Not surprisingly Spencer was the first to speak up. He explained that he and Keith had been roommates in college and had quickly discovered they both believed in ghosts. Their ghost hunting adventures started one weekend as a lark but eventually became a more organized endeavor.

"And Drew and I have worked at the same oil and gas company for almost seven years now," Keith explained. "One day at lunch, he asked me what I had done the weekend before and I told him. Since he'd had a few experiences with ghosts as a kid, it was only natural that he eventually started joining us on our ghost-hunting outings."

"You mentioned that you'd had some encounters," Claire said to Drew, trying not to seem overly interested. "But what about everyone else? Who's had the most experiences?"

"Drew," the other three said in unison.

Claire chuckled and turned to look at him. The frown on his face made it clear he wasn't keen on the topic.

Claire picked up her water glass again to take a sip. "It's none of my business really. I was just curious."

"No, it's okay," he said, forcing a smile. "It's not exactly my favorite topic of conversation." He shifted slightly in his seat and cleared his throat. "When I was a kid, I had an imaginary friend who turned out not to be so imaginary. My parents pretty much freaked out when they realized I was actually playing with the ghost of a woman who had lived in the house years before. She wasn't any kind of a threat and nothing bad ever happened, but my parents weren't okay with it and eventually we moved to a whole different town."

Claire looked at Luke. "Did you see the ghost, too?"

He shook his head. "No. I played along with them because I didn't want to be left out, but I never actually saw the Blue Lady."

Claire looked from one brother to the other. "Why did you call her that?"

Drew shrugged. "Because she was blue."

The other ghost hunters chuckled.

"Drew always sees the ghosts as colors," Keith explained.

"Colors?" Claire repeated. "Interesting." She looked at Drew. "And Bettie was green?"

He nodded.

"This little talent of his is actually pretty helpful," Keith said.

"How's that?"

Luke answered. "Because it helps us know when to get the hell out of dodge."

"How does it do that?" Claire pressed.

"The evil or negative spirits," Spencer said, "you know the ones that really mess with your emotions or physically hurt people, those spirits are red, or sometimes black."

Claire nodded as pieces began to fall into place. She had wanted to know what his acumens were, but there was no way she could have expected this. "And the rest are blue or green?" she confirmed.

"Most of the time," Drew said. "Sometimes there are other colors, too, but we haven't figured out exactly what that tells us about the spirits yet."

"I'm sure you'll figure it out." And if he didn't, the Bureau training officers would certainly explain it all to him after he was recruited. Claire didn't want to dwell on that, though, so she decided to take the conversation in another direction. "Have you guys had a lot of experiences with red or black spirits?"

"Enough to know we need to take them seriously," Spencer said dramatically.

"In fact, we generally try to avoid them altogether," Keith added. "When there's a Code Red, that's when we pack up and get out."

"Good idea," Claire said.

"That's why we pray before our investigations," Luke added. "We learned the hard way that it's important to have as much spiritual protection as possible on our hunts."

Claire looked around the table. "What happened? Did someone get hurt?"

"Not on one of our investigations," Luke told her, "but Drew was scratched once when we were kids." Drew gave him a look that clearly told him to shut up. "Sorry, bro. She asked."

"I didn't mean to pry," Claire said.

Drew sat up straighter in his seat. "It's okay," he assured her. "It was just a stupid high-school dare that went farther than it should have."

Claire decided it was best not to press him any further. "So, Luke," she said, taking the spotlight off Drew, "how did you get in the group?"

"Their ghost hunting tools needed some high-tech tweaking, so Drew brought me on board." He smiled proudly. "I have a master's degree in computer science and a bachelor's in mechanical engineering."

"Impressive," she told him, and she meant it.

"We'd be lost without him," Drew said, ruffling his hair.

Claire felt a twinge of regret as she thought about her own relationship with her brother. Even with their five-year age difference, she and Zach used to be so close. But that was before the fiasco in San Francisco.

She clamped off the emotions and forced a smile. "It's good that you two can hunt ghosts together."

"And what about you?" Drew asked, turning the spotlight on Claire. "How did you get started leading ghost tours?"

All eyes at the table turned in her direction.

"Well, believe it or not, it's kind of a family business."

"Your family leads ghost tours?" Keith asked, clearly skeptical.

Claire laughed. "Well, that's not all we do. Our focus is actually on preserving the history of significant locations. The ghost tours are one way to do that."

"That's awesome," Drew said. With a wink, he added, "I love history…minored in it in college."

She smiled back at him, though she definitely couldn't relate. During the semester she had spent in college, the last thing she had wanted to do was study history.

She looked at her watch and stifled a yawn. "It's getting pretty late. I've got a busy day tomorrow, so I guess I better get going."

She wasn't actually tired, but the direction the conversation had taken made it the perfect time to bow out. This was another part of her job she hated. She couldn't even have a casual conversation with new friends without having to choose her words carefully or else flat-out lie to them.

Claire stood up and Drew did, too.

"You're right," he said. "It's late. Let me walk you to your car."

She nodded and he followed her toward the door.

"I had a great time on the tour tonight," he told her once they were outside.

She smiled at him. "Even though Bettie got a little frisky with you?"

"Maybe it was *because* Bettie got frisky with me?" He wiggled his eyebrows and gave her a mischievous wink.

Claire laughed in earnest. "She'll be happy to hear that."

They reached her car and she pressed the button to unlock the door. Drew looked like he wanted to say something else, but Claire cleared her throat, saving him the trouble.

"Thank you for walking me to my car. I'll give Spencer a call when I have the next tour confirmed."

He nodded. "Thanks. I'll let him know."

It was probably a curt way to end the evening, but she didn't know what else to say. She desperately wanted to spend more time with

Drew, but every ounce of her agent training was protesting, warning her not to let her heart get carried away. At best, Drew would be recruited by the Bureau and most likely get a job working at headquarters in Boston, or possibly even Paris, thousands of miles away. If not, he would leave and go back to Beaumont in a week. Either way, there wasn't a future for any relationship between them, so there was no point entertaining the impossible.

(Excerpt from A Concise Accounting of the Conservancy of Energy-based Metaphysical and Transcendental Entities: The History of the Bureau for Historical Preservation (1680-1973))

Chapter 15 – Bureau finances

One of the earliest projections contacted by Pierre Abelard and the other scientists was that of a Templar knight who had been killed in 1307. In that year, King Philip IV of France ordered the arrest and torture of many members of the Templar order. This particular knight refused to give a false confession, so he was executed. When Abelard encountered him in the south of France in 1685, the knight disclosed the location of the portion of the Templar treasure he had been assigned to guard and welcomed the four scientists to use those resources to help other projections find their way.

When the team of surveyors landed in the New World in 1740, they quickly recognized the profit that could be made through wise investments there. A portion of the Templar treasure was used for that purpose, and the return on investment was significant.

Today, the Bureau continues to invest wisely, and these investments fund the majority of the operating costs of the Paranormal Assistance and Monitoring Division.

Chapter 14

The next morning, Claire met Aaron at a restaurant on the Seawall that was known for its amazing breakfasts. She had no idea what to expect from their conversation that morning, which made her more than a little nervous. Even after working together for close to a year, Aaron remained something of a mystery. And she still needed to finish his evaluation, a fact her brother had reminded her of twice in the past two days. Hopefully this conversation would help her with that.

By the time Claire walked into the restaurant, Aaron was already waiting at a table. He had ordered them both coffee, which helped alleviate some of her apprehension. At least she wouldn't have to wait too long for the caffeine to kick in.

"Good morning," she said as she slid into the seat across from Aaron.

He smiled probably the most genuine smile she had ever seen from him. "Good morning to you."

Claire nodded toward the coffee cup as she set her purse on the seat next to her. "Thanks for looking out for me."

"No problem. Thanks for agreeing to meet with me."

She smiled. "Of course."

He watched as she took her first glorious sip of coffee, savoring the steaming liquid and letting out a contented sigh. He chuckled at her reaction. "So, how did the tour go last night?"

Claire rolled her eyes. "They had a spirit box."

"I'm sure Bettie had a field day with that."

"Unfortunately."

The waitress came and they placed their orders. There were a few seconds of awkward silence once she left. Claire seriously considered making a run for the restroom to get away from the tension, but then Aaron broke the silence.

"After you left the restaurant the other day, I realized I must have sounded like a complete jerk, and I don't want you to think that about me. I'd really like the chance to explain why I feel the way I do about rogues."

"I've read your file," Claire told him. "I know you had some negative experiences when you were a kid."

He cleared his throat. "The file doesn't tell the whole story."

Claire raised her eyebrows. "In that case, I'm all ears."

Aaron took a deep breath and let it out slowly. "When I was eight years old, my family moved to a new town because of my dad's job. From the first moment I entered the new house, I knew something was off, but at that age I had no idea what the problem was, much less how to explain it to anybody." He looked out the window at the tourists walking up and down the Seawall for a few seconds before continuing. "We had only been in the house for a few days when I saw the projection for the first time. He looked right at me and we made eye contact, but that was all. I told my parents about it, but they thought I was making it up because I missed our old house and our old life." He shook his head. "My brother was thirteen years old at the time, and he wasn't about to let an opportunity to tease me pass by. He was pretty merciless about it, so I decided not to bring it up again."

The waitress brought their food to the table and Aaron paused. Once they were alone again, he resumed his story.

"Several days passed and I saw the projection a few more times. I didn't tell anyone about it, but that didn't keep my brother from continuing to tease me." He pushed his eggs around on his plate but didn't take a bite. "Though I was uneasy knowing our house was haunted, there weren't any problems until one night about a month after we moved in. My brother had been particularly mean to me that day, and that night, while we were watching a movie, my brother felt someone pull his hair. He yelled and we all turned around, but I was the only one who could see the projection behind him. I didn't dare tell anybody what had happened, though, because I knew they wouldn't believe me, and it would only give my brother more ammunition to tease me with."

He set down his fork and looked out at the water.

"After that, the projection started really harassing my brother. At first it was just things like pulling the sheets off him at night while he was sleeping and causing objects to fall off shelves or fly across the room, but it gradually got more and more intense until eventually we started seeing scratch marks on him. My parents thought my brother was hurting himself, so they sent him to a therapist. I told them it was the ghost, but they said I was only making things worse by encouraging my brother's delusions. They said my brother was sick and needed help, and I wasn't helping him by putting those kinds of ideas into his head. I let it drop, but I knew they were wrong."

Claire took a bite of her toast and tried to chew quietly. Her breakfast was getting cold, but somehow it felt disrespectful to dig in while Aaron was sharing something so personal.

After several seconds, he looked away from the window and continued. "Over the next year or so, my brother really began to withdraw into himself. He believed what everyone else was telling him, so he started to think he was crazy." Aaron looked at Claire. Their eyes met for a second before he looked away again. "When he got into high school, he started doing drugs, I guess maybe to try to get away from everything. Eventually my parents had him admitted to a rehab facility that was also a psychiatric hospital in the hope it would help him sort things out. It seemed to work, but as soon as he came home, the harassment started again, only much worse than it ever had been before."

Aaron closed his eyes and swallowed hard. "He was only home from the hospital a week before we found him in the bathroom. He had slit his wrists."

Claire started to reach across the table for Aaron's hand but stopped. Her heart hurt for him, but she didn't know how to offer any encouragement. Her upbringing was so different from what he was describing.

As close as she and Zach used to be, Claire couldn't imagine what she would have done if she had lost her brother like that.

Aaron took another deep breath and let it out slowly.

"With my brother gone, the projection shifted his attention to my mom. She was home by herself during the day, and little by little things started to happen. After a few weeks, she realized that my brother and I hadn't been imagining it after all and she called a paranormal investigation team to come check out our house. We didn't know it at the time, but it was a Bureau P.I.D. team operating out of a store front in a nearby town.

"When they got to the house, they asked us all to leave while they conducted their investigation. I was curious, though, so I snuck back into the house while my parents were at the neighbor's. I was watching from a closet in the hallway when they finally confronted and eventually dispatched the projection. I was terrified and fascinated at the same time. My curiosity got the better of me, and I came out of my hiding place and asked them what had just happened. I guess at that point they realized I was a sensitive because they didn't seem angry with me for being there. One of the agents handed me a business card and told me to call the number on the back when I turned eighteen if I was still curious."

"Obviously you did," Claire said.

He nodded. "It took me a few years to decide that I actually wanted to join the Bureau, though. I blamed myself for what happened to my brother and I really wanted to forget about it. Learning the truth about projections only added to the guilt."

"You can't blame yourself," Claire tried to assure him. "You were just a kid, and nobody believed you."

He shook his head. "I've made peace with it now. But I still can't help wondering if things could have been different if I would have been more insistent about what was really happening."

"That rogue knew what he was doing," Claire told him. "He left you alone because you could see him. It's much scarier to be harassed by something you can't see. He probably targeted your brother because of all the negative energy from him teasing you, and he certainly targeted your mom because of her grief at losing your brother. It's doubtful anyone would have believed you even if you had pushed the issue. Until a person experiences it for themselves, it's hard for them to believe it."

"I know you're right, but even so, joining the Bureau feels like a sort of penance, which is one reason why I've worked so hard to get accepted to P.I.D. The best way I can help prevent another tragedy like what happened to my brother is to get out there and stop dangerous rogues from harassing other people."

Claire sat back in her seat and studied him. "Not all rogues are like the one that went after your family. You know that, right?"

"I know," he assured her. He held her gaze for several seconds before he added, "But they all have the potential to be."

Claire couldn't argue with him. In the right situation, almost any projection could regress and deteriorate into a hostile presence.

They sat in silence for several seconds.

"Thank you for sharing this with me," Claire eventually told him.

He nodded. "I wanted you to know. I'm not against all rogues, but hopefully now you can understand why I have such a problem with them."

She definitely could. She smiled at him as she took another bite of toast.

The rest of their breakfast together wasn't nearly as awkward as Claire had feared it would be. In fact, it was surprisingly pleasant. When they said their goodbyes an hour later, she felt certain completing his evaluation wouldn't be a problem, and maybe she could even recommend him for a position with P.I.D.

Chapter 15

After her breakfast with Aaron, Claire stopped at the Hotel Galvez to talk with Isabel. The Galvez was one of the most "haunted" locations on the island and Spencer was keen for a tour. Unfortunately, while there was a Bureau agent assigned to the location, they didn't have any legal jurisdiction there. If a private tour was going to be given, Claire would need special permission.

She walked through the front doors of the lobby and smiled. The Hotel Galvez, nicknamed "The Queen of the Gulf," was built a decade after the 1900 hurricane devastated the island. It was one of many efforts to revitalize the island as it recovered from the deadliest natural disaster in American history. In 2011, the hotel underwent extensive renovations to restore it to its original splendor. One look around the lobby confirmed the project had been well worth the time and effort.

Claire spotted Isabel at her desk next to the front windows, the phone receiver pressed against her ear. Isabel waved and Claire responded with a smile. She crossed the lobby and waited for her friend and fellow agent to finish her phone call.

"Yes, ma'am, and thank you for calling the Hotel Galvez." Isabel hung up the receiver and turned her attention toward Claire. "Hey there. How was the tour last night?"

Claire rolled her eyes. "Bettie and a spirit box. You can probably figure out the rest."

Isabel laughed. "I can't wait to watch the episode." She folded her arms on her desk and leaned forward. "Do I even need to ask why you're here?"

"Probably not, but I'll tell you anyway." Claire forced an overly enthusiastic smile. "The ghost hunters would like a tour of the Galvez, if there's any way you can arrange it."

"I don't think that'll be a problem, but I'll ask my supervisor when she gets in later to be sure. I'm pretty sure she'll be as excited about promoting the hotel's haunted history as the higher-ups at HQ seem to be."

Claire frowned. "I figured you'd say that." She had hoped it wouldn't be so simple. "Just let me know when we can do the tour and we'll be here with bells on."

"Sounds good." Isabel held up a hand. "Hey, before you go, I need to talk to you about something." She looked around the lobby to make sure no one could overhear them. "I'm a little concerned about Jackson. I haven't been able to make contact with him for about a week now."

Leon Jackson was one of the more infamous projections lingering at the Galvez. He was known to haunt the women's restroom near the spa center on the ground floor of the hotel, blowing in guests' ears while they did their business or playing with their hair while they were at the mirrors. He had even appeared reflected in the mirror of several ill-advised selfies in recent years.

Though Jackson was a rogue and not officially under the Bureau's jurisdiction, Isabel was more sympathetic than most agents and did her best to help him whenever she could. It was one of several reasons she and Claire were friends as well as co-workers.

"Sometimes he can be evasive," Isabel told Claire, "so I didn't think anything of it at first. Plus, I was kind of harsh with him the last time we made contact, so he's probably pouting and avoiding me."

Claire looked down the broad, spacious hallway toward the hotel's spa. Normally she wouldn't have been too concerned either, but after the conversation she'd had with Jean Lafitte, this definitely deserved some attention.

"You said it's been about a week?"

Isabel made a face. "Actually, it might even be longer than that. I have to confess I usually steer clear of that bathroom and let him do his own thing. I know an agent shouldn't admit this, but he creeps me out."

Claire chuckled. "I can't say I blame you."

Since energy projections didn't have to worry about any of the concerns that plague the living, like paying bills or going to work or needing to sleep, they tended to be purified and amplified versions of the personality they had when they were alive. Since Jackson had chosen to tether himself to a women's restroom, that spoke volumes about the nature of his projection energy.

"You might have better luck contacting him," Isabel suggested. "I mean, since you're a higher level sensitive than me and he's not mad at you."

"I'll go check it out."

Claire started down the hall toward the restroom, focusing her thoughts and energy on sensing any projections that might be nearby. She certainly didn't fault Isabel for being creeped out by Jackson. Unfortunately, there was no way to predict or control what kind of person left behind an energy projection. The person's energy output level when they were alive played some part, but it was only a part of it. Even after more than three hundred years of Bureau activity, there was still a lot to learn about the whole process.

As Claire approached the women's restroom without feeling any sense of a projection nearby, her apprehension grew. Even if Jackson was trying to avoid her, she should still be able to feel his presence.

She entered the restroom and stood next to the mirror for a full minute. Still no sign of Jackson. A huge knot began to form in the pit of her stomach. This would have been cause for concern under normal circumstances, but in light of Jean Lafitte's missing crewmen...

She left the restroom and made her way to the fifth floor where Audra, one of the Galvez's most active projections was tethered. In the 1950's, Audra and her fiancé were frequent guests of the hotel and always stayed in the same room, room 501. While her fiancé, who was a sailor, was away at sea, Audra would go up to the hotel's west turret every day to look for any signs of his return.

One day she received word that his ship had gone down with no survivors. In her grief and despair, she went to the turret one last time and took her own life. The real tragedy of Audra's story was that the report she received was wrong. Her fiancé hadn't died, but by the time he returned to the island, it was too late. The deed had already been done.

Audra's spirit wasn't particularly problematic, though guests had reported all sorts of strange occurrences in the rooms on the fifth floor. More often than not, the electronic hotel keys didn't work in the lock of room 501, and doors had been known to slam repeatedly when no one was there to close them.

The elevator doors opened and Claire stepped out into the empty hallway. She was relieved to immediately sense Audra's presence. A gentle wave of sadness washed over her as she made her way to room 501, further confirmation of Audra's presence on the floor. Since the projection had never moved past the intensity of her final, pre-death emotions, sadness was her default emotional state. A fact that often made it difficult to have a productive conversation with her.

Claire readied herself as she slipped the master key into the electronic lock. To her surprise, she heard the lock disengage as the light immediately turned green. As soon as Claire pushed the door open, she saw Audra standing next to the window, looking out at the water.

"Hello, Audra," she said quietly.

The projection turned to look at her and let out a heavy sigh. "Hi, Claire. It's so nice of you to come see me today."

"Of course." Claire smiled sadly, allowing her emotions to mirror Audra's as she closed the door behind her. "How are you doing today?"

Audra floated away from the window and took a seat on the edge of the bed. "I'm alright." She let out another sigh and turned her attention back to the window. "We've got lovely weather today."

Claire sat down next to her on the bed. "We certainly do." She joined the projection in looking out the window for several seconds.

"Audra," she finally ventured, "I wanted to ask you if you've had any interactions with Jackson lately or if you've talked to anyone who has. We haven't been able to make contact with him in his usual places."

Audra raised her eyebrows. "Jackson? I'm happy to say that I haven't." She scrunched up her face. "I appreciate the fact that there are five floors between us."

"I understand," Claire assured her. "He can be very unpleasant. But we need to see if we can find him. If something has happened to him, it's best for everyone if we know about it."

Audra thought for a few seconds. Claire could feel her emotions shifting from sadness to genuine concern.

"Why would you think something has happened to him?" Audra eventually asked.

"I'm sure it's nothing," Claire lied, being careful to mask her true emotions. "We're just considering all the possibilities right now as we look into it."

Claire sensed the projection's apprehension waning.

"I guess I can ask the others if they know anything about it," she offered.

"Thank you, Audra," Claire said with a smile. "That would be great. I should be back to lead a tour later this week, so I'll check in with you then if that's okay."

Audra nodded. "I'll see what I can find out."

Claire thanked her again and left the room. The further she got from the room and from Audra's presence, the more her forced optimism faded. If rogues were going missing, then history was repeating itself, and this time nothing would keep her from finding out the truth.

Chapter 16

After Claire left the Galvez, she reported to the candy store for the afternoon shift. The rest of her day was relatively uneventful, though she couldn't stop thinking about the missing rogues. After her shift ended, she stopped by her house to quickly change clothes before the tour on the Strand that night with the ghost hunters. She didn't have time to look into what might be happening with the rogues, so she asked the house projections if they had heard anything about it.

"Oh, a mystery," Thelma squealed, shimmering with excitement. "I'm on it!"

"I wasn't asking you to investigate," Claire told her. "I was just asking if you had heard anything."

"And how am I supposed to hear anything if I'm stuck in this neighborhood until the end of time?"

Claire sighed. As much as she wanted answers, she still wasn't willing to give Thelma permission to venture past her tether zone. At least not yet.

"So, I guess that means you haven't heard anything about missing rogues?"

Sarah looked at April then back at Claire. "Do you think we should be worried?"

Claire shook her head, carefully masking her own feelings of concern. "I don't think so. Since rogues don't follow the same accountability system as Bureau projections, sometimes it's harder to keep up with them. I'm sure they'll turn up soon and there's a perfectly logical explanation for where they've been."

The three projections didn't seem convinced.

"I'll try to talk to some of the projections on the Strand during the tour tonight," Claire told them. "We'll figure it out."

"You know," Thelma said, "there's a way we can find an explanation sooner rather than later."

Claire gave her a look, but she knew Thelma was right. She took a deep breath and let it out slowly. "I'm not going to give you permission to go to the cemetery, but if you could please see what you can learn from the Ghost Net, that would be very helpful." She pointed a finger at her. "Don't leave the neighborhood though."

Thelma shimmered and a pulse of excited energy poured over Claire. "I'll see what I can find," she said before blinking out of sight.

April frowned. "I don't like the idea of Thelma going out by herself, especially not if projections have been disappearing."

"Do you want to go with her?" Claire asked, unable to hide her surprise.

"I don't want to, but I feel like I should."

Claire nodded and April faded from view as well.

"Well," Sarah said when they were alone, "it looks like I'm on my own tonight."

"It's going to be quiet and boring," Claire said with a smile.

The projection slowly faded from view. "And I'm going to love it."

****

Later that night Claire had arranged to meet the ghost hunters at the Railroad Museum on the Strand. It was the best place to start their private tour as far as both location and the level of activity was concerned. The building was the home of several projections, both rogues and Bureau-sanctioned, who liked to make appearances whenever they had the chance.

Claire arrived at the museum a few minutes before the ghost hunters were supposed to get there so she could have a few minutes to talk to the projections. Her best bet was to find Diego, a Bureau-sanctioned projection who had worked as a train conductor for more than twenty years before his death. He loved his job driving trains, so not surprisingly he had chosen to tether himself to the building that used to house the headquarters of the Gulf, Colorado, & Santa Fe Railroad, the company he had worked for. Diego had a friendly and warm personality, and he regularly interacted with rogues as well as other Bureau projections.

Claire entered the darkened building and locked the door behind her. She was scheduled to meet the ghost hunters in about fifteen minutes, so she needed to move fast. She had only taken a few steps across the lobby when the air rippled around her and the translucent form of Stanley, the museum's notorious headless train engineer materialized in front of her.

"Hey, Stanley," she said. "Have you seen Diego?"

Stanley spread his hands out to either side in a "What the hell?" gesture.

Claire cringed. "Sorry. Poor choice of words."

He folded his arms across his chest in agreement.

"I need to talk to Diego," she told him. "It's really important. I don't suppose you know where he is?"

He held up four fingers on his right hand.

"The fourth floor?" she asked.

He gave her a thumb's up.

"Thanks," she told him as she headed toward the bank of elevators. "We'll talk again soon." She cringed again at her own insensitivity but didn't stop to apologize.

When she stepped off the elevator on the fourth floor, she was hit by a wave of sadness and fear. It was coming from Diego. The sickening knot returned to her stomach. She had never known Diego to be anything but cheerful and upbeat. Something serious must have happened.

"Diego?" she called out, feeling her way down the darkened hallway. "I need to talk to you. Can you come out here, please, so I can see you?"

There was no response. Claire could feel the heavy emotions pulling on her, threatening to drag her under. She was about to call out to him again when the air began to ripple a few feet in front of her. The glow of Diego's projection was faint, as if he couldn't, or didn't want to, expend the energy necessary to make an appearance.

"Hey, Diego," Claire said, trying her best to project positive emotions his way.

"Hi, Claire," he said softly. He let out a heavy sigh and looked away from her.

"Diego, what's wrong?" she asked. "You seem so sad."

He sighed again, floating listlessly in the middle of the hallway, but didn't respond. The deep despair he was projecting brought tears to Claire's eyes.

"Diego, please tell me what happened," she pressed.

"It's Greta," he eventually said. "She's gone."

Claire's heart began to pound in her chest. Greta was another projection that made her home in the Railroad Museum. She was the rogue projection of a woman who had committed suicide by jumping out a sixth story women's restroom window.

"What do you mean she's gone?" Claire asked. "Did someone help her move on?"

Diego shook his head vigorously and another wave of sorrow rolled over Claire. "They took her," he sobbed.

"Who took her?"

"The agents. They dispatched her. Right there in front of me."

Claire frowned. No one had told her about a P.I.D. team being on the island. That would explain the missing rogues, but she couldn't imagine her brother would send a team without letting her know about it, especially when there had been no reports of troublesome rogues in the area.

"How do you know they were agents?" Claire asked.

"They had the tool."

Claire's frown deepened. "What offenses did they accuse Greta of?"

He shook his head again. "None. They just dispatched her."

It was against Bureau policy to dispatch troublesome rogues without making them aware of their offenses and giving them the opportunity to explain themselves. It was the metaphysical equivalent of a legal trial, and it was an absolute, non-negotiable requirement.

"And you saw it?"

"I was right there next to her when it happened," he insisted. "And I couldn't do anything to stop them."

Another breech in protocol. No other projections were supposed to be present when a rogue was dispatched.

Claire took a step toward him. "What do you mean, Diego? Are you saying they wouldn't answer your questions?"

A wrinkle of confusion creased his brow. "Not exactly," he eventually said. "I don't think I *tried* to interact with them."

"You don't *think* you tried?" Claire pressed.

He stared at her for several seconds, clearly trying hard to remember.

"Diego, this is important," Claire told him. "I need to know if the P.I.D. illegally dispatched Greta, and if they ignored your protests about it."

"It's all a little fuzzy," he admitted. "I remember I was on the sixth floor talking to Greta, and then those men came in the room." He paused, reliving the moment. "And then I just stood there as they drained her. I couldn't move."

"Did the men say anything before they dispatched her?"

Diego shook his head. His face clouded over and the wave of sadness in the room swelled. "I was so afraid they'd dispatch me next. but they just left once Greta was gone."

Claire had more questions than she could begin to ask, but it was clear Diego was in no condition to help her find any answers. She was sorry for the pain he was experiencing, but it would eventually wear off. Projections retained the emotions of their previous lives, but any new emotions experienced in their current existence rarely stuck. That meant whatever happened to Greta had happened very recently.

"I'm so sorry you had to witness that," Claire said. "I promise you I'll get to the bottom of things."

Diego nodded half-heartedly and faded from view. The cloud of sadness clung to Claire as she made her way back to the elevator. She had come there that night hoping Diego had some information about missing rogues and she had gotten more than she'd bargained for.

There was no time to make any calls before her tour with the ghost hunters. It would have to wait until the morning. But if there was a P.I.D. team on the island indiscriminately dispatching rogues, there was going to be hell to pay.

Chapter 17

By the time Claire returned to the lobby, Spencer and his team were waiting on the steps in front of the building. She'd hoped the museum would be a good stop for them on their tour, but with Stanley feeling offended and Diego in his current condition, it was best to leave it for another time.

As Claire crossed the lobby, she spotted Drew through the window of the front door. He was dressed in a pair of jeans and a dark hoodie, but he still looked amazing. She mentally slapped herself across the face to get her head back in the game, but it didn't seem to do much good. With a resigned sigh, she took a deep breath and pushed the door open.

"There she is!" Spencer said as Claire stepped out onto the landing.

Claire smiled. "Hey, sorry I'm late. I needed to check on a few things in here before we started our tour. They've got a lot of renovations going on throughout the building, so it looks like we'll need to start someplace else."

Spencer looked completely dejected, as if he had just heard about the death of a loved one. "Oh man, I really wanted to see if we could make contact with the headless train engineer."

"Not tonight," she told him. "Sorry."

"That's okay," Drew said. "I'm sure there are plenty of other haunted places we can check out around here."

"Definitely," Claire assured them all.

She descended the stairs and led them across the street and down a block. The first location she wanted them to visit was the Hutchings-

Sealy Building. They stopped on the sidewalk in front of the building and Claire turned to face the group.

"This building was built in 1895. It's one of the earliest examples of a steel-framed structure in the entire state. It has survived every single hurricane and flood that has hit the island, including the 1900 hurricane. And it's that storm in particular that's to thank for most of the paranormal activity we have here."

She unlocked the door and led the way inside. She could feel the presence of several projections that were tethered there, but there was an undercurrent of apprehension around them as well. Was it possible they had already heard about what happened to Greta?

Claire led the ghost hunters to the second floor where the projection of Mona spent most of her time. Mona was a school marm who had found herself trapped in the Hutchings-Sealy building during the 1900 hurricane. It was unlucky for her, but lucky for the dozens of people she pulled out of the flood waters to safety throughout the course of that fateful night.

Claire suggested Spencer and his team set up in one of the rooms then excused herself to go to the restroom. They weren't the only ones who had an investigation to conduct.

She stepped into a nearby room and waited, though she didn't have to wait long. The air rippled in the room as Mona and two other projections, Malcolm and Lorenzo, materialized in front of her. Claire had jokingly nicknamed the two projections Mona's lackeys since they accompanied her everywhere. Their devotion was an expression of gratitude for having been pulled from the flood, even though neither one of them had lived through that fateful night.

"Oh, Claire, we're so relieved it's you!" Mona exclaimed. "We were so worried!"

"Hey guys," Claire said softly. "I guess you heard about what happened to Greta."

They all three nodded in unison.

"It's just horrible," Mona said. "I can't believe the Bureau would dispatch her like that."

"Let's not make any assumptions," Claire said, though she knew how ridiculous it sounded given the circumstances. "I promised Diego I'd look into it and I will. First thing tomorrow."

The three projections seemed to relax a little.

Malcolm nodded toward the other room. "So, what's this you've brought us? A private tour?"

Claire gave him a look. "I'm sure you know that's exactly what it is."

Lorenzo smiled. "Ghost hunters." He elbowed Malcolm. "This should be fun."

Claire pointed a finger in his direction. "Be nice. Give them some good readings, but don't go overboard."

Malcolm frowned. "How come Bettie gets to have all the fun?"

"Bettie received a firm reprimand," Claire assured him. They didn't seem intimidated. "Seriously, though. Don't go overboard with this."

Malcolm nodded reluctantly and Claire returned to the room where she had left Spencer and the team. They already had several pieces of equipment out and fired up.

"You ready?" she asked.

"As we'll ever be," Drew replied.

Claire smiled and led the way into the hallway. "On the morning of September 8, 1900, the residents of Galveston Island were all going about their day just like they would any other day, even though the island had already begun to flood. The skies were clear for the most part, and children were even out playing in the flood waters. At that time, scientists didn't have a way to forecast tropical cyclones, which is what they called hurricanes back then, so the island's residents had no idea what was barreling toward them out in the Gulf of Mexico."

She stopped in the doorway to one of the rooms in the southeast corner of the building. "By that evening, the entire island was underwater. The highest natural spot on the island at that time was only eight or nine feet above sea level, so there was no place for residents to escape the fifteen-foot storm surge." She entered the room and the ghost hunters followed. "That day, a school marm named Mona had sought refuge here on the second floor of the Hutchings-Sealy building.

As the storm raged through the night, she could hear people crying out for help in the storm surge outside. In the darkness, she reached her hand out that window," she pointed across the room, "and began pulling in whoever she could, whether they were alive or dead. She saved dozens of people that night, though not all of them made it to see the next morning."

"That's incredible," Drew said. "What a heroic story."

"This place is hopping with activity," Luke said, studying his K2 meter. "We're getting spikes all over the place."

"How many ghosts are in the building?" Spencer asked Claire.

"Several," she told him, "but Mona is by far the most active."

"Did she die here, too?" Drew asked.

Claire shook her head. "No, we don't know exactly when and where she died."

That wasn't entirely true. The Bureau did know the details of Mona's death, but those details weren't written in any historical records that could be verified. The information came from Mona's projection herself, but Claire couldn't exactly tell the ghost hunters that.

Luke scanned the room with a thermal imagining camera, hoping to pick up significant changes in temperature, mainly any cold spots that might indicate the presence of a ghost. This bit of technology actually had the right idea for spotting projections. If a projection chose to manifest, they had to pull energy from the air around them, leaving behind a cold spot. Thermal imaging devices allow non-sensitives, or sensitives who lacked Visual Acumen, to see the heat signatures.

Drew tapped Luke on the shoulder. "Point it toward the window. I feel like we've got some activity over there."

Claire smiled. He was right. Mona and Lorenzo had indeed chosen to manifest by the window.

"I think I've got something," Luke said, looking intently into his camera. "There are two figures over by the window, just like you said."

"What are they doing?" Spencer asked, moving slowly to join Luke, clearly not wanting to spook the ghosts.

"I think they're just standing there," Luke said. "No, wait, now they're bent down, like they're reaching out the window, just like Claire said Mona did."

Claire shook her head. Re-enacting the events of that night was a bit melodramatic, but the ghost hunters were clearly eating it up. She'd have to thank Mona and her lackeys later.

"I'd like to do an EVP session in this room, if that's okay," Drew said. "I feel like they've got some things to tell us."

Claire nodded. "Of course. This is your investigation. You guys can do whatever you like."

Drew turned on his digital recorder and began asking questions in hope of recording an electronic voice phenomenon. Claire knew this was a favorite tactic employed by ghost hunters, as well as sensitives who lacked the Communicative Acumen, but it wasn't a very reliable means of communication. Projections had to expend a great deal of energy to manipulate the recording devices, and often their utterances were incomprehensible, which left any interpretation susceptible to listener bias.

Drew clicked off the digital recorder and smiled at Claire. "If we get anything good after we check the data, would it be possible to come back later to follow up?"

Claire shrugged. "Sure, if that's what you want."

When they left the Hutchings-Sealy building, the hunters were pumped up. Thanks to Mona and her lackeys, they had gotten all kinds of readings and data. Claire stood on the sidewalk for a few seconds, trying to decide where to take them next. In their excitement, they were all talking at the same time, so she didn't even try to ask for their input.

They had walked about a block from the Hutchings-Sealy building when she spotted a large group of people standing on the sidewalk about fifty feet ahead of them. The figure standing in the center of the crowd told her immediately that it was another tour group, and it was being led by a rival company to the Bureau's. The owner of this company was flashy and over-the-top, and Claire definitely didn't feel like dealing with him that night.

She stopped in the middle of the sidewalk, debating the best course of action. Up ahead, a car full of drunken tourists drove past the other tour group, making loud ghost noises out the window as they did.

Tremont House it is, she thought. The old hotel definitely had its share of projections, and it was only a block south of the Strand, which made it close enough to be worth the walk.

As Claire led the way to the other side of the street, Spencer pointed to the large tour group. "What's that?"

"Nothing I have the energy to deal with tonight," Claire told him.

Chapter 18

As they made their way to the Tremont House hotel, Claire began to feel apprehensive. She hadn't originally planned to take the hunters to the hotel because Marshall, the projection of the gambling salesman that was tethered there, could be pretty ornery. So far Drew and his team had mostly had positive interactions with the island's projections. Odds were very good that was about to change.

As they approached the intersection of Mechanic and 23rd, Claire had just begun her history lesson when someone rounded the corner ahead of them coming in their direction. She was so surprised to realize who it was that she almost forgot why she was there in the first place.

"Philip?"

He stopped short, clearly as surprised to see Claire as she was to see him. "Claire!" he exclaimed, recovering his composure. "How good to see you." He took in the sight of the ghost hunters behind her. "Are you leading a tour? You don't usually work during the week, do you?"

"Not usually, no, but this was a special assignment."

"Lucky you."

Claire smiled. It was strange to see Philip away from the candy store. "So, what are you up to at this hour of the night?"

He looked down at his watch then looked back toward the hotel entrance. For the first time since Claire had met him, he seemed uncertain what to say next. "Um, well, I met a friend for dinner and drinks at the Tremont House. I guess the time got away from us."

It was a perfectly reasonable explanation since the Tremont House was famous for its rooftop bar. Claire couldn't understand why Philip seemed so uncomfortable answering the question, until a thought struck her. Perhaps Philip's friend wasn't of the male variety, and perhaps the dinner and drinks had ended a while back and their activities at the hotel might not have been the kind that he wanted to share them with her.

Claire could feel her face getting warm. "Well, it was great to see you," she blurted out, not wanting to prolong the awkward moment. "We better get on with our tour."

"You have a good time," Philip said, clearly just as relieved to end the conversation.

As he passed by them on the sidewalk, Claire realized that a part of her was slightly hurt at the thought that Philip might have a lady friend. She blamed Monica and all her romantic notions for putting even the slightest thought of it into her head.

She turned to the ghost hunters behind her and smiled, probably broader than she needed to. "So," she said, motioning to the building next to them, "this section of the hotel was built in 1817. It served as a brothel for decades, and at one time it was even owned by the famous pirate Jean Lafitte."

"Does Jean Lafitte haunt this place?" Keith asked enthusiastically.

Claire chuckled. The mention of Jean's name always piqued people's interest. "Unfortunately, no, but there are several interesting and active spirits that linger here." She led them around to the front of the building. "The one that's spotted the most often is the ghost of a gambling salesman…"

Chapter 19

When Claire finally returned home after the Strand tour, it was close to three in the morning. She had the afternoon shift at the candy store the next day, so she was looking forward to sleeping in a little. As soon as she walked in the front door, the drowsiness poured over her. Maybe it was the quietness of the house with two of the three projections out investigating, but she went straight to her room and flopped into bed.

Claire had only been asleep for about an hour when a noise woke her.

"Psst!"

She refused to open her eyes, hoping it had been her imagination. Since projections had no need to sleep, they often forgot how desperately the living needed their rest.

"Psst, Claire!" someone said in a stage whisper. "Are you sleeping?"

Claire groaned and rolled over, covering her face with her pillow. "I *was* sleeping."

"Well, now that you're up," Thelma said, her translucent form hunched over so her face was right next to Claire's, "we've got some news about the missing rogues."

Claire moved the pillow and stared up at the ceiling. "What did you find out?"

"Jackson isn't the only projection on the island that's missing," April announced from behind Thelma.

Thelma glared up at her. "I wanted to tell her!" She turned her attention back to Claire before April could ruin any more of her presentation. "There are at least a dozen rogues missing around the island."

By that time, Claire was sitting up in bed. "Are you serious?"

Thelma nodded enthusiastically. "That's why all the rogues have been meeting at the cemetery. It wasn't a party after all." Her face took on a somber expression. "This sounds pretty serious. You probably should have told the Bureau about those meetings."

Claire didn't even acknowledge the comment. Instead, she laid back onto her pillow and put her arm over her eyes.

"I'll make some phone calls in the morning," she assured them.

"That's not all," Thelma insisted.

Claire sighed. "I feel like I'm going to regret asking…"

"Bettie said that woman was on the tour *again* tonight."

"What woman?" Claire asked, moving her arm to look at Thelma, though she was pretty sure she already knew the answer.

"That Ann woman." Thelma wrinkled her nose in disgust. "The one that gave you those books. She's quite the dingle dangler."

Claire let out another sigh. "I'm going to tell you the same thing I've told Bettie a dozen times. Ann is harmless. I don't know why you keep getting all worked up about it."

"Well, it's ridiculous," Thelma insisted. "I mean, what more can the woman possibly think she's going to learn on those tours? You guys say the same thing every time."

Claire gave her a disapproving look but let the jab slide. "I don't understand why it upsets you all so much. So what if that she was on the tour again?"

"She's been poking her nose into Bureau business for months," April said, as if it were Claire's fault. "I'm afraid she won't give up until she learns the truth about us." She shivered, even though she couldn't possibly be cold. "Every time that woman pops up somewhere, it sets us all on edge."

Claire covered her eyes again, hoping the projections would both get the message.

"It's like she's a stalker or something," Thelma continued dramatically, clearly missing Claire's hint.

Claire peeked out from underneath her arm. "If she's stalking anyone, it's me. Besides, you guys should be flattered Ann is showing so much interest in the haunted history of the island. It means we're doing our jobs."

Thelma shook her head. "I don't trust her. She knows too much about the Bureau."

"She *thinks* she knows about the Bureau," Claire corrected. "All she has is conjecture and speculation, and no self-respecting agent is going to confirm any of her ideas."

Thelma leaned in close. "But what if she really does find out the truth and she tells the whole world? What will happen to us all then?"

"Absolutely nothing," Claire tried to assure her. "You know as well as I do that there is a whole division within the Bureau whose job is to discredit people like her. The rest of the world will just think she's crazy. The Bureau has managed to maintain secrecy for centuries. I seriously doubt it'll get derailed by one over-zealous writer."

"I think you should ask Craig to ban her from the tours," April suggested.

"He wouldn't," Claire told her, "and I wouldn't ask him to." She rolled onto her side so her back was facing them. "And besides, right now Ann is the least of my concerns."

Claire closed her eyes but knew sleep would evade her. Eventually she felt the energy from the two projections leave the room. She opened her eyes and stared into the darkness. Yes, Ann Menefee and her overly enthusiastic pursuit of the island's ghosts was the least troubling thing Claire had to deal with. If rogues were disappearing again, she needed to find out why. But before she reported anything to anyone at the Bureau, she needed to conduct some extensive research of her own. She couldn't afford to go off half-cocked. This time, she needed to be sure.

Chapter 20

Later that day, while Claire was on a break during her shift at the candy store, she made a call she really didn't want to make. She had to proceed with caution, but she also needed to know if the problem of missing rogues was limited to Galveston or if it was more widespread. There were only a few people connected to the Bureau that she felt comfortable looping in, so she made the call.

As the phone in her hand continued to ring, she held her breath. Finally, the call connected and a familiar voice answered.

"You've got Jeff."

"Hey friend," Claire said, a genuine smile on her face. "How're things in The Big Easy?"

"Oh, you know, same ol', same ol'."

Claire chuckled. She and Jeff had gone through agent training together, which meant they had known each other for close to ten years. They had dated for most of their time in the training program, and when their service assignments were handed out, they were thrilled to be assigned to the same city.

Their first year in San Francisco had been great, but then Claire had messed everything up, both for her career at the Bureau and for any potential relationship she and Jeff might have had. When the Bureau's official investigation into the missing rogues failed to turn up any explanation, or even any real evidence, Claire was reassigned to Atlanta. Shortly thereafter, Jeff had asked for a transfer to New Orleans, where he had been serving ever since.

"So," Jeff asked after a few moments of silence hung across the phone line, "is this a business call or a social call?"

Claire smiled again. Straight to the point, as always. "Unfortunately, this is a business call," she admitted. "I wish we had time to catch up, but right now I need to know if you've had any reports of strange things going on there in New Orleans."

"I guess it depends on what you mean by 'strange'," he said. "Normal person strange, or Bureau strange?"

"Bureau strange."

"I can't think of anything out of the ordinary." He was silent for a few seconds. "Is there something specific you're wanting to ask me about?"

She took a deep breath. "I was wondering if you guys have had any disappearances."

Jeff let out a loud sigh. "Claire, please tell me you're not starting this up again."

Claire's defenses immediately went up. "We both know I wasn't wrong before." She felt hot tears threatening to spill as the memories rushed back. "The investigation wasn't conclusive."

"I know it wasn't," Jeff said, his tone softer than it had been before. "But I'm not sure your career with the Bureau can take another hit like it did in San Francisco. I don't want to see you throw away everything you've worked so hard for."

"I'm not going to," she tried to assure him. "I'm being very careful this time. I'm seriously looking into it before I talk to anyone at headquarters."

"Does that include your dad?"

Again, she felt defensive. "That's not fair. My dad only did what he thought was right."

"Still, going over Zach's head like that..." Jeff paused. "It may have been the right thing to do, but that doesn't make the consequences any easier to accept."

Claire took several deep breaths. She couldn't afford to let her emotions about the past cloud her judgment in the present. "So, no disappearances then," she pressed ahead, bringing the conversation back to the problem at hand.

"None that I've heard of." Jeff thankfully followed her lead and let the past drop. "But I'm pretty sure you aren't asking about registered projections, are you?"

Claire frowned. "Well, that would concern me, of course, but no, I'm not asking about registered projections."

"I didn't think so." He was silent for several seconds, probably weighing how involved he wanted to get this time. "Give me a few days to look into it."

Claire smiled despite the seriousness of the situation. "Thanks, Jeff. You're the best."

They disconnected the call and Claire sat in the break room, considering her options. It would be torture to wait a few days without taking any actions, but this time she needed to be careful. If headquarters needed to be brought in, she couldn't be the only one involved in the initial investigation.

She dropped her phone back into the pocket of her apron and returned to the front of the store. She had barely made it back to her station before she spotted Ann passing by the front window. Claire groaned, debating whether to make a run for the break room or simply duck down behind the counter until she left. Since she wouldn't be able to explain either action to any of her co-workers, she decided to stay put.

Not surprisingly, Ann spotted Claire as soon as she walked in the door and headed straight in her direction.

"Hey, Ann," Claire said, trying not show her irritation. "What can I get for you today?"

Ann waved an accusing finger in Claire's direction. "You didn't lead the Ashton Villa tour last night. We were stuck with boring old Aaron." She shook her head. "There was no chance Bettie was going to make an appearance with him leading the tour."

Claire chuckled. "Sorry. I was on the Strand with another assignment."

Ann looked confused. "The Strand? I didn't see that tour on the website. I definitely would have signed up for it."

Claire cringed. "Well, it wasn't exactly open to the public."

Ann's eyes grew wide. "A private tour? You said you guys don't give private tours."

"Normally, we don't," she assured her, "but this was kind of a special case. My boss assigned it to me, and I didn't really have a choice about it."

"Friends of the boss, huh?" Ann asked with a wink. "Can I meet them? Maybe I should give them a copy of my book and see what they think."

Claire thought for a second. The idea of unleashing Ann and her theories on Spencer was tempting. It might be fun to watch, but ultimately, she decided against it.

"Still clinging to your conspiracy theories, huh?" she said instead. "It was just a group of ghost hunters with a web series. My boss thought it would be fun, and good publicity for our company. That's all."

"If you insist." Ann picked up a bag of taffy and handed a $20 bill across the counter. "I still want to hear your thoughts when you finish my books."

"Of course," Claire partially lied, accepting the money and ringing up the purchase. "I'm waiting for a little free time so I can read them."

Ann smiled as she accepted her change, though not as enthusiastically as she had in the past. Claire felt a twinge of guilt as she watched her leave the store. She couldn't keep deflecting the woman forever without seriously hurting her feelings. One of these days, she was going to have to actually read her books.

Chapter 21

A few minutes before Claire's shift was about to end that afternoon, she felt what was becoming a familiar sensation. An involuntary smile crept across her lips as she focused a little too much attention on straightening the decorative boxes of candy behind the counter.

"Hey, Claire," Drew said as he approached her station.

She turned around, feigning surprise. "Oh, hey Drew. What are you up to?"

"I was heading back to the hotel and I thought I'd stop and pick up some candy for the guys. It looks like it's going to be another late night sorting through all the data and recordings." He studied the candies in the display case. "What do you recommend?"

"I think we've got just the thing."

She came out from behind the counter and headed toward the bins of taffy. He followed her across the store and selected a large bag of assorted flavors, then they returned to the counter so Claire could ring up his order.

"Would you like to go get some coffee or something when you get off work?" he asked as she handed him his change.

Claire looked at her watch. Officially her shift didn't end for another ten minutes, but if there was ever going to be a time to clock out early, this was it.

"Give me a minute," she told him before crossing the store to Monica's station. "Hey," she said, sidling up to her coworker. "I'm going to clock out a few minutes early if that's okay with you."

Monica raised her eyebrows. She looked around the candy store and spotted Drew. With a knowing smile, she said, "Sure. That won't be a problem."

"Thanks." Claire gave her a wink and a huge smile as she untied her apron and headed back to the counter where Drew was waiting.

A few minutes later, Drew held the door open for her as they stepped out onto the sidewalk. "My truck is around the corner if you don't feel like walking."

Claire shrugged. "The weather's pretty nice today. I wouldn't mind a little exercise." She pointed down the street. "There's a cute little café a few blocks down."

"Sounds perfect."

In typical Gulf Coast fashion, the temperature had warmed back up from the cold front they'd had earlier in the week. Where people had been wearing jackets and coats a few days before, today they were dressed in shorts and t-shirts.

Though the sidewalks weren't crowded with tourists, the Strand district was still bustling with activity. They hadn't walked an entire block before Claire spotted one of the local projections peering at them through a shop window. Claire frowned. Projections were as bad about gossiping as old ladies in a knitting bee. It wouldn't take an hour before word got around the island that she was taking a walk with one of the ghost hunters.

"Is everything okay?" Drew asked, studying her face.

She smiled up at him. "Yeah, everything's fine. I was just thinking about work."

"Which work? Candy store or ghost tours?"

Claire chuckled. "Not a lot of stress at the candy store."

Drew frowned. "I hope we're not causing you any stress."

Claire shook her head. "No, I don't mind leading your tours." To her surprise, she realized she wasn't lying, and she suspected Drew's presence had something to do with that. She spotted another iridescent face watching as they approached the next building and sighed again. "It's just some of the people I work with can be a little childish sometimes."

He nodded. "I know what that's like. Think about who I've been hanging out with for the past week."

They stopped at an intersection next to the café and Claire glanced at Drew from the corner of her eye. "Can I ask you a question?" she said as they waited for the light to change.

"Of course. You can ask me anything."

She turned to look at him. "Why do you do this? The ghost hunting, I mean. You've taken two weeks off from your real job to come down here and investigate these places. I can't help but be curious as to why."

The light changed and they started to cross the street. He took her hand as he stepped out of the way of a group of passing tourists, pulling her along with him until they were safely out of the flow of traffic. She couldn't tell if he was being a gentleman or if he was avoiding her question.

They reached the café and Drew glanced at the menu posted outside. "Can I answer your question over coffee?"

She smiled. "Of course."

They ordered their drinks then sat down at one of the tables arranged on the sidewalk.

"Alright," he said after he had taken a sip. "Here we go. I guess the simplest answer is that I want to understand the spiritual world better." He shook his head. "There's so much we don't know about ghosts and why they exist and how they operate and how they interact with us. I'm hoping to get a better understanding of all that."

Claire nodded, feeling like a complete jerk for keeping the truth from him. "That makes sense," she said instead. A warm breeze blew a few strands of her hair into her face and she brushed them aside. "Do you think your need to understand is because you got scratched when you were younger, or maybe because of your blue lady?"

He thought for a second. "Probably a little of both, though obviously one experience was much more pleasant than the other."

Claire smiled. "What do your parents think about you and Keith chasing ghosts?"

He shrugged. "Honestly, they think it's kind of silly. After we moved when I was a kid, they never talked about the blue lady again, at least not with me. I don't think they've ever put much stock in the idea of paranormal things. My dad used to be a science professor at Lamar University, so he prefers dealing with things he can test and prove in a lab."

"That makes perfect sense for a professor."

Drew's expression clouded over. "Well, he's not a professor any-more." He cleared his throat. "He teaches high school biology now."

Claire nodded, confused by the sudden change in his demeanor. It was clearly a touchy subject and she got the feeling she shouldn't pry. When he didn't offer any more details, she decided to change the subject.

"Would you tell me a little more about the colors you see when there are spirits around? I didn't want to press the issue the other night, but I'm really curious about that."

He seemed hesitant to go into it. She didn't want to seem like she was interrogating him, but she desperately wanted to know more about him. Honestly, she wanted to know everything about him.

She was about to tell him, "Never mind," when he finally answered.

"Like I said the other night, most of the spirits we interact with usually show up kind of like a green or blue cloud. I can sometimes make out a human-like shape, but not always."

Claire nodded slowly, convinced her earlier suspicions were correct. Drew had Force Perceptive Acumen, the most rare and highly valued acumen. In Bureau circles, sensitives with Force Perceptive Acumen were often referred to as unicorns. Claire had only met one other person in her entire life who had it and he served in a very high po-sition in the Bureau, largely due to possessing the coveted ability. Once she submitted Drew's name to her superiors, they wouldn't waste any time trying to recruit him.

"Was Bettie a green cloud the other night?" Claire asked. "Or could you see a human form?"

He smiled. "No, she was a cloud…a frisky green cloud."

Claire looked at the buildings around them. "And what about now? Do you see any clouds here?"

He looked around. "The sun's too bright. I see the colors best when it's dark. But I can tell these buildings are full of spirits. I can feel them." He smiled at her. "I wish we could've seen more of the Strand last night so we could have interacted with them."

Claire took another sip of her coffee. "Maybe next time."

The waitress brought their bill and Drew insisted on paying. She was happy to let him, even though it meant their time together might be coming to an end. He set a few bills on the table, then took her hand as they started walking again. Clearly, she wasn't the only one who wanted to spend a little more time together.

They walked a few blocks in silence. Claire was surprised that it didn't feel awkward at all. When they arrived at the intersection of the Strand and 21st St, she suggested they have a seat next to the fountain there.

"Tell me more about the red spirits," she said as they sat down. She wasn't ready to drop the subject of the colors yet.

Drew chuckled and Claire could feel her face flush. She hadn't intended to interrogate him about it, but Force Perceptives were so rare she couldn't help being curious.

"If you don't want to talk about this anymore, I completely understand," she told him. "It's no big deal."

"No," he said, "it's fine. I don't mind talking about it with you." He chuckled again. "It's just that I asked you out so I can get to know you better, but we've spent most of our time talking about me."

Claire couldn't hide her smile. "Next time we'll talk about me," she lied.

That seemed to appease him, though Claire knew it would never happen. What could she possibly have to tell him about herself? Her whole life revolved around the Bureau and projections, and those weren't topics she could go into without proper authorization.

"And the red spirits?" Claire prompted, returning the conversation to a topic she was more comfortable with.

Drew's expression grew serious. "Unfortunately, yes, I've encountered more of those over the years than I would have liked." He fidgeted slightly in his seat. "And like we said the other night, those are the ones we try to avoid."

Claire couldn't be certain, but she was pretty sure she knew what type of projection he was describing. They were usually left behind by people who had been involved in dark forces, like demonic activity or voodoo or witchcraft, and the projections that remained were simply pure evil. The Bureau labeled them as Malevolent Entities, and P.I.D. teams had little tolerance for them. As an agent, Claire avoided interaction with them unless absolutely necessary, like if one of her registered projections was in trouble.

"Was it one of those entities that scratched you when you were in high school?"

He took a deep breath. The other night he hadn't seemed keen on talking about it, but she needed to understand the extent of his interactions with projections.

He nodded slowly as if remembering the whole event. "There was an abandoned house in our town that everyone said was haunted. I always felt like there was something off about the place, but I had no idea how to explain it to people. I told myself I was just letting the stories freak me out." He paused. "One Halloween, a bunch of us were driving past the house and one of the other guys dared me to go in." He shrugged. "I didn't want to look like a wuss in front of this girl I had a thing for, so I took him up on the dare. I knew as soon as I entered the house there was an evil presence there, but I couldn't exactly run back out again." He frowned. "I had been in the house for about thirty minutes when I heard this deep, gravelly voice say, 'Get out!' That's when I felt this burning sensation across the back of my neck. I left as fast as my feet would carry me. When I got back to the car, the others saw some bright red marks, three parallel scratches, on my neck, right where I had felt the burning sensation."

"That must have been terrifying," Claire said honestly. She'd had plenty of negative interactions with projections in her life, but she'd also been taught from a young age about the true nature of the entities she was dealing with. She could only imagine what it would be like to encounter them without knowing the truth.

Drew shrugged again. "The whole experience definitely taught me to be more cautious, and to trust my instincts. I knew something wasn't right then, and I certainly don't ignore those feelings now."

Claire nodded again. "That's good."

He studied her face for a few seconds. "You know, it's not only spirits that have colors."

She raised her eyebrows. "Really?'

He nodded. "Most *people* have a faint blue or green glow around them, too, kind of like a halo around their whole body, or when the picture isn't clear on a TV screen. Some people are other colors, too, mostly purple and orange and yellow, but I don't come across those very often."

"What color am I?" Claire wanted to know. She prayed he wouldn't say, "Yellow." She looked horrible in yellow.

A smile slowly crept across his lips. "Honestly, I've never met anyone like you before."

Claire frowned. "What do you mean?"

His smile widened as he turned to look at her. "I've never met anyone who's your color."

"What color am I?"

He shrugged. "I don't even know how to describe it." He studied her for a few seconds. "Actually, you're not one single color. You're more like a mix of a bunch of colors, like what you see in a soap bubble."

Claire laughed. "I'm a soap bubble?"

He looked embarrassed. "I can't think of a better way to describe it. You've got a bunch of colors that keep shifting and moving all around you. It makes me think of a soap bubble."

Claire thought about it for a few seconds. "And you've never met anyone with those kinds of colors before?"

He shook his head.

Claire nibbled at her bottom lip. Her knowledge of Force Perceptive Acumen was limited, so she could only speculate about what he was telling her. It made sense that the various colors probably corresponded to a person's sensitivity level or acumens, though Claire couldn't say for sure. If that was the case, it would explain why Claire wasn't one single color. Since she was a high-level sensitive who possessed almost all of the acumens to one degree or another, it would make sense that her colors could be confusing to him.

She looked across the street and spotted several translucent faces peering through the windows of one of the buildings. She had completely forgotten that Hendley Green, where they were sitting, was directly across from what used to be a Civil War hospital. If news of her outing with Drew hadn't already made its way around the island, it wouldn't be a secret much longer.

"Okay," Claire said standing up quickly, "I think I should probably be getting home." She couldn't think of a reasonable-sounding excuse, but since she certainly couldn't tell him the truth, this lamely abrupt ending to their "date" was the best she could manage.

Drew looked confused. "Um, yeah," he said, standing up as well, "I guess I need to get back to the hotel anyway. We've got another long night of sorting through data, and Spencer is probably getting pretty frothy about how long I've been gone already."

They made their way back to the candy store where both of their vehicles were parked. Claire forced herself not to ask any more questions about his acumens or his experiences with projections. For the rest of their time together, short though she had ensured it would be, she wanted to pretend she was a normal single woman on a coffee date with an attractive man. The truth of her crazy life would come flooding back soon enough, but at least for a little while she could pretend.

Chapter 22

"Tell us all about him!" Thelma squealed before Claire had even taken a step inside the house.

Claire pushed past her, shivering at the contact. "What are you talking about?"

"The ghost hunter," April said. "We heard you had a date with one of the ghost hunters."

Claire sighed. "It wasn't a date. We just went for coffee."

"Well, from what we heard, you two looked pretty friendly with each other," Thelma insisted. "Everyone said so."

Claire rolled her eyes. The Ghost Net had struck again. "Even if we were," she said, "it really isn't anyone's business."

"Can he talk to us?" Thelma asked.

"I don't know."

"If he's as strong a sensitive as everyone's saying," Thelma said, "I bet he definitely can talk to us."

"Unfortunately, you'll probably never know, because you're never going to meet him."

"That is so unfair!" Thelma stuck out her lip in an exaggerated pout. "All the Strand projections have met him."

"Not exactly," Claire said. "They only participated in a single paranormal investigation. There wasn't a whole lot of interaction last night."

"Claire, you know you have to be careful with men like that," Sarah said as she floated toward her.

Claire frowned. "Men like what? You don't even know him."

"Maybe not," Sarah admitted, "but he's a ghost hunter and you work for the Bureau. He's already knocking at the door of the paranormal, and you can't risk breaking Bureau secrecy."

Claire set her purse on the table in the entryway and headed for the kitchen, the three projections right on her heels. She poured herself a glass of juice and leaned against the counter.

"I don't think Bureau secrecy is going to be a problem for long." She took a sip of her drink. "He's a Force Perceptive."

"Ooooh," Thelma said in a hushed voice. "I've never met one of those before."

Sarah nodded. "You're right. The Bureau will definitely snatch him up as soon as he's on their radar." She looked at the other two projections. "He'll probably be offered a position at headquarters."

Claire didn't say anything. What was there to say? Sarah was right. Drew would certainly be a hot commodity once the Bureau found out about him.

"A Force Perceptive," April said thoughtfully. "I've never met one of those before either."

"If you ask me," Thelma gushed, "that makes him even sexier."

April frowned. "We didn't ask, and you don't even know what he looks like."

Thelma huffed. "Maybe not, but the descriptions of him were very…well…descriptive."

"Have you already turned his name in to the Bureau?" Sarah asked.

Claire shook her head.

Thelma looked confused. "Why not? You're goofy about him, aren't you?"

Claire took another sip of her drink, not wanting to throw any fuel on the fire.

"That's the problem, isn't it?" April asked.

Claire set her glass down on the counter and began preparations to make dinner. There was little chance the projections would drop the issue, but she could hope.

"What do you mean?" Thelma asked April, as if Claire wasn't there.

"How many agents are on the island already?" April asked.

"Three."

April gave Claire a sympathetic look. "If this ghost hunter joins the Bureau, they're not going to assign a fourth agent here."

Thelma's face fell. "Oh, Claire, I was so hoping your luck with men had changed. We really wanted to see a handcuff on that ring finger of yours." She floated over to where Claire was standing next to the stove and placed a hand on her shoulder. "It's so sad. You finally find love only to have him snatched away from you."

Claire slammed the frying pan down on the stove with more force than she had intended. "It's not love," she insisted. "It was just coffee." She looked down at the pan, suddenly not in the mood to make dinner anymore. "I'm ordering a pizza."

"And then maybe we can watch a movie," Thelma suggested. Her heartbreak over Claire's shattered love life forgotten.

Claire sighed as she picked up her phone. "Sure, we can watch a movie, too."

Claire was thankful the subject of the conversation had changed, but unfortunately, she couldn't switch off her emotions as easily as the projections could. Of course, she knew Drew would be an asset to the Bureau, and it was her responsibility to turn in his name for possible recruitment, but Sarah had hit the nail on the head. There was no way the Bureau would assign a fourth agent to the island, which meant there was no future for her and Drew.

Chapter 23

The next morning, Claire had the early shift at the candy store. She had just clocked in when her phone rang. It was Jeff.

"Hey," she said, stepping toward the back of the break room so she wouldn't be in anyone's way. "Did you learn anything?"

He let out a heavy sigh. "Unfortunately, yes."

"Oh no." She sat down in a nearby chair. "Who's missing?"

"Well, nobody right now, but about two years ago several rogues in the area disappeared."

Claire searched for words. "How come we didn't know about this?" she eventually asked.

"Because nobody reported it. The Bureau projections didn't think any of the agents here would help the rogues, so they didn't say anything."

Claire lowered her voice as a coworker walked past. "That's awful. I hate that they felt like that."

"I know. Me too." The sincerity in his voice was clear. "What kills me is that the Bureau projections said they were terrified back then too, but they didn't feel like there was anything they could do either. They didn't think anyone would listen."

Claire smiled. "Well, they're talking to you now, so at least that's something."

"Yeah." He cleared his throat. "Look, Claire, if the same thing is happening there with the rogues, you need to proceed with caution. Whatever it was, it had all the projections here really worked up. I want you to promise me you'll be careful, for your personal safety as well as for your career."

"I will," she assured him.

She disconnected the call and immediately pressed the speed dial for Isabel, who answered after a few rings.

"Hey Claire, what's up?"

"I need your help."

"With what?"

"It turns out Jackson isn't the only rogue on the island who's gone missing. I think we need to look into it."

Isabel didn't respond right away. "I don't know what you think we can do. That's not our jurisdiction."

"I know," Claire said, "but we both know nobody at headquarters is going to pay any attention to this unless we have some solid evidence that there's actually something going on here." She paused. "You're the only other agent I know who doesn't completely ignore the rogues."

"I don't know, Claire. We could get into a lot of trouble if anyone at the Bureau finds out we're spending our time and resources on something like this, especially if it turns out to be nothing."

"I promise that nobody at the Bureau will know about this unless we find definitive proof there's cause for concern." Isabel didn't answer, but Claire felt like she was considering it. "Besides, if something is happening with the rogues, there's always the possibility it could eventually affect the registered projections as well. It would be better if we could get ahead of whatever this is before that happens."

"Okay," Isabel finally said, "I guess it can't hurt to look into it. But promise me we'll only take it to the Bureau if we find something definitive."

Claire let out a sigh of relief. "I promise."

"So, when do you want to get started?"

"Is tonight too soon?"

"Not if we can work my normal rounds in. I'm supposed to check up on a couple of my projections tonight."

"Sounds good."

They said their good-byes and hung up. Claire dropped her phone back into her pocket and returned to the front of the store. She was feeling pretty good about her plan of action until she saw who was standing at the counter waiting for her.

"Claire!" Spencer called out when he saw her. "We were hoping we'd find you here. We wanted to show you some of the footage from the Ashton Villa investigation before our tour tonight."

Oh crap! She had completely forgotten she was supposed to take the ghost hunters on a tour of Moody Mansion that night.

"Hey guys," she said, trying to avoid making eye contact with Drew. "I'm really sorry, but an emergency has come up. I can't do the tour tonight. Can we switch it to tomorrow night instead?"

Spencer looked devastated.

"I promise I'll make it up to you," she told him. "I'll even get you an overnight lockdown at one of the historic homes, maybe even the Bishop's Palace."

"A lockdown?" Spencer said.

"Absolutely."

"Okay," he conceded, "tomorrow night then." With a wink he added, "And a lockdown."

"Definitely."

The rest of the team turned to leave, but Drew stayed behind. "Is everything okay?" he asked, studying Claire carefully.

"Yeah," she tried to assure him with a smile. "Everything's fine. I just have to help a friend with something." She couldn't tell if he believed her.

"Well," he eventually said, "let me know if there's anything I can do to help."

"Thanks. I will." She took her phone out of her pocket and held it up. She didn't want to seem like she was trying to get rid of him, but she had a lot on her plate. "I need to set up your lockdown, so I guess I'll see you tomorrow night."

He nodded. "Okay, tomorrow night then."

She watched as he crossed the shop to where the rest of his team was waiting for him. She was dying to tell him the truth, but there was no way she could. No matter how much she hated lying to him, until he was officially approached by Bureau recruiters, he had to stay in the dark.

Chapter 24

That night after sundown, Claire met Isabel outside the Hotel Galvez.

"I spoke to Audra today," Isabel said, a frown of concern wrinkling her forehead as she fastened her seatbelt. "She confirmed what you told me. Jackson isn't the only rogue that's gone missing."

Claire put the car in gear and pulled out of the circular drive. "Did she have any idea what might be happening to them?"

Isabel shook her head. "No, but they're all very concerned about it." She turned in her seat to look at Claire. "What do you think is going on?"

Now it was Claire's turn to frown. The investigation into the events in San Francisco had never provided an explanation, and she had more theories than she could begin to sift through. "I have no idea," she admitted, "but hopefully we can get some answers tonight."

"Where do you want to start?" Isabel asked. "I only know of a few other rogues on the island that we could check in with. What about you?"

Claire trusted Isabel not to rat her out to their superiors at the Bureau, but she still didn't want her fellow agent to know how far or how often she had ventured outside their jurisdiction. Claire knew of several rogues on the island, but they didn't have time to try to track each one of them down. Thankfully, there was another possibility.

"Thelma told me that some of the rogues have been meeting at the Old City Cemetery. She thought they were having parties there, so she was pestering me to get permission for her to join them."

"I hope you didn't do it."

"Of course not. But it turns out their meetings weren't parties after all. Apparently, they've been meeting to discuss these disappearances."

"Will they be there tonight?"

"I hope so. But either way, I think it's the best place to start."

"Sounds like a plan."

They pulled up to the cemetery gate and got out of the car. What's often seen as one giant cemetery is actually comprised of seven separate sections that have merged over the years.

After the 1900 hurricane, the cemeteries were raised along with the rest of the island, though many of the graves and markers weren't. If a family couldn't afford to pay for the grave raising, the ground was filled in on top of, or in the case of the mausoleums around, the existing gravesite. Not only did this cause the cemetery to be developed in layers, it also resulted in the roofs of many mausoleums sticking out only a few feet above the ground. When Claire was a girl, she had accompanied her dad on a business trip to Galveston and thought the short structures must have been intended for very short people, a fact her father still enjoyed reminding her of every time they passed one of the cemeteries together.

During the day, when the gates were open, Avenue K was a city thoroughfare running straight through the middle of the cemetery complex. Though locked gates prevented cars from driving through at night, they didn't do a very efficient job of keeping people out. Due to city budget cuts, maintenance of the cemetery had been lacking in recent years, so sections of the fence and brick retention walls had fallen into disrepair, allowing vandals and ghost enthusiasts relatively easy access to the cemetery. Even so, Claire decided it would be best if they entered the legitimate way.

Since the cemetery was part of their regular ghost tours, Claire had a key to the gate. If anyone asked any questions, she would explain that they were planning out some new routes through the cemetery to keep the tours fresh.

"Good evening, ladies," Tony, the night watchman, said as Claire unlocked the gate and pushed it aside.

"Thanks so much for meeting us here," she told him, extending her hand in greeting.

He shook it and nodded to Isabel. "Anything for our best customers. It gets pretty boring here at night when there aren't any tours coming through. Our residents aren't the liveliest bunch of people, you know." He laughed at his own humor as he closed the gate behind them.

Maybe not for you, Claire thought. She and Isabel shared a look. Clearly her fellow agent was thinking the same thing.

"Do you feel them?" Isabel asked quietly once they were out of Tony's earshot.

Claire frowned. "I'm not sure."

When they first entered the gate, Claire had sensed a large amount of energy nearby, but there was something strange about it. It didn't feel like the usual projection energy. Perhaps if there was a large meeting of rogues that night, their combined energy signature could be the source, but Claire couldn't be sure. Adding to the challenge was the fact that the energy source seemed to be on the move. She was struggling to pinpoint its location.

"Maybe they decided not to meet tonight," Isabel suggested.

"Maybe." Claire wasn't convinced. "I don't feel any individual projections, but there's definitely something here giving off a powerful energy signature."

They started their search in the Old City Cemetery section of the complex. Claire wanted to find Uncle Newton, a Bureau-registered projection who had chosen to be tethered to the cemetery. In life, Newton had been one of the city's grave diggers, having dug hundreds of graves by hand during his lifetime. The cemetery had been a logical choice for his tether location.

As they searched the massive grounds, Claire could feel the strange energy pulsing through her. It grew in intensity then ebbed, only to grow stronger once again. It was unlike anything she had ever experienced before.

They made their way through the maze of grave markers, not really knowing what they were looking for. Claire hoped Isabel was right and the rogues had decided not to meet that night, but her instincts were saying something else. There were actually only a few rogues who called the cemetery home, but many of the others on the island frequented the place from time to time in order to mess with thrill seekers who ventured onto the property after dark.

Claire's heartrate quickened as she sensed they were drawing closer to the strange energy signature. It seemed to have stopped moving a few rows over from where they were, though the abundance of above-ground grave markers and mausoleums blocked their view of whatever it was. Claire held out her hand, signaling for Isabel to slow down as they reached the end of their path.

When they turned the corner, Claire froze. The scene before them was so surreal and unexpected, it took several seconds to process what she was seeing. She counted six figures that appeared to be human standing in a semi-circle around a single projection. The living people were wearing jackets with their hoods up so Claire couldn't make out any of their faces.

One of the figures was holding something that resembled a large hairdryer, pointing it at the projection. Claire recognized the device immediately. She had witnessed more than one P.I.D. team dispatch a troublesome or dangerous projection. But while this tool resembled the others, it was larger than any Claire had seen before.

"What the hell?" Isabel exclaimed, not too loudly, but loud enough to draw the group's attention.

The man holding the dispatching tool turned and said something to the men next to him. Claire couldn't hear what was said, but the meaning was clear when the two men began moving in their direction. Her first reaction was to run, but the sight of the projection kneeling only a few feet away held her in place. Already his energy had dimmed to where she could barely feel him. It wouldn't be long before he had been drained completely.

Claire didn't sense any other projections in the area, but she didn't know if that was a good thing. Had they already been dispatched, or had they been able to get away safely?

As the two men approached, Claire couldn't get her feet to move, torn between wanting to help the fading projection and wanting to run for her life. Next to her, Isabel took a step away from the approaching men but tripped over one of the grave markers, landing hard on her backside. One of the men grabbed her arm and pulled her back to her feet. She struggled against his grip, but he was clearly stronger than she was.

Claire didn't resist as the other man took hold of her arm as well. If she couldn't help this projection, maybe she could get some answers to keep any others from being dispatched.

She felt tears threatening to spill over as the last of the rogue's energy was drained. It felt like she was watching him die all over again. The projection hadn't expressed any feelings of fear or anger or sadness, emotions that frequently accompanied a forced dispatchment. Still, it was a difficult process for Claire to witness.

The hooded figure with the dispatching tool motioned to the man holding Isabel. Worried for her friend's safety, Claire struggled against her captor's grip, trying to break free. Just because she hadn't seen any weapons among the hooded men, that didn't mean there weren't any. She watched helplessly as the man practically dragged Isabel toward the rest of the group, stopping in the place where the projection had been only moments before.

As the man pointed the dispatching tool in Isabel's direction, Claire stopped struggling. Obviously, these men weren't part of a Bureau-sanctioned P.I.D. team, otherwise they would have known the tools didn't work on the living. Claire frowned as she heard the familiar hum of the tool activating, then watched in shock and horror as Isabel let out a loud scream and doubled over.

"Stop it!" Claire yelled, struggling once again to free herself from her captor's grip. He held on tight.

Hot tears began to roll down Claire's cheeks as she realized Isabel was in serious trouble. The dispatching tool shouldn't to be able to drain her energy, but that seemed to be exactly what it was doing.

As Claire watched Isabel fall to the ground, her body limp, she could feel a volcano of anger and frustration and fear building up inside of her. She shut her eyes and gave in to the powerful emotions. She didn't stop to think about what happened next. A strong pulse of energy coursed through her entire body, boiling up from somewhere in the center of her being. "Nooooooo!"

She could feel the energy surge out of her as she screamed until her throat was sore. Collapsing to the ground, exhausted, she listened to the sound of her scream echoing through the cemetery before eventually fading away.

Whatever had just happened left her with barely enough energy to open her eyes and take in the scene around her. Isabel was lying motionless where she had fallen while the hooded men were slowly picking themselves up off the ground. They seemed to have been knocked backwards several feet from where they had been standing before.

The man holding the dispatching tool was looking in Claire's direction, though his hood shielded his face from view. He took a step toward her, but the sound of voices coming from a few rows away stopped him. He motioned to the other men and they all quickly left the area.

Claire could hear voices drawing closer and prayed Isabel was still alive.

"Call 9-1-1," a familiar voice said.

Claire was shocked and relieved when Drew knelt down next to her. Convinced she was hallucinating, or dead, she smiled up at him and let the darkness engulf her.

Chapter 25

"How are you feeling?"

Claire forced her eyes to open, turning her head away from the harsh glare of the fluorescent lights overhead. She squinted up at the face of Dr. Bethany Russell, an attending physician at the University of Texas Medical Branch, one of the major hospitals on the island. Like Deputy Martens, Dr. Russell worked with the Bureau to help identify new projections when they formed.

"I'm fine," Claire said softly, bringing her hand up to her forehead. "I've just got a monster headache."

"That's understandable given the circumstances." Dr. Russell briefly examined the bandage on Claire's forehead then removed a pen light from the pocket of her white coat.

It had been several hours since the incident at the cemetery and Claire's condition was steadily improving. It seemed that whatever energy she had expended was gradually replenishing itself, and just as slowly, the fog around Claire's thoughts and memories was beginning to clear as well.

Claire let out a grunt of disapproval as Dr. Russell shone the pen light in her eyes. "How's Isabel?"

"She's stable, but still in a coma." Dr. Russell clicked off the light then took a step back to study Claire. "Is there anything else you can tell me about what happened to the two of you? Anything you remember about the tool they used on you?"

Claire closed her eyes and tried to push her way through the fog in her mind. The details were slowly coming back to her, but she wasn't ready to share everything with Dr. Russell, or anyone else. The final moments of the encounter felt surreal. If she didn't fully understand what had happened to her, how could she possibly explain it to anyone else?

Finally, Claire shook her head. "I wish I could tell you more. I've never seen anything like that. A dispatching tool shouldn't be able to harm a living person, but that's exactly what it did. I have no idea what that thing was."

Dr. Russell nodded. "Well, as long as Isabel continues to improve, that's the important thing."

There was a knock on the door and Drew stepped into the room carrying two Styrofoam cups. "Is it okay if I come in?"

Claire had asked him to see if he could find some coffee, and now her knight in shining armor had returned. She and Isabel had started their investigation at the cemetery around ten the night before. Now the sun was up, and Claire needed something to keep her awake a little longer.

Claire looked at Dr. Russell and she nodded. As Drew handed one of the coffee cups to Claire, she tried to play it cool. She wasn't ready for him to know how addicted she was to the stuff.

"I'll come back to check on you in a little while," Dr. Russell said, nodding to Drew before turning to leave.

Claire slowly sipped her coffee, partially because she desperately needed it, but also because she had no idea what to say to Drew. He had filled in some of the gaps in her memory, since she had faded in and out of consciousness while waiting for the ambulance. She desperately wanted to tell him the truth about what had really happened, but that was impossible. So instead, she sipped her coffee.

"Keith and Luke went back to the cemetery to get your car," he told her as he sat down in a chair next to the bed.

"That's nice of them." Claire was genuinely pleased. She appreciated the practicality of the gesture. In all the craziness, she hadn't even thought about her car.

"If you're okay with it, I'd like for them to drop it off at your place rather than bringing it up here."

"How will I get home if they do that?"

He smiled and nodded toward the bandage on her temple. "I don't think you should be driving, so I'd like to take you home when you get released."

Claire could feel her face turning red. His suggestion was the most logical option, but the intimacy of the gesture both touched and terrified her. She only hesitated for a few seconds, though, before nodding in agreement.

"That might be for the best." She gave him her address, which he texted to his brother. She set the cup of coffee on the tray next to the bed and waited for him to finish his text. "Thank you again for what you guys did last night. We're lucky you were there."

A nagging suspicion had begun nibbling at the corners of her mind, but she couldn't bring herself to say it out loud. How had Drew and his team found them so quickly at the cemetery? She hated to be suspicious of the ghost hunters, and especially Drew, but the men who attacked them had all been wearing hooded jackets to hide their faces. She had no way of knowing who they really were, or who else might be working with them, and she couldn't write their appearance off as mere coincidence.

"It's a good thing you told me about the broken-down section of fence that first day we met," Drew said. "Otherwise, we wouldn't have been at the cemetery at all."

Claire nodded. She had completely forgotten about that conversation. "It's crazy how things work out sometimes, isn't it?"

She couldn't tell if Drew had registered suspicion in her question, but it didn't seem to faze him if he did.

"I guess it was fate," he said with a wink.

Before their conversation could lapse into another awkward silence, there was a knock on the door. Deputy Martens stepped inside and smiled at her.

"Hey, Claire. How're you feeling?"

She nodded. "Better and better."

"You feel up to answering some questions?"

Drew looked concerned. "More questions?"

The Galveston police had already questioned them all extensively. Claire stuck to her original cover story about planning out new tour routes, but she left out most of the details about what had really happened. As far as the local police knew, they had apparently surprised a group of vandals or grave robbers. The men had attacked them, and luckily Drew's ghost hunting team showed up before anything worse could happen.

"I need to follow up on a few things," Deputy Martens assured Drew. "It won't take long."

Drew didn't seem entirely convinced, so Claire placed a hand gently on his arm. "It's okay."

"Do you need anything else?" he asked, concern still clearly etched in his face.

She smiled at him and held up her coffee cup. "I'm good, thanks."

Once Drew had left the room, Deputy Martens took out a notepad and sat down next to the bed. "Okay, I know what you told Galveston P.D., and I've spoken to Dr. Russell. Now tell me what really happened."

Claire told him everything she could remember, stopping just short of the final details. She trusted Deputy Martens, but for the time being, she still wanted to keep those to herself.

"You were unconscious when the ambulance got there," he told her. "Did they use the weapon on you as well?"

"I don't remember," she lied. "But they must have, right? I mean, since I was unconscious."

He nodded. "That seems most likely, and it could also help explain your lapses in memory."

He asked a few more questions, which Claire unfortunately couldn't answer honestly. She knew she wasn't helping his investigation, but that wasn't her concern at the moment. This was a matter the normal police were ill-equipped to handle anyway.

"Has the Bureau been contacted yet?" she asked as the deputy stood to leave.

"Now that I've got your statement, I'll call Craig as soon as I leave here." He patted her leg. "I'm sure they'll want to talk to you as well, but for now just rest."

Claire nodded. Once Craig knew about what had happened, he would contact headquarters. She stared at her cell phone on the table next to the bed. She knew she needed to call Zach, and probably her parents as well, before too many people at headquarters heard the news, but she couldn't bring herself to do it. Her energy was slowly returning to normal levels, so she decided it could wait a little longer until she was back to full strength.

Chapter 26

When Claire was finally discharged from the hospital, Drew was true to his word and drove her home. The more time they spent together, the more comfortable she felt around him, and the more acclimated she became to their energy connection. When they got to her house, he insisted on walking her to the door, though she told him repeatedly she was fine.

Claire unlocked the front door but didn't open it immediately. "Would you like to come in?" she asked after a long pause. Even as she said the words, she wasn't sure why she had.

Drew seemed surprised as well. "Sure."

As soon as the door closed behind them, a ripple of excited energy filled the room. Claire groaned. She had probably made a huge mistake.

Drew stood in the entryway for several seconds, most likely trying to get a read on the sensations he was feeling and wondering what he had walked in to.

"Would you like something to drink?" Claire asked casually, as if the whole situation was perfectly normal.

"Sure," Drew said again as he slowly followed Claire to the kitchen.

He sat down at the island while Claire got the coffee maker going. She glanced over at him, trying to read the expression on his face. So far, the house projections hadn't actually made an appearance, but that shouldn't matter. With his sensitivity level, there was no way he had missed their energy.

When the coffee was ready, Claire handed Drew a mug. He took a sip and studied her.

"You know you have a presence here, right?"

Claire nodded as she blew on the hot liquid in her coffee mug.

"More than one, if I'm not mistaken."

She nodded again. "They're harmless though."

Now it was his turn to nod. "I know." He set his cup down and leaned forward, arms folded on the counter in front of him. "I get the feeling there are some things you're not telling me."

Claire raised her eyebrows. "What do you mean?"

"Well, for starters…" He spread his arms out wide. "You live in a haunted house."

She scrunched up her face. "Actually, 'haunted' isn't the best way to describe it. They're more like roommates that most people can't see."

He looked around the kitchen. "Most people?" he repeated. "Does that mean you can see them?"

"Sometimes," she said reluctantly, "but only when they want me to."

Drew shook his head. "That's awesome. I just see colored mists, but you get to see the real thing."

"It's not always awesome. Sometimes it's a big pain in the butt." She chewed on her bottom lip for a few seconds, debating how far she wanted to take him down the rabbit hole. "Have you ever tried to see the ghosts during your investigations? I mean, have you ever tried to see past the mist?"

He leaned forward. "Do you think I can learn how to do that? Like, *really* see them?"

Claire nodded slowly but didn't elaborate. She didn't want to think about all the things he would learn how to do once the Bureau recruited him and he entered the agent training program.

Before she could say anything else, she heard a faint sound coming from somewhere near the dining room table. She looked at Drew, but he gave no indication he had heard it, too.

"Psst!" the sound came again, a little louder this time.

It had to be Thelma. Claire cleared her throat in what she hoped the projection would take as a warning. This was not the time to try to figure out if Drew had Communicative Acumen.

Drew took a drink from his coffee mug and studied Claire. He looked like he had something to say but was trying to find the right words. Claire held her breath. Had he actually heard Thelma's less-than-subtle attempt at communication?

After several seconds, he took a deep breath and looked Claire straight in the eyes. "Last night in the cemetery, we heard a lot of shouting and screaming before we found you and Isabel. We didn't tell the police about it because I didn't want to contradict your story, but I think we both know those guys weren't there just to vandalize graves."

Claire shrugged. What explanation could she possibly give? She wanted to tell him the truth. God, she wanted to tell him everything, but she couldn't. As it was, she had already gone against Bureau procedure by not immediately submitting his name to her superiors as a high-level sensitive. If she told him the truth about projections now, it really could be the end of her career at the Bureau, no matter how high her family connections went.

She opened her mouth but then closed it again, completely at a loss for words. There was no good way to handle this. They stared at each other for a few seconds before finally Drew slowly began to nod.

"I get it. You just met me." He took a final sip of his coffee and stood up. "I understand if you don't feel like you can trust me with whatever is going on here."

"It's not that," she told him, reaching out and placing a hand on his arm. She looked him in the eyes. "If I could tell you, I would..."

"But you can't," he finished the thought for her. "And I get it." He leaned over and kissed her on the forehead, carefully avoiding the bandage. "You need to get some rest. I'll stop by later to check on you."

Claire could tell he genuinely wasn't angry with her, but seeing his disappointment felt like a little piece of her had died. More than anything, she wanted to trust him with this, but at this point it wasn't her secret to tell.

She didn't follow him to the door to see him out. Like an idiot, she stood next to the kitchen island, holding her coffee mug and debating if she should chase after him.

The air rippled next her as she heard the engine of Drew's truck rev to life.

"Are you going to let him leave like that?" Sarah asked.

Claire didn't answer.

"You should have told him everything," Thelma said.

"You know I couldn't do that." Claire pointed an accusing finger at her. "And you were pushing it, young lady."

"What?" Thelma batted her eyes innocently. "He already knew we were here, so it was the perfect opportunity to see if he could communicate with us. Where's the harm in that?"

Claire gave her a look. "Knowing you're here, and knowing the truth about you being here, are two different things."

Thelma completely ignored Claire's warning. "Did it seem like he heard me?"

Claire folded her arms across her chest. "He didn't even flinch."

Thelma frowned. "Well, no surprise, the way you were throwing all that static his way I couldn't get a word in edgewise, even if he could hear me."

"You two definitely have a connection," April announced, materializing on the opposite side of the island.

Claire let out a heavy sigh. "Believe me I know it, but that doesn't change the fact that I'm an agent and he's a ghost hunter."

"Maybe one day he'll be an agent, too," Thelma suggested with a glimmer in her eye.

"Maybe," Claire said, "but until then, he stays in the dark."

Sarah floated across the kitchen and reached out to touch the bandage on Claire's forehead. "You've had a rough night," she said, a wrinkle of worry creasing her brow.

"I'll be fine," Claire insisted as she sidestepped the projection's touch. She couldn't allow herself to accept Sarah's sympathy. She had failed to get any real answers at the cemetery, which meant she had let down every projection on the island. The fact that one of them would be concerned about her at a time like this only added to her guilt.

Claire set the two coffee mugs in the sink then turned back to face Sarah. "I really appreciate your concern," she assured her, "but I'm not the one everyone needs to be worrying about right now. We still don't have any answers, and until we do, I'm afraid more rogues are going to go missing."

Sarah nodded, but didn't say anything. Claire could tell she had hurt the projection's feelings, but the hurt would soon pass and be forgotten.

As Claire left the kitchen, she spotted her cell phone lying on the counter and sighed. She was dreading calling her parents, especially since she already felt so much better, but she knew how upset they'd be if they heard about what happened from someone else. It was late enough in the morning that she couldn't use the time difference as an excuse any longer. Resigned to what had to be done, she picked up the phone and headed to the living room, pressing their speed dial number on the way.

"Claire Bear!" her dad's chipper voice answered after only two rings. "You're up early this morning."

"Hey, Dad," Claire said as she curled up on the couch. She tried to hide the weariness in her voice but apparently failed.

"Is everything okay?"

"I'm fine," she assured him, "but there's been an accident."

She filled him in on the details, trying to make it sound less serious than it was. When she had finished, he was silent for several seconds.

"Your mother and I are already booked on a flight out later this morning."

Unlike many people his age, Claire's father wasn't crippled when it came to technology. Clearly, he had gotten on his computer while she was speaking, probably before she even finished the word "accident."

"Dad, there's really no need for you to come down here. I'm feeling better by the minute."

"I'm glad to hear that, but we'll see for ourselves when we get there. Our flight lands in Houston at two o'clock."

Claire sighed. Part of her wanted to talk him out of it, but a larger part wanted them both there. Her dad was also a high-level sensitive and he shared her attitude toward rogue projections. If anyone would be willing to help with the investigation, it was him.

"Okay, Dad," Claire finally conceded. "Let me know when you land."

He paused for a second. "You need to call your brother."

"Deputy Martens said he would notify the Bureau."

"You need to call Zach because he's your brother, not because he works for the Bureau."

Claire sighed. She didn't have the heart to tell him the call wouldn't be made. "I love you, Dad," she said instead. "I'll see you when you get here."

All three projections shimmered with excitement.

"Noah and Leila are coming?" Sarah asked, beaming broadly.

Claire chuckled. Her parents, and her dad in particular, were always favorites with the projections. "Yes," she told them, pulling the afghan her grandmother had made off the back of the couch and covering herself with it. "They'll be here later today."

Thelma squealed. "Well, that's just the cat's pajamas!"

Her unbridled excitement was contagious. Claire smiled despite her exhaustion. She had to admit the idea of having her parents there put her mind somewhat at ease. There were still so many questions left unanswered, but she didn't have the energy to worry about them right then. All she could think about was sleep.

Chapter 27

As hard as she tried, Claire was only able to get a few hours of sleep that morning. Her thoughts kept returning to the missing rogues and the mysterious group at the cemetery. How had they been able to drain Isabel's energy? She couldn't believe the Bureau had developed a tool that worked on the living, but what other explanation could there be?

The quickest way to get answers would have been to call Zach, but that wasn't going to happen. She needed solid evidence first.

With a resigned sigh, she slung her feet off the edge of the couch. If she wasn't going to get any sleep, there was no point lying around wasting time. She crossed the living room and rummaged through her desk until she found a notebook with a decent number of blank pages.

"What're you doing?" Thelma asked, materializing a few feet away.

"I'm looking for some paper. I need to try to get my brain around all this."

"Can I help?"

Claire gave her an appreciative smile. "Well, this is going to require a lot of writing, so I'm afraid that's going to be all on me." Thelma looked genuinely crestfallen, so Claire added, "But you can keep me company while I work. I'm sure it will help if I can talk this all out."

That seemed to cheer the projection up. She followed Claire to the couch and took a seat next to her as she settled in. "So, what do we know so far?"

Claire took a deep breath. "Rogues have gone missing." Thelma nodded and Claire wrote the words "MISSING ROGUES" in bold letters on a piece of paper. "It happened in San Francisco five years ago, and according to Jeff it happened again in New Orleans two years ago." She wrote both city names on sheets of paper as well.

Thirty minutes later, Claire had filled several pages with bits of information she thought were important to the investigation. It wasn't nearly enough, but at least it was a start.

"Now let's see if we can put this all together," she told Thelma.

Claire crossed the room to the wall next to the kitchen. Using thumbtacks, she began posting the pages in what she hoped would be an organized fashion, or at least one that would help her see any possible connections.

When the last piece of paper was stuck to the wall, she took a few steps back and surveyed her work. Unfortunately, she didn't feel any closer to solving the mystery than when she had first begun.

Thelma floated next to the wall, examining each piece of paper closely. "Who do you think those men were?" she asked, pointing to the piece of paper that read HOODED MEN DRAINED ISABEL.

Claire shook her head. "I have no idea." She ran her hand through her sleep-mussed hair. "Honestly, I'm not even certain they were all men. I couldn't see under their hoods."

Thelma continued perusing Claire's notes. "Are there any other cities where rogues have gone missing? I mean, besides San Francisco and New Orleans."

Claire shrugged. "I don't know, and I don't know how I could begin to find out. I'd have to call all the agents I know, and that wouldn't be a very wise move."

Thelma smiled at her sadly. "After what happened the last time you investigated missing rogues?"

Claire scowled at her. "Obviously."

Thelma nodded then returned her attention to the papers on the wall. After a few seconds, she pointed to a piece of paper and frowned. "Why do you have such a big question mark next to the words 'GHOST HUNTERS?' I thought they rescued you."

"I thought so, too," Claire admitted. "But it still feels a little suspicious that they were even there in the first place. At this point, I don't think I can afford to rule out any theories, no matter how much I hope I'm wrong about them."

Thelma shook her head. "There's no way Drew was involved. He's too dreamy." She glanced at Claire and shrugged. "I think you're trying to sabotage your relationship before it even has a chance to get started."

Claire stared at the back of Thelma's translucent head. How could someone so flighty and self-absorbed come up with such an insightful theory?

"I'm not sabotaging anything," Claire insisted, though not as emphatically as she wished she could have. "But it's definitely something to consider in light of the evidence."

"If you say so."

Thelma floated back to where Claire was standing. They both stared at the pages for a few more seconds without reaching any conclusions.

"There has to be some connection I'm not seeing," Claire eventually said. She pulled up a chair and sat down, jostling her desk in the process and knocking a package to the floor.

With a sigh, she bent over to pick it up but stopped when she noticed its contents. She had set Ann's books to the side without giving them much thought, but now she unwrapped the package the rest of the way. She held each book up for Thelma to see.

"Look at this," she said, barely able to contain her excitement. "Ann's first book is titled 'San Francisco Hauntings' and her second one is 'New Orleans Hauntings'."

Thelma stared at her. "So?"

"Where do we know rogues have gone missing?"

Recognition dawned on Thelma's face, followed by confusion. "But what could she have to do with any of this? She's not even a sensitive."

"I don't know," Claire admitted, "but it's too much of a coincidence to overlook. Ann was in San Francisco working on her first book when I was there five years ago. We've talked about that more than once." She quickly opened the second book and checked the publication date. "And it's very likely she was in New Orleans when the rogues went missing there, too."

Claire sat down in the chair she had pulled over. She couldn't fathom Ann's involvement with the missing rogues, but it had to mean something. It couldn't be a coincidence, and it was the only lead she had.

"How could she have gotten her hands on a dispatching weapon?" Thelma asked. "She doesn't work for the Bureau, does she?"

Claire shook her head. "No, and that's just one of a hundred questions I have about all this."

She set the two books back on the desk, regretting that she hadn't read them like Ann had asked her to so many times over the past few weeks. She could take the time to read them now, or she could go straight to the source. After staring dumbly at her information board for several seconds, she finally decided, "I need to go talk to her."

Thelma followed Claire as she headed to her bedroom to change clothes. "What are you going to say? You know you can't tell her about the Bureau."

"If she's the one behind this," Claire said without slowing down, "then maintaining Bureau secrecy is going to be the least of my problems."

Chapter 28

Claire pulled up in front of the rental house Ann had been staying in since the beginning of the summer. She knew the address because Ann had written it on the inside cover of one of her books, along with an invitation to coffee. Though she hadn't read Ann's books, Claire suspected she was about to get a firsthand explanation of the woman's theories.

As Claire looked up and down the empty street, she considered the wisdom of such an impulsive action. If Ann really was behind the missing rogues, and more disturbingly the draining of Isabel's energy, it might not be the best idea to confront her alone. She briefly considered waiting until her parents arrived later that day so she could have some back-up, but something inside her refused to believe Ann was actually a threat. And Claire needed answers.

With one last look around, she took a deep breath and crossed the street. The house was in a neighborhood that was known for vacation rentals. Since this was the off-season for vacationers, there wouldn't be anyone to come to her assistance should the need arise. All the same, she climbed the large staircase to the front door and knocked.

"Claire!" Ann exclaimed as she opened the door. She seemed genuinely pleased to see her. "Does this mean you read my books?"

"Not exactly," Claire admitted. "I've been busy with other things." She pointed to the bandage on her forehead. "I had to spend the night in the hospital last night."

"Oh, you poor dear." Ann leaned forward to get a better look, then took a step back and motioned for Claire to come inside. "What happened?"

Claire stepped into the stylishly furnished living room and waited for Ann to join her. "There was an accident at the cemetery."

Ann looked genuinely confused as she passed by. "The cemetery? What on earth were you doing there?"

Claire's resolve wavered. If Ann was faking her reactions, then she was the best actress Claire had ever seen. Claire reminded herself of the facts that had brought her to the woman's doorstep that afternoon. Despite her appearance of innocence, Ann had to know more than she was letting on.

"Some of the ghosts around the island have gone missing," Claire said, choosing her words carefully. "I was at the cemetery looking into the disappearances."

Ann frowned and headed toward the kitchen. "How could they disappear? Aren't they made of energy?"

"Yes, they are," Claire assured her. "So, someone would need very specialized equipment to make them disappear." She paused as Ann began filling a tea kettle with water. "You wouldn't know anything about that, would you?"

"Me?" Ann stopped mid-motion. Again, her surprise seemed genuine. "Why would you think I'd know anything about that?"

"Because this isn't the first time something like this has happened." Claire took a step toward her. "It happened in San Francisco five years ago and again in New Orleans two years ago."

Understanding slowly showed on Ann's face. "I see, and because I was working on my books then, you think I had something to do with it."

"It does seem a bit coincidental."

Ann set the kettle on the counter and looked at Claire for several seconds. "You're right. It does seem like a bit of a coincidence. But let me ask you this – how did you know ghosts had gone missing in those cities?"

Claire's heart began to pound. She hadn't even considered needing an explanation for that. There was no logical way she could have such information if the Bureau didn't exist. She stood stupidly for what seemed like an eternity, trying to come up with a response.

"It's okay," Ann assured her, returning to the task of putting the kettle on to boil. "I already know the answer to that question."

Claire shook her head. "I don't know what you think you know…"

Ann looked her in the eyes. "We both know that I know about the Bureau, Claire. There's no point being evasive anymore."

Claire again tried to formulate a response, but her brain wouldn't work fast enough. "I don't know what you're talking about," was all she could manage. After a lifetime of keeping Bureau secrets, lying about this should be as natural to her as breathing.

Ann sighed. "Really, Claire. This is ridiculous. I know all about the Bureau, and your continued attempts to deny it are a waste of time." She folded her arms across her chest and leaned back against the kitchen counter. "Yes," she admitted, "I was in San Francisco and New Orleans at the times you mentioned. I'm not surprised ghosts were going missing." She cleared her throat. "But I didn't have anything to do with it."

Claire weighed her options. It was clear secrecy was a moot point now, but years of training made the words stick in her throat. Still, if Ann knew what was happening to the rogues, it was worth breaking protocol to get some answers.

"So, if you aren't the cause of the disappearances, then who is?"

"A group of people you don't want to have anything to do with." Ann's face grew serious. "Ghosts aren't the only things they can make disappear."

Chapter 29

Claire frowned at Ann across the kitchen island. "What are you talking about? What group of people?"

Ann shook her head. "I can't tell you that. I'd be putting your life in danger, just like mine is. The Bureau isn't the only organization that takes secrecy seriously."

Claire let out a disbelieving chuckle. "So, you're telling me there's *another* secret organization out there and they're the ones responsible for the missing ghosts?"

Ann nodded. "I know it sounds far-fetched, but it's the truth."

"But I can't know any more about them or else my life would be in danger?"

Ann nodded again.

Claire struggled to think of anything else to say. Her brain was too busy trying to process what she had just heard. Several questions ran through her mind, but she finally settled on the most obvious one.

"So, if this organization is so secretive, how do you know about them? Do you work for them?"

Ann looked out the window. "No, but my husband did."

Claire couldn't hide her surprise. Ann had never mentioned a husband before. Realization slowly dawned on her. "Did?" she repeated.

Ann nodded.

"But he doesn't anymore?"

"No," Ann's face clouded over. "I told you. Ghosts aren't the only things these people can make disappear."

Claire couldn't hide her shock. "What did they do to your husband?"

The tea kettle on the stove began to whistle before Ann could answer. She removed it from the burner and poured the steaming liquid into two cups. She handed one cup to Claire then made her way over to the kitchen table. Uncertain what else to do, Claire followed.

Ann sat down at the table and cleared her throat. "About six years ago, Peter came home from work one day very agitated. At first, he didn't want to tell me what was wrong, but I wouldn't let it drop. I could tell something was seriously bothering him. Eventually he told me that the company he had worked for the past fifteen years wasn't what it seemed. He had seen something on his boss's computer that day, something he wasn't supposed to see, and it scared him to death."

"What did he see?"

She smiled sadly. "That's not something I'm ready to tell you just yet, at least not until I'm sure I can trust you." She slowly stirred the drink in her cup and returned to her story. "About a week later, my husband told me he had made a decision. He needed to expose the company for what it really was. He said that was the only way to stop them. He didn't know how he was going to do it, but he knew he had to do something, even though it would be dangerous for him to start snooping into areas of the company where he didn't have authorization."

She let out a heavy sigh. "A few days later, he came home from work even more agitated than he had been that first day. He gave me a USB drive and told me he had managed to collect the evidence he needed to expose the company, but he suspected they knew what he had done. He told me to keep the drive safely hidden, and if anything happened to him, I was to run. I asked what he meant, and he said he wanted me to leave town and change my name. I thought he was being paranoid, but when he didn't come home from work the next day, or the next, I knew he had been right. I called his office, but nobody had seen him for two days. I didn't let on that I suspected them of anything, but that afternoon I did exactly what Peter told me to do. I ran."

Claire's heart hurt for her, but she still wasn't sure she believed the story. "Did you ever find out what happened to him?"

Ann shook her head, her eyes filling up with tears. "While conducting research for my books, I've tried to make inquiries without drawing too much attention to myself, but I haven't had much luck."

"Did you ever look at the information on the drive?"

Ann nodded. "At first, I didn't want to have anything to do with it, but eventually I realized it might be my best chance of figuring out what had happened to Peter. When I saw the evidence he had collected, I knew why he'd been so scared." She looked down at her hands. "That's why I started writing about haunted locations. It seemed like the best way to get close to that world without drawing too much attention to myself. Even then, I've used a pen name to make sure no one could connect me to my husband."

Claire reached out and placed her hand on top of Ann's. "Ann, if it's really that terrible, I think your best option is to let me help you. The Bureau has resources."

She shook her head vigorously. "I don't know if I can trust the Bureau either. For all I know, they're just as bad as this other group. Peter called them The Syndicate." She pulled her hand away from Claire's. "That's one reason I kept pressing you about the Bureau. I need to know more about how it operates before I can be sure I can trust anyone there."

Claire sat back in her seat. "Trust goes both ways. I shouldn't even be talking to you like this, not without some kind of confirmation that this other group actually exists and actually poses a threat of some kind."

"So much secrecy is rarely a good thing," Ann told her.

"Well, I can assure you the Bureau isn't dangerous like you say this other group is. We want to preserve history. We would never hurt someone because they learned the truth about us."

"Maybe not physically," Ann said. "You just discredit them and make them look like a crazy person, which is almost as bad." She frowned. "Trust me. I have firsthand knowledge about that."

Claire cringed. She couldn't argue with her, so instead she decided to change the subject.

"So, if you didn't have anything to do with the rogue disappearances, how did you happen to be in those two cities at the right time? Doesn't that seem like a bit of a coincidence?"

"I didn't say it was a coincidence," Ann pointed out. She wrapped her hands around her coffee mug. "As I worked my way through the evidence Peter had collected, I noticed that The Syndicate's plans all seemed to center around one man. His name was Donald Burch, or at least it was at the time Peter went missing. The man has had several aliases over the years, so it's been a challenge for me to follow him. I first tracked him down in San Francisco, then Chicago, then New Orleans, though he was only in those places for a few months at a time. I lost his trail for close to a year after that, but eventually I tracked him here to Galveston."

She looked out the dining room window. "I started following him because I thought maybe he could lead me to Peter, or at least help me find out what happened to him." She closed her eyes. "But I gave up hope of that a long time ago." She was quiet for several seconds. "I still want to finish what Peter started, but to do that I need to find a way to stop The Syndicate somehow."

Claire leaned forward in her chair. "Let me help you. I understand you're hesitant to trust the Bureau, but we have resources you don't have. I don't know what this other group's plan is, but if it involves making ghosts disappear, I'll do whatever I can to help you stop them."

Ann didn't respond, and Claire didn't know what else to say to convince her. They sat in silence for what seemed like an eternity.

Eventually, Claire stood up. "I'm going to be honest with you. I don't know if I believe all of this. I can't just take your word for it, and clearly you're not willing to trust me with any proof to back up your claims. But I do know this, if you know what's going on with the disappearances here on the island, then you might be the only one who can help us put a stop to it." She felt hot tears threatening to spill over. "That might not mean anything to you, but it means everything to me."

Ann stared into her cup and remained silent. Frustrated and angry, Claire turned on her heel and headed for the door. She paused with her hand on the knob then turned around slowly.

"I really am sorry for your loss. Obviously, I didn't know your husband, but from what you just told me, I'm pretty sure he would want you to do whatever you could to help us now. He didn't hesitate to take action, and I'm sure he would want you to do the same."

This time Claire didn't wait for Ann's response. With tears of frustration stinging her eyes, she stepped out into the warm afternoon sun, slamming the door behind her.

Chapter 30

Later that afternoon, Claire's parents arrived. They landed in Houston and insisted on renting a car to come to the island. Knowing they were less than an hour away made Claire feel like a little girl who desperately needed her mommy and daddy to help make things right again.

After her conversation with Ann, Claire wanted to get her dad's take on what the woman had told her. She couldn't imagine a secret organization could exist without Bureau leadership knowing about it, but she also couldn't believe they would keep something so colossal from the agents.

When Claire's parents arrived at her house, she met them at the front door. Immediately her mom pulled her into a firm embrace. After several seconds of squeezing her daughter like a boa constrictor, she held Claire at arm's length and examined her, frowning as she gently touched the bump on Claire's forehead.

"Are you sure you shouldn't still be at the hospital?"

Claire smiled. "I'm fine, Mom. Really."

Leila Abelard placed a hand on either side of her daughter's face and looked straight into her eyes. "You're exhausted," she announced after a few seconds. "You need to get more sleep."

Claire's mom's Affective Acumen was off the charts. Unlike most sensitives, though, Leila's acumen wasn't limited to tuning in to the emotions of projections. She could always tell what another sensitive was feeling, and the stronger the sensitive, the stronger her connection to their emotions. It was a handy skill for the mother of two sensitives, and it had made it almost impossible for Claire and Zach to get away anything as kids.

Leila had never been an agent herself, though her family's history with the Bureau dated back to the 1920s when her grandfather became an agent. She worked as a secretary at headquarters in the early eighties, which was where she had met Noah Abelard. There were few female agents in those days, and Leila's interests lay elsewhere anyway. All she wanted was to be a wife and mother, so a career with the Bureau wasn't a priority for her. Claire always believed her mom would have made an incredible agent, though, had the circumstances been different.

Claire removed her mother's hands from her face and gave her a kiss on the cheek. "I think exhausted is my new norm."

"It's the job, Leila," Claire's dad reminded her, moving in to wrap his daughter in an embrace. "You know sleep is a luxury an agent can rarely afford."

Claire fought back tears as she nestled into her dad's embrace. As ridiculous as it sounded, with his arms wrapped around her, she could actually convince herself everything was going to work out.

The room rippled with energy as all three house projections shimmered into view.

"Noah! Leila!" Thelma squealed, floating up and down as if bouncing on non-existent toes. "Oh, I wish I could hug you, too!"

Claire couldn't help but smile. Their excitement would have been contagious for even the mildest of sensitives. It had been less than a year since her parents' last visit, but the sensation of time passing was different for projections than it was for the living. For them, it could have been ten years or ten days, and their excitement level would have been the same.

"Good afternoon, ladies," Noah said with a gentlemanly bow in their direction. "You're all three looking very fine today."

The projections beamed at him.

"Leila," Sarah said, floating forward and extending both hands toward her, "you haven't aged a bit."

Claire's mom reached out and let Sarah's hands hover over her own. "Thank you, Sarah," she said with a gracious nod. "And you look as lovely as ever."

"Did you bring us any presents?" Thelma asked, pushing her way to stand in front of the other two projections.

"Of course," Noah assured her, reaching into his carry-on bag and pulling out a heat lamp. Claire could only imagine what the security agents at the airport had thought when they screened his luggage.

"Oh, that's a nice one," Sarah said, examining the lamp.

"Will you plug it in for us?" April asked, her eyes beaming.

"Of course." Noah crossed the room and set the lamp on the desk. He laughed as all three projections hovered close around him, watching intently as he plugged it in to the wall socket. With a wave of his hand, he turned the lamp on and stepped back.

Thelma reached her hand out toward the glow. "Oh, that's the bee's knees."

"Only the best for my girls," Noah said with a huge smile.

This was one of the things Claire loved most about her parents. Unlike many connected to the Bureau, Noah and Leila Abelard treated all projections as if they were still living people. This show of respect was one of the things that had made Noah such an exceptional agent, and it was a quality Claire tried to emulate.

Noah left the projections to enjoy their gift. He turned to join his daughter and wife on the other side of the room but stopped when he saw the wall plastered with Claire's notes.

"Let us get settled in, and then you can fill us in on everything that's happened." He motioned toward the pieces of paper. "Clearly you left a few things out when we talked earlier."

"That ain't just static," Thelma remarked, glowing more brightly as she absorbed the heat from the lamp. She winked at Leila. "I can't wait to tell you about the ghost hunter."

Claire's parents both looked at her, eyebrows raised in an unspoken question.

"Thelma, really," Claire said, rolling her eyes. "You're not helping."

"They said they wanted to know everything," the projection said defensively.

As Noah and Leila took their bags to the guest room, Claire retreated to the kitchen to make some more coffee. Her father shared her addiction to the brown liquid, and with the conversation that was about to take place, she figured they would both need plenty of it.

When Claire's parents finally joined her again, Noah didn't waste any time getting to the point. "Okay, spill it. What about this ghost hunter?"

"Seriously," Claire told him. "That's the least of our concerns right now."

She took a deep breath and told them everything, beginning with her conversation with Jean Lafitte and finishing with her visit to Ann's house earlier that afternoon. The only detail she skirted around was the means by which she and Isabel had actually escaped the hooded men. Until she had a better idea of what had happened to her, she wasn't ready to tell anybody about it, not even her parents.

When she finished, they sat in silence for several seconds, processing the information.

"So, this Ann person told you there's another organization out there, this Syndicate, that knows about projections," Noah said.

Claire nodded. "She never called them projections, but, yes, that's what she claims."

Noah shook his head. "I'm sorry, but I find that hard to believe."

"That's what I thought, too," Claire admitted, "but she seemed very sincere, and very convinced that this organization is dangerous."

"But she wasn't willing to show you any evidence to prove any of this?" Leila asked.

Claire shook her head. "She said she didn't know if she could trust the Bureau. She was afraid we might be as bad as The Syndicate." She turned to face her dad. "Is there anyone you could ask about this? Maybe someone at HQ has heard about this group, but it just isn't common knowledge."

Noah frowned. "Sweetie, not to sound too full of self-importance, but if I've never heard even a whisper about this group during my time at headquarters, then it's not knowledge around the Bureau, common or otherwise."

"Could you make some phone calls?"

"I don't even know who I would call."

A knock at the door brought their conversation to a halt. Claire wasn't expecting any guests, so the interruption was a little unnerving. Ann's warning about The Syndicate rang in her ears as she crossed to the front door.

When Claire peeked through the peephole, she froze. She had completely forgotten Drew's promise to stop by to check on her. His timing couldn't have been worse. She cringed inwardly as she opened the door.

"Hey," he said with a big smile. "How're you feeling?"

Claire stood frozen in the doorway, debating if she should join him on the porch or simply ask him to leave. The last thing she needed or wanted right then was for him to meet her parents.

"Who is it, Sweetie?" Leila's voice asked from over her shoulder, taking the decision out of her hands.

"Um, Mom, this is Drew Mitchell." Claire took a step to the side so he could come in. "Drew, these are my parents, Noah and Leila Abelard."

They all shook hands while Claire stood awkwardly next to the open door.

"It's nice to meet you," Drew said. He turned his attention back to Claire and asked again, "How're you feeling?"

"I'm good. I got some rest, so I'm almost back to 100%." She turned to her parents. "Drew and his friends scared that group of thugs away at the cemetery. He stayed with me at the hospital then made sure I got home okay."

Noah shook Drew's hand again. "We can't thank you enough for looking out for our Claire like that."

Leila stepped in and gave him a firm hug. "No, seriously, we can't thank you enough."

Drew looked slightly embarrassed by all the attention. "It was no trouble at all. I'm glad we were there to help."

"Would you like to join us for dinner?" Noah asked. "We haven't made any definite plans yet, but you're more than welcome to join us when we do."

"I'd love to," Drew said, "but I'm on my way to meet my team. Claire got us a lockdown at the Bishop's Palace, so we're heading down there a little early to get everything set up."

"A lockdown?" Noah asked innocently.

Claire gave him a warning look over Drew's shoulder, but he ignored her.

"I'm sorry," Drew said. "I just assumed." He looked at Claire then back to her parents. "I'm part of an amateur paranormal investigation team. We're here in Galveston shooting a few episodes for our web show, and Claire has been taking us on some private tours."

"Oh yes," Noah said, enjoying himself a little too much. "Claire loves those ghost stories."

Claire was still glaring at her dad when Drew turned around.

"The guys are really excited about this lockdown tonight. Thanks for setting it up."

"I believe you have Craig to thank for that," she told him. "He was really grateful for what you guys did, too."

"Again, it was my pleasure." He turned back to Claire's parents. "Well, I better get going. I just wanted to check on Claire." He shook Noah's hand again. "Enjoy your dinner."

"And you enjoy your lockdown."

Claire followed Drew out the door onto the front porch then closed the door behind them. "Sorry about that," she said once they were alone. "They can be a little excitable."

"No need to apologize," he assured her. "Your parents seem great." He took a step toward her, looking closely at the bump on her head. "Are you sure you're okay?"

Claire smiled and shrugged it off. "I really am fine. I promise. I should be as good as new in no time."

"That's good to hear." He cleared his throat. "Actually, there was another reason I wanted to stop by."

Claire raised her eyebrows. "Really? What's that?"

He smiled an almost boyish smile. "I wanted to know if you'd like to have dinner with me sometime. Like, maybe tomorrow night?"

Claire smiled back at him. Ignoring all the logical reasons why she should say, "No." Instead she said, "I'd love to, and tomorrow night sounds perfect."

"Great!" He leaned over and kissed her on the cheek. "I'll give you a call tomorrow."

"Sounds good."

She watched him get into his truck then went in the house. When she opened the front door, her parents were standing in the entryway, and they weren't alone. Three shimmering projections stood looking over their shoulders.

"So," Leila said. "I assume that was the ghost hunter Thelma mentioned earlier."

"Obviously." Claire moved past the five of them into the living room. She still didn't want to have this conversation with any of them, but clearly it couldn't be avoided.

"I told you he was dreamy," Thelma said with a shimmer of excitement.

"But you didn't tell us he was a sensitive," Noah pointed out, "and a high-level one at that."

Claire didn't respond. What was there to say?

"Have you turned his name in to the Bureau yet?" Leila asked.

"I've been a little busy," Claire said defensively. "He's only been in town a few days, and I've had a lot of other things going on." She pointed at the bump on her head, but no one seemed to buy her excuse.

"Are you going to turn his name in?" Leila pressed.

"Of course," Claire said with a shrug. "Why wouldn't I?"

"I don't know. You tell me."

"Stop doing that," Claire told her, even though she knew her mom couldn't help it. "Can I please have my emotions to myself for once?"

Leila smiled at her serenely but didn't say anything else.

"I know why she hasn't done it," Thelma answered for Claire. "She's goofy for him, and she's afraid that if he joins the Bureau, they won't be assigned to the same city."

Claire gave her a disapproving look as she sat down in the recliner. "Mind your own business." Five sets of eyes studied her. Clearly, Claire was the only one who wanted to drop the subject. She sighed. "Honestly, it doesn't matter anyway. He'll only be here for a few more days, then he'll go back to Beaumont and I'll probably never see him again."

"And how do you feel about that?" Noah asked, looking at Leila when Claire didn't answer right away.

"It doesn't matter how I feel about it," Claire eventually said, hoping she sounded more confident than she felt. "It is what it is."

"Are you still going to have dinner with him tomorrow night?" Sarah asked.

Claire frowned. "Eavesdropping is *not* okay." She squared her shoulders defiantly. "And, yes, I'm going to dinner with him."

"Claire, honey, you need to be careful here." Noah looked to Leila to back him up, but she kept her face neutral.

Claire groaned. "I'm not a teenager. I know what I'm doing. It's just dinner." Her parents didn't say anything else, but she could tell they wanted to. She let out a heavy sigh. "Look, I'm exhausted. I'm going to go get some sleep. We can talk about this later."

She felt a little childish for making such a quick escape, but she also wasn't lying. The few hours of sleep she had gotten over the past two days wasn't healthy, even for someone who was used to operating with mild amounts of sleep deprivation. The fact that taking a nap would also allow her to avoid facing the reality of her situation with Drew was just a bonus.

Chapter 31

Claire woke up a few hours later with a better attitude and a renewed determination to complete her investigation into the missing rogues. Her mom had prepared dinner, but she had decided to let Claire sleep, and Claire was grateful for the consideration.

As Claire used a piece of bread to mop up the last bit of spaghetti sauce from her plate, she said, "I really think I need to go back to the cemetery." Her full belly was clearly adding fuel to her renewed fire.

Noah raised his eyebrows. "You want to go *back* to the cemetery? Don't you think that's a little dangerous?"

"Not really," Claire told him. "I seriously doubt those men will make another appearance there after everything that's happened." She couldn't tell him that she wanted to look for clues that might help explain exactly what had happened and how she had managed to shoot out a massive blast of energy. Instead, she said, "That's where the rogues have been congregating, so that's still where we're most likely to find answers."

"That may be true," Leila said, sharing another look with Claire's dad, "but I'm still not sure it's such a good idea." She pointed at Claire's investigation wall. "If this Syndicate group is behind these disappearances, and if they're as dangerous as that Ann woman said they are, you need to be careful." She closed her eyes and shook her head. "I hate to think what could have happened to you if those ghost hunters hadn't come along when they did."

Noah nodded in agreement. "You're lucky they didn't drain your energy like they did Isabel's." He took Leila's hand. "Drew and his team definitely saved your lives last night."

Claire got up from the dining room table and carried her plate into the kitchen. She stood by the sink for several seconds, her heart racing at the idea of telling them the truth. The worried looks she had seen on their faces tore her apart. She couldn't remember ever having kept a secret from them, and especially not one as big as this.

She turned back around to face them, and said, "Let's go into the living room. I've got something I need to tell you."

When they were both seated on the couch, Claire sat down in a chair across from them. "I'm afraid I haven't told you everything that happened in the cemetery last night." Her nervous energy wouldn't let her sit still, so she stood up again and began pacing around the living room. How would she even *start* to explain this to them? Eventually, she cleared her throat and turned to face them.

"Claire, you're scaring me," Leila said, gripping Noah's hand tightly.

Claire sat back down, desperately trying to find the right words to explain something she didn't even understand herself. "I know and I'm sorry. I just don't know exactly how to explain it." She took a deep breath and gave it her best shot. "Those men didn't run away just because the ghost hunters showed up." She stood up again. "When I realized they were draining Isabel's energy, I felt helpless to stop it. I was so scared and angry, and all of those emotions built up inside me until…"

"Until what?" Noah prompted.

Claire closed her eyes. "Until it all just came out in a huge blast of energy." She opened her eyes but couldn't bring herself to look at her parents. "I don't know how it happened, but when it was over, I felt like all the energy had drained out of my body. When I looked around, it seemed like all the men had been knocked off their feet." She sat back down. "And that's when Drew and the others came on the scene."

Noah and Leila were quiet for what felt to Claire like an eternity. Finally, her dad cleared his throat. "So, you're saying you shot out some sort of energy blast that knocked the men off their feet."

Claire nodded, knowing it sounded ridiculous, even impossible.

"That's incredible." Noah shook. "In all my years at the Bureau, I've never heard of anything like that happening before."

Claire stared at him in disbelief. "So, you believe me?"

Leila reached for her hand. "Oh, honey, of course we do. Why on earth would you make something like that up?"

Her whole life, Claire had always known she could count on her parents for support, but she had been certain something like this would strain even their parental sensibilities. She almost cried from relief. "So, what do you think that was?"

Noah furrowed his brow. "I'm sorry. I can't even begin to explain something like that."

Claire swallowed hard. "Can you think of anyone at the Bureau we could ask? Maybe there's some obscure case somewhere that can offer at least *some* kind of explanation."

"I don't think that's such a good idea," Leila said hastily.

"You don't think what's a good idea?"

"Asking people at the Bureau about it." Noah shifted in his seat. "That's probably not a good idea."

"Why not?"

Her parents exchanged a look.

"I'm afraid we haven't been entirely honest with you either," Noah eventually said.

Claire looked from one parent to the other. "What do you mean?"

Leila took a deep breath and let it out slowly. "Sweetie, you're not a Level-5 sensitive."

"What are you talking about?" Claire gave a short laugh. "Of course I'm a Level 5. I couldn't interact with the projections like I do if I wasn't."

"Well, that's not entirely true."

What Claire was hearing made no sense. "If I'm not a Level 5, then what am I?"

Noah shrugged. "I guess you could say you're a Level 6, if the Bureau's rating scale went that high. Honestly, though, that might not even be a high enough ranking either."

She stared at them, unable to put any words together. Finally, she came up with a question to ask. "How many millivolts do I put off?"

Noah shook his head. "We don't know. The readings were off the charts so tests couldn't accurately register it."

"We always suspected you had a special gift," Leila said. "The way you and Emma Lynn played together was unlike any interactions we had ever seen from a child before. To you, she was literally like any other flesh-and-blood playmate."

"As you know, that's extremely unusual for children," Noah pointed out. "I used my position at the Bureau to have you tested when you were five years old. We were stunned by the results."

"We figured it would be best to keep it all a secret, though," Leila said. She looked at her husband. "I was afraid Bureau researchers would want to study you if they knew how strong your sensitivity was."

Noah cleared his throat. "When you decided to enter agent training, I again used my connections at the Bureau, but this time to make sure you weren't tested along with the other applicants. It was already common knowledge around headquarters that your skills were impressive, so nobody ever pressed the issue. After all, most of the Bureau's leadership had known you since you were a little girl, and they knew you possessed most of the acumens." He shrugged his shoulders. "You had already gotten the attention of the Bureau's leadership, so I doubt anyone ever even looked at your scores anyway. All the same, I convinced the assigning board that you needed a few years as an agent in the field before they approached you for any additional assignments higher in leadership, which would have led to additional tests."

Claire sat quietly for a long time, her thoughts reeling. She was stunned, but she had to admit it actually explained a lot of her childhood. Maybe she should have been angry with them for keeping something like this a secret, but she couldn't see how her life would have played out any differently if they had told her the truth.

She cleared her throat. "So, you think I should keep what happened in the cemetery a secret then."

Leila nodded. "At least for now. At least until we have a better idea of what might be going on with you."

"Obviously it's your decision, though," Noah said. "If you want to bring in Bureau resources to help figure things out, that makes perfect sense. Just tread cautiously."

Claire nodded several times then began shaking her head. "It's too much to think about right now." She took a deep breath and stood up. "After we figure out what's happening to the rogues, then we can figure out what's going on with me."

"That's reasonable," Noah said, standing as well. "But you know we aren't going to let you investigate this alone." He pulled the keys to his rental car out of his pocket. "If you're determined to go back to the cemetery, we're coming with you."

Claire smiled. That was the best news she'd heard in days.

Chapter 32

When Claire woke up late the next morning, she didn't immediately get out of bed. Instead, she just stared at the ceiling, wallowing in frustration and discouragement. The investigation she and her parents had conducted at the cemetery the night before had been a complete bust. The only information Newton had been able to tell them was that the rogues had been meeting at the cemetery for weeks, but that wasn't anything they didn't already know.

Claire picked her phone up off the nightstand and looked at the time. It was after eleven o'clock. She debated for a few seconds, then dialed Drew's number.

After only a few rings, Drew picked up.

"Good morning," he said, a little too chipper for Claire's liking first thing in the morning.

"Good morning," she replied. "How did the lockdown go last night?'

"Ummm…" he hesitated, "It wasn't great."

Claire sat up in bed. "What happened?"

"Nothing, honestly."

"What do you mean?"

"Well, nothing happened. We didn't get any readings… at all." He paused. "If I hadn't sensed the presence of a couple of entities, I would have said the place wasn't even haunted."

Claire cringed. "I'm sorry. Usually, the Gresham's are really active for visitors."

The line was silent for a few seconds. "It may have just been my imagination," Drew finally said, "but it seemed like the ghosts were actually scared of us." He chuckled. "I know it sounds crazy, but that's the feeling I got from them."

"That doesn't sound crazy," she assured him, though she couldn't tell him how reasonable it actually was. With everything that had been happening to the rogues, it was no surprise the Bureau-registered projections were on edge, too.

"Please, tell the guys I'm sorry," Claire told him. "Hopefully, the tour at the Galvez will be better."

"I'm sure it will be," he assured her. "And don't worry about us. It's not the first time one of our investigations has fallen flat."

There wasn't much else to say about it, so they said their good-byes and ended the call.

Claire got out of bed, then took a shower and dressed before joining her parents in the kitchen. After they had finished eating lunch, Claire and her parents sat around the dining room table, reviewing the facts as they knew them and trying to find some sensible explanation for what was happening on the island.

"You said the man at the cemetery used something that looked like a dispatching tool, but it worked on Isabel?" Noah asked, restating what they had already discussed numerous times. Claire nodded and he frowned. "That's what bothers me the most about this."

"Why is *that* what bothers you most?"

He sat back and folded his arms across his chest. "There used to be a scientist who worked for the Bureau back in the forties, a specialist in bioelectrical studies, named Werner Vogel."

"The guy who invented the dispatching tool," Claire said, nodding in recognition of the name. They had learned about him during agent training.

Noah cleared his throat and stood up. "Well, that wasn't the only tool he was working on during that time." He left the kitchen and went into the living room, talking over his shoulder as he continued. "Vogel theorized that it could be possible to drain the energy from a living human. In fact, his experiments in that area, among other things, are what got him dismissed from the Bureau."

Noah returned to the kitchen with a familiar thick, leather-bound book in his hand. Claire immediately recognized it as the official Bureau history book. As instructed during training, her copy of the book was kept well hidden, though, of course, Noah knew where to find it. The book's title, *A Concise Accounting of the Conservancy of Energy-based Metaphysical and Transcendental Entities*, was intentionally confusing and vague in order to repel any non-Bureau personnel who might stumble across it by accident.

All agents were given the book at the beginning of their training and were expected to study it. One of the major tests for becoming an agent assessed their knowledge of the hundreds of years of history. Personally, Claire had never even opened her copy of the book. Having grown up in a deeply Bureau-connected family, she had heard enough of the history over the years that she passed the test with flying colors without reading a word.

Noah began thumbing through the pages as he talked. "The details of Vogel's dismissal are not widely spoken of in Bureau circles, but your grandfather was head of the research division back then. He told me everything when I took my first position at headquarters."

He found what he was looking for and set the book on the counter, turning it so Claire and her mom could see the black-and-white photo on the page. There was a group of about twenty men in lab coats standing stiffly together, smiling into the camera. Claire leaned in to study the photo and immediately recognized her grandfather. She looked up from the photo as her dad continued.

"After Vogel left the Bureau, he was recruited by the Nazis. World War II was in full swing, and Hitler was obsessed with the occult and all things supernatural and paranormal. The Nazis were keenly interested in Vogel's work, and they pretty much gave him free rein to conduct his research however he saw fit." Noah shook his head. "Your grandfather tried to keep tabs on him as much as he could, but when the war ended, Vogel was one of the many in Nazi leadership who fled Germany. No one knows what happened to him after that." He tapped the photo several times. "But from what you've described, it sounds like he might have passed on his research to a protégé."

Claire frowned as she considered the possibilities. Turning her attention back to the photo, she asked, "Which one is Vogel?"

Noah pointed to a man standing not far from Claire's grandfather. Claire leaned in closer and felt her blood run cold. The face smiling back at her was shockingly familiar. She picked up the book and brought it closer, unable to believe what she was seeing.

"He looks *exactly* like Philip," she said, continuing to stare at the picture.

"Who's Philip?" Leila asked.

Claire set the book back on the counter but couldn't take her eyes off the photo. "He's one of our regulars at the candy store. He's been on the island for a few months studying the coastal ecosystem, and he comes in pretty much every day to get taffy."

Noah frowned. "Is his last name Vogel?"

Claire shook her head. "No, it's Graham, but I would bet anything they're related. He looks as much like the man in that photo as you look like grandpa, maybe even more so."

"We need to talk to him," Leila said, folding her arms across her chest. "If he's somehow connected to Werner Vogel, maybe he knows what's happening to the rogues."

"Do you know where we can find him?" Noah asked.

Claire shook her head again. "No." She thought for a second. "But maybe somebody at the candy store does."

"Then that's where we'll start," Leila said.

Noah took his cell phone out of his pocket. "First, I think we need to get a little more intel about Werner Vogel and his family."

"You're not calling Zach, are you?" Claire still wasn't ready to bring her brother in to the investigation until they had more information.

"No, but I do want to get the Bureau's resources involved, especially if there's a weapon out there that can drain the energy from humans." Noah smiled at her and winked. "Besides, your brother isn't my only connection at the Bureau, you know."

He went into the living room to make his call, leaving Claire and her mom alone in the kitchen. Claire kept staring at the picture, still unable to believe what she was seeing.

"So, are you ever going to tell me about this ghost hunter," Leila asked, swirling the remains of the coffee in her mug, "or am I going to have to depend on Thelma for all my intel?"

Claire let out a heavy sigh. "There's nothing to tell. Thelma just likes to stir up drama."

She could tell her mom wasn't convinced, but thankfully she let the matter drop when Noah came back into the kitchen.

"Alright, Harlan is looking into it for me," he announced proudly. "He said he'll put it on the top of his list and get back to me later today."

"That's good." Claire picked her purse up off the table by the door and pulled the strap over her shoulder. "I'll run by the candy store and see if anybody knows where to find Philip."

"You're not going by yourself," Noah insisted. Leila was already heading toward the front door.

Claire let out another sigh but didn't protest. She didn't see how this outing would be dangerous, but honestly, she was starting to enjoy investigating as a family.

Chapter 33

When they arrived at the candy store, Noah and Leila checked out the assortment of candies while Claire talked to Monica. She waited until her friend had finished with her customers then approached the counter.

"Can I help you, ma'am?" Monica teased.

"I hope so," Claire said honestly. "I don't suppose you know how to get in touch with Philip Graham?"

Monica gave an exaggerated pout. "Did you lose your boyfriend again?"

Claire smiled feebly. She wasn't in the mood to joke around. "Not exactly. I just need to ask him about something." She looked around the candy store. "Do you think anyone else might know?"

"Deshaun might. They talk about marine wildlife sometimes when Philip comes in and you're not here."

Claire thanked her then crossed the shop to where their coworker, Deshaun, was getting ready for his next taffy pulling demonstration.

"Hey," Claire said casually. "I know you're busy right now, but I need to ask you something."

He straightened up, wiping his hands on his apron. "Shoot."

"You wouldn't happen to know how I could get in touch with Philip Graham, would you?"

He gave her an odd look. "It's funny you should ask. He was in here a little while ago looking for you." He reached into the pocket of his apron and pulled out a piece of paper. "He asked me to give you this the next time I saw you."

Claire took the piece of paper with a smile, hoping her hesitation wasn't obvious. She waited to look at it until she had returned to the front of the store where her mom and dad were paying for their large supply of candy.

Noah pointed at the piece of paper. "Is that good news?"

Claire frowned. "I think it's his phone number. Deshaun said he was in here earlier looking for me, too." She put the note in her pocket. "Hopefully, he'll have some answers for us."

"Let's hope so," her dad agreed.

Claire started toward the door, but Leila stopped her. "Are they about to pull the taffy?" she asked with an expectant smile.

Claire chuckled. "Do you want to stay and watch?"

Leila smiled sheepishly. "I know it's important we find this man, but this won't take long, will it?"

They returned to the back of the store and took their place among the crowd of tourists already gathered there. Claire had seen the demonstration more times than she could count, so she stayed to the back of the crowd. As Deshaun began his routine, some of the children who were gathered cheered.

Deshaun was a few minutes into the familiar procedure when Claire suddenly felt a swell of energy begin to pull on her. She looked around the store, trying to locate the source of the sensation, but nothing seemed out of the ordinary. She made eye contact with her dad. Clearly, he was feeling it, too.

She closed her eyes and tried to isolate the sensation. Her heart began to pound as she recognized the energy signature. It was the same one she had felt in the cemetery, and it was close by.

But there was something else, a more natural and more familiar signature that seemed to be entangled with the stronger one. She opened her eyes. Mona.

Claire looked at her dad. His eyes mirrored her concern. She made a motion with her head indicating the building across the street and he nodded. She took a few steps back from the crowd, motioning for him to stay put as she made her way to the front of the store then out into the warm autumn sunshine.

She waited for traffic to clear then hurried across the street. When she stepped into the front lobby of the Hutchings-Sealy building, she spotted Mona hovering near the ornate staircase. There was a strange expression on her face, and she didn't seem aware Claire was even in the room.

"Mona?" Claire said, taking a step in her direction.

The projection didn't respond. She simply turned and floated out of the room.

Claire could feel the other energy signature in the building. She couldn't explain it, but it seemed to be getting stronger. Her heart began to pound harder and faster as she weighed her options. It probably wasn't the wisest move, but she had more questions than she apparently had sense, so she took a deep breath and cautiously followed Mona.

When Claire entered the next room, Mona was hovering near one of the windows on the outside wall. Claire was so distracted by the projection's strange behavior that it took her a few seconds to realize they weren't alone. She startled when she turned and saw Philip standing in the doorway on the opposite side of the room.

"Philip," Claire said breathlessly, "what are you doing here?"

He smiled at her. "I think the better question is, what are *you* doing here?"

It took Claire a few seconds to recover from her shock. "What do you mean?"

He looked at Mona and then back at Claire. "You followed this ghost in here, didn't you?"

Claire made a face, feigning confusion. "Ghost?" she scoffed. "I don't know what you're talking about."

"Oh, I'm sorry." He took a step toward Mona. "It's been so long I sometimes forget the preferred nomenclature is 'projection'."

Clearly there was no point pretending anymore. Claire's expression grew serious. "How do you know about projections?"

"Oh, I know a lot more than that." He paused and turned toward her. "In fact, I'm pretty sure I know significantly more about the nature of all this than you do."

Claire watched him closely, worried what he might do to Mona. She didn't see a dispatching device, but that didn't mean he wasn't hiding one somewhere. She drew in a deep breath. Again, Philip's energy signature seemed to be getting stronger, though Claire knew that wasn't possible.

"Are you the reason the rogues have been disappearing?" she asked. No point beating around the bush.

Philip nodded. "I'm afraid it's a necessary evil." He had almost reached Mona by this time.

"Necessary?" Claire repeated. "Why is it necessary? We haven't received any reports that the rogues on this island have been causing any problems."

Philip frowned and shook his head. "Such a limited view of things. It's a pity really." He turned to Mona. "Thank you, dear. You can go now."

Without a word or a blink of her eyes, the projection turned and floated out of the room. Claire stood speechless for several seconds, trying to find a logical explanation for what she had just witnessed.

"How did you do that?" she finally asked when she found her voice again. "It was like you were controlling her."

He seemed surprised by the question. "I was."

Claire let out a derisive laugh. Bureau scientist had proven years before that controlling projections, what they had labeled as Beguiling Acuity, wasn't scientifically possible.

"You can't be serious," she told him. "Beguiling Acuity is a myth."

"Oh, of course it is," he said with feigned solemnity. "I mean, the Bureau couldn't possibly be mistaken." He paused. "Unless they knowingly lied to everyone about it all these years."

Claire frowned. "Why would they do that?"

He studied her for several seconds. "I don't think you'd like the answer to that question."

"Were you really controlling Mona?" she pressed, refusing to be baited.

He weighed his response. "Yes," he eventually said, "but I assure it isn't as big of a deal as you're making it out to be. Honestly, it's nothing you couldn't do."

She narrowed her eyes at him. "What are you talking about?"

"As I think you showed us the other night, with enough energy, you can do all kinds of things."

He closed his eyes and Claire felt a surge of energy build in the room around them. She gasped as the weight of it pressed on her.

"How can you be doing this?" She took several deep breaths to try to slow her heart rate. "All those times you came into the store, I felt your energy signature. You were a Level-3, at best."

He held up his hand. It took a few seconds for Claire to figure out what he was holding. It was the ring she had been admiring only a few days before.

"It's an energy-dampening device," he told her, "and a gift from an old friend." He carefully placed the ring back on his finger and the energy level in the room subsided. "Sometimes it's helpful to fly under the Bureau's radar."

He slowly slid the ring off again and the energy level began to increase, as did Claire's irritation. His deception, and the hollowness of all those months of friendly interaction at the candy store, stung more than she wanted to admit.

She scowled at him. "Is this some kind of game to you?"

His expression grew serious. "I assure you, it's not."

Claire wanted to ask him to elaborate, but honestly, she was terrified to hear what he would say. "What was that tool you used the other night?" she asked instead. "How were you able to drain Isabel's energy?"

He shrugged. "I'm afraid I can't tell you that, at least not yet."

Claire was so tired of hearing that. First Ann, now Philip. She glared at him. "You almost killed her."

He nodded slowly. "Regretfully, yes, but you put a stop to that, didn't you?" He snapped his fingers as if he had just remembered something.

"And that's precisely what I wanted to talk to you about." He looked her straight in the eyes. "How did you manage to pull off that little trick of yours?"

Claire hesitated. "I don't know what you're talking about."

A knowing smile spread across his lips. "That's what I thought. You don't know how you did it, do you? That's interesting." He took a step toward her. "I would love to help you figure it out. This kind of thing is sort of an area of expertise for me."

Claire took a step back, desperate to take the spotlight off herself and what had happened in the cemetery. "So, clearly you've been carrying on your father's research then."

He looked confused. "My father?" Slowly a light of recognition dawned. "Oh, you mean Werner Vogel." He nodded. "Yes, I *have* been continuing his research." He looked like he wanted to say something else but was interrupted.

"Claire?" Her dad's voice called out from the building's lobby.

Philip slipped the ring back on his finger. "I'll be in touch," he told Claire as he began moving toward the building's back exit. "We still have much to talk about."

She watched him leave, overwhelmed by the urge to follow him. She had so many questions, and still no real explanation for the missing rogues. Even so, the past few minutes had made her keenly aware of how ill-equipped she was to handle the situation on her own. With a resigned sigh, she hurried to the front of the building where her parents were waiting for her.

"Are you okay?" Noah asked, his face mirroring the concern Claire saw in her mom's eyes. He looked over her shoulder. There was no way he had missed the energy surges Philip had created.

Claire nodded. "I'm fine," she said. "But boy have I got a lot to tell you."

Chapter 34

Once they were all in the car, Claire filled her parents in on her encounter with Philip.

"How was he able to control Mona like that?" Claire asked, still unable to get her head around what she had just witnessed. "It was like he was using Beguiling Acuity, but that's just a myth. Bureau researchers concluded the science was impossible."

Neither of her parents responded.

Claire couldn't read their faces from the backseat, so she cleared her throat loudly. "Hello? Did you hear me? I said it looked like he was *controlling* Mona, but that isn't possible, right?"

Noah looked at Leila, then found Claire's eyes in the rearview mirror. "We're almost back to your place. Let's talk about it when we get there."

Claire shook her head. "Oh no, there's no way I'm waiting another minute. You need to tell me what you know."

Noah let out a slow breath. "Beguiling Acuity isn't a myth," he said. "It's a very real and very dangerous possibility for a strong enough sensitive."

Claire found it difficult to put coherent thoughts together. "But they told us in training it was a myth," she said stupidly. "Why would they lie to us about it?"

"Because it's too dangerous," Noah explained. "The door swings both ways. If it's not done correctly, or if the projection is stronger than the sensitive, rather than pushing their energy out toward the projection, the projection's energy can be absorbed into the sensitive."

"What happens then?"

"In mild cases the sensitive absorbs all the personality traits and memories of the projection. They can't distinguish between the projection's thoughts and memories and their own. From the outside, it's almost like they have multiple personality disorder." Again, he met her gaze in the mirror. "In severe cases, the foreign energy has a physiological effect on the sensitive's brain and causes severe neurological damage, like dementia, or worse."

Claire shook her head. "Why would the Bureau cover that up? Why wouldn't they just tell us how dangerous it is?"

"They didn't want anyone to even try it," he explained. "Besides, controlling projections requires a huge amount of energy, and the average agent doesn't have enough juice to pull it off. Bureau leadership decided years ago that it was better not to even put the idea into agents' heads. That way no one would be tempted to try."

"Well," Claire told him, "somehow Philip has mastered it." She shook her head again. "He was giving off so much energy without that dampening ring. I've never felt that much energy from a single sensitive before."

"I can't explain that," Noah admitted, "but I'm not surprised he had acquired Beguiling Acuity. It was one of the areas of study that Werner Vogel was fascinated with. If Philip is his son, it's perfectly reasonable to assume he carried on his research in that area as well."

Claire sat quietly in the backseat as they turned on to her street, still stunned by everything she had learned in the past twenty-four hours. "How could you keep all this from me?" she finally asked. "I'm your daughter."

"And you're also an agent," Noah pointed out. He pulled the rental car into the driveway and put the car in park before turning in his seat to look at her. "Even though I'm retired from the Bureau, I could still get into a lot of trouble for telling you all this even now."

Before Claire could ask any more questions, Noah's cell phone began to ring. He hesitated, then reached into his pocket and retrieved it. Claire let out a frustrated sigh.

"It's Harlan," Noah said, looking at the caller ID. "He may have some helpful information for us about Werner Vogel. I should take this." He connected the call then exited the car.

Claire looked at her mom once he was gone. "Did you know Beguiling Acuity was a real thing?"

She folded her hands in her lap. "I know a lot of things I probably shouldn't, but this is a conversation you and your father need to have."

Claire let out another sigh and opened the car door. Noah was standing on the porch with a frown on his face. Clearly, he didn't like what he was hearing. Claire knew this call from Harlan was important, but curiosity was eating at her, and she wanted to know more about Beguiling Acuity.

She moved past her dad and unlocked the front door, but he didn't follow her inside. After what seemed like an eternity, he finally joined Claire and her mom in the living room, a concerned look on his face.

"So?" Leila asked. "Is this man Vogel's son?"

Noah shook his head. "It doesn't look like it. Werner Vogel does have children, and grandchildren, but they're all still living in Germany. And there's no evidence that any of them have followed in his footsteps, either scientifically or with the Bureau."

"Are you sure Harlan checked all of them?" Claire pressed. "Maybe he missed one."

Her dad gave her a look. "You really think Harlan would let any detail fall through the cracks?" He stopped by her desk and picked up her notebook before joining them on the couch. "Like I said earlier, Vogel fled with the rest of the Nazi leadership after the war. There were possible sightings of him in the years that followed, but nothing definitive. He's one of the few who was never found, but it's presumed he died either in Argentina or Canada."

"Well, then it's possible he had a second family from when he was on the run." Claire was excited by the possibility. The resemblance between the two men was too uncanny for them not to be related somehow. "We can't assume he didn't have a second family somewhere."

"Of course, that's a possibility," Noah admitted, looking up from the page he had been writing on, "but we've got no way of knowing that for sure."

"I'll have to press the issue the next time Philip and I meet," Claire said with a determined nod.

Leila put her hand on her daughter's knee. "Honey, I think that's a very bad idea. It's too dangerous for you to meet with him again."

"I don't think so," Claire told her. "If he wanted to hurt me, he had a perfect opportunity when I followed Mona into that building. I think he genuinely wants to know how I did what I did." She let out a heavy breath. "Honestly, so do I."

Noah stood up and crossed the room to pin some more pieces of paper to the investigation wall. "Well, whatever this man's connection to Vogel, I think the situation has definitely reached a point where we need to loop your brother in."

Claire felt sick to her stomach at the idea. "Are you going to tell him everything?"

Her dad smiled down at her. "Only what he needs to know." He kissed her on top of her head then turned to leave the room. "We don't have much of a choice here. If this Philip person has a weapon that can drain the living, and he has also figured out how to use Beguiling Acuity, then this is bigger than any of us realized."

Noah was on the phone with Zach for close to an hour. When he finally rejoined his wife and daughter in the living room, he pointed his phone in Claire's direction and gave her a disapproving frown.

"You didn't call your brother. He was very upset when he found out you'd been hurt and everyone else knew about it before he did."

Claire shrugged. "What can I say? It was a crazy time. I'll call him later and apologize."

"No need," Noah assured her. "You can tell him you're sorry when he gets here this afternoon. He's coming with a P.I.D. team."

Claire groaned. "Is that really necessary?"

"What? The team coming or Zach coming?"

"Both."

"Well, this is some pretty serious stuff. He wants to make sure everything is handled correctly." Noah crossed to the investigation wall and pinned up another piece of paper with information on it about Vogel. "And I'm sure he also wants to make sure his little sister is okay."

"You mean, he wants to make sure his little sister isn't imagining things."

Noah gave her a sympathetic smile. "If we want to get to the bottom of this, we need to get Bureau resources involved."

Claire knew he was right, but that didn't mean she had to like it. She stared at her investigation board with all its unanswered questions. Of course, she wanted to find out the truth behind the rogues' disappearances and Philip's involvement and the existence of the Syndicate. Though it was childish, she just really wished it could happen without her brother having to get involved.

Chapter 35

Later that afternoon, Claire and her parents were at Claire's house, waiting for word from Zach that he had landed in Houston with the P.I.D. team. Because of the attack at the cemetery, Claire's boss at the candy store had given her another day off and she had gladly taken it. Leila was sitting at the kitchen table with Sarah and April, discussing favorite recipes while Thelma hovered from room to room, making everyone nervous.

"They're not coming *here*, are they?" Thelma asked, peeking through the front window curtains.

"No, dear," Noah assured her. "They're going to call us, and then we'll meet them at their hotel."

"I don't like it when there are P.I.D. agents running around. I don't trust them." She looked at Claire. "Those guns they carry. They could use them on me at any moment and I'd just be gone."

"They wouldn't do that," Claire said. "You aren't a threat to any livings."

"You know that, and I know that, but they don't necessarily know that."

"Well, if they want to dispatch you," Noah assured her, "they'll have to come through me."

His gallant declaration seemed to calm Thelma's nerves a bit, though she continued to hover near the window.

Claire tried to keep herself occupied by playing a game of solitaire on her phone while they waited, but she couldn't stop thinking about Philip and how he had used Beguiling Acuity. She had gone over it at least a hundred times, and she'd probably go over it a hundred more. The image of Mona clearly under his control, and his assertion that Claire could beguile a projection as well, kept replaying in her mind.

Claire watched Thelma float back and forth in front of the window. The projection's fidgety behavior was starting to wear on her nerves. Her dad's warning about the dangers of Beguiling Acuity continued to ring in her ears, but she couldn't help being intrigued. Though she had no idea where to actually begin, would there be a better time to test the waters?

She leaned forward in her seat and focused her thoughts on Thelma. She took several deep breaths to make sure her own emotions were calm, then tried to push those peaceful feelings across the room. *Calm down,* she thought. *Everything's going to be okay.*

Thelma turned in her float-pacing and their eyes met. As best she could, Claire focused all her positive energy toward the projection, continuing to send calming thoughts her way. They stared at each other for several seconds.

Claire's heart began to race. Was her attempt at Beguiling Acuity working?

"Claire, honey," Thelma finally said. "Are you constipated? You look like you're in pain."

Claire sighed and sat back on the couch. "No, I'm not constipated. I was just trying something."

"Well, whatever you're doing, stop it. It's giving me a headache."

Noah stared at her. "Claire, please tell me you weren't trying to use Beguiling Acuity."

Thelma gasped. "You were trying to control me!?"

"Thanks, Dad," Claire said with another sigh. "That was so not helpful."

He ignored her protest. "Didn't you listen to anything I said earlier about how dangerous it can be?"

"Yes, Dad, I heard you," she assured him. "I was just trying to help Thelma calm down."

The air around them pulsed and the temperature in the room dropped several degrees.

"I am so disappointed in you, Claire Abelard," Thelma said, planting her hands firmly on her hips.

Leila leaned her head in from the dining room. "What's going on? I felt the temperature drop."

"Your daughter was trying to control me," Thelma informed her. "You need to tell her how wrong that is."

Leila gave Claire a stern look, but there was amusement behind her eyes. "Claire, that was very wrong of you. You need to apologize to Thelma."

"Sorry, Thelma," Claire said begrudgingly. "I won't do it again."

Claire picked up her phone and pretended to check her email, ignoring the two sets of glaring eyes in the room.

A few seconds later, Thelma turned back toward the window and gasped. "Oh, Lord, they're here!" A second later, she shimmered out of sight, with April and Sarah quickly following her lead.

Claire stood and looked out the window. A black SUV was parked in the driveway with two more on the street next to the curb.

Noah set down the book he had been reading and headed toward the front door. "Well, so much for giving us a call when they landed."

"You know Zach," Claire said as she joined him at the door. "He's got to keep everybody on their toes."

They went out on the porch and waited as Zach and the rest of the P.I.D. team piled out of the SUVs. For an organization that flew under the average person's radar, this display was anything but inconspicuous.

Claire waved at one of her neighbors walking down the street with her dog. The woman eyed the men and the SUVs suspiciously. Claire could only imagine the rumors that would be flying around the block before the day was done.

Claire smiled at Zach as he walked up the front steps. She wasn't sure if she should hug him or punch him, so instead she said, "Hey."

"Claire," Zach said, nodding back at her then shaking hands with their dad. He frowned at the bandage on Claire's forehead. "I'm pretty upset with you. I don't like having to hear from one of my subordinates that my baby sister got hurt."

"It wasn't a big deal," she insisted. "Just a bump on the head."

"Are you sure that's all it was?"

Claire had no idea what Deputy Martens or Dr. Russell had reported to the Bureau, so she decided it was best just to nod and change the subject. "The black SUVs are a nice touch. Not exactly subtle, though."

"We needed to transport a lot of men and equipment quickly," he told her. "They were the most efficient mode of transportation we could find."

Claire opened the front door then stepped out of the way. "Why don't you guys come on inside before my neighbors hurt themselves trying to figure out what government agency you work for."

"And then you can fill me in on everything that's been happening around here."

She forced another smile as Zach passed by and entered the house.

"I know that look," a familiar voice said. "Please don't tell me I'm going to have to break up another fist fight."

Claire turned toward the speaker and her smile broadened genuinely. "Blake!" she said, stepping forward to hug him. He wrapped her up in a bear hug, easily lifting her feet off the ground as he squeezed.

Blake Crawley was like a second brother to Claire, only without all the baggage that accompanied actual family ties. They had grown up together in Boston, their two families linked by connections to a secret world of energy projections. As a child, making friends outside of Bureau circles hadn't been easy. It was hard to host sleepovers with schoolmates when your house was "haunted," so your closest friends tended to be the ones who already knew the truth.

Blake's family's roots with the Bureau traced back to the first colonists recruited for the American Branch in 1740. Though two of his uncles had been expelled during the schism of 1955, his father and grandfather had remained with the Bureau. So, like Zach and Claire, it was only natural Blake would enter the family business, too. When

Zach got promoted, so did Blake, so for the past few years he had been Zach's right-hand man.

"Wow!" Claire said, punching Blake playfully in the arm once he had set her down again. "All the good agents must be busy with something else if HQ pulled you away from your cushy desk and put you back in the field."

Though Blake's promotion had been well deserved, Claire knew he wasn't cut out for life stuck in an office. Any opportunity for field work would be a welcome break for him, and Claire was glad he had come. Though he didn't share her views on rogues, she was certain he would help provide a balance to the investigation that might otherwise be lacking.

Blake nodded toward the house. "You know your brother. He'd be lost without me." He took a step back and examined her, like Zach had, gently touching the bandage on her forehead. "Of course, we're going to take this seriously, Claire. You were attacked."

Claire nodded and motioned toward the door. "Then, by all means, let's get started."

Blake ruffled her hair and entered the house, followed by the rest of their P.I.D. entourage. Claire and her dad stayed back on the porch until the last agent had crossed the threshold.

"Is it too late for me to run?" Claire asked.

Noah laughed. "I'm afraid so. You're our star witness."

She scrunched up her face. "That's what makes me want to run."

Chapter 36

Claire spent the next two hours telling Zach and his team everything that had happened over the past few days, though once again she left out the details about her part in their escape from the hooded men. There was also no mention of Philip's apparent use of Beguiling Acuity. Such a taboo topic would be discussed later, when the room wasn't full of mid-level Bureau agents.

"How's Isabel doing?" Claire asked when she had finished. "I haven't gotten an update since yesterday."

Zach looked up from the tablet where he'd been entering notes. "We received word this morning that she's out of the coma. She says she doesn't remember anything, but I don't know if that's true or if that's just the story she's telling the police. We're going to go by the hospital and talk with her as soon as we leave here."

Claire nodded, relieved to hear Isabel's health was improving. With the amount of energy that had been drained from her, it was a wonder she had woken up from the coma at all.

"So, what do you think we're dealing with here?" Noah asked after Zach had spent a few more seconds typing notes into his tablet.

"I really couldn't venture a guess right now," Zach replied, this time not looking up. "We haven't even started our investigation yet."

"What do you mean you haven't started your investigation?" Leila said. "You just spent two hours grilling your sister."

"Yes," Zach replied, "but that's only one witness's account. We're going to need a lot more information before we can even begin to formulate any theories. We need to talk to Isabel and take readings at the cemetery, and that's just a start." He motioned to one of his team members as if a thought had just occurred to him. "I'm wondering if we need to talk to any of the rogues. Maybe Jean Lafitte." The other man nodded enthusiastically as if it were a brilliant suggestion and Zach looked at Claire. "Do you think you could have the house projections get word to him if we decide we need to talk to him?"

Claire stared at her brother. "Of course, you should talk to the rogues," she said, "if there are any of them left. They're the ones who've been disappearing."

The P.I.D. agent Zach had been speaking to smiled at her condescendingly. "We don't know that they're missing. There are any number of possible explanations for what's happened to them."

Claire stood up, indignant. "I *saw* what's happening to them! I saw Philip drain that projection of its energy, and then turn the weapon on Isabel."

"Let's not call it a weapon," Zach cautioned. He wasn't the least bit fazed by Claire's outburst. "I think that's a little inflammatory."

Out of the corner of her eye, Claire saw her mom give her dad an all-too-familiar signal. Even without her Affective Acumen, Leila knew her children well enough to know where this conversation was headed.

Noah stood up and crossed to where Claire was standing. "I think we should take a break from the questioning for now." Taking Claire by the arm, he looked at Blake and suggested, "Maybe we could order some take out for everybody. I'm sure you guys are hungry."

Blake nodded as he pulled his cell phone out of his pocket. "That's a great idea."

With a gentle but firm hand on Claire's back, Noah led his daughter toward the door before she could say something she would regret later.

Claire shoved the front door open and stepped out onto the porch, still seething. Her dad followed.

"They're acting like I'm making this stuff up," Claire fumed before the door had completely shut behind them. "I didn't imagine what I saw in the cemetery, or what Philip was able to do to Mona. They need to take this seriously."

"They *are* taking it seriously," Noah tried to assure her. "They just have to follow certain procedures in conducting their investigation. It's not that they don't believe you, but they need to find evidence to support what you've told them."

Claire knew what her dad said made sense, but she couldn't shake the feeling they were wasting too much time wading through the Bureau's red tape. They stood on the porch together in silence for several minutes, waiting for Claire's frustration and anger to subside.

Noah put his arm around Claire's shoulders. "You about ready to give this another try?"

Claire nodded, but neither of them made a move to go back inside. Before too much longer, the front door opened and Zach stepped out onto the porch.

Noah cleared his throat. "I'll let you two talk."

Before he went back inside, he gave his son a stern look. A smart man would have recognized the warning to handle Claire with kid gloves.

"Claire," Zach began instead, his tone no less condescending than it had been before, "you're blowing this all out of proportion. Don't you want us to do a thorough investigation? If this Philip Graham person really is harming projections, we need to get to the bottom of it, but we need to do it the right way."

She turned to look at him. "There's no 'if' here, Zach. I saw it with my own eyes."

"And at this point you're the only person who has. There's no way I can authorize the kind of action necessary to deal with what you've described based solely on one agent's statement."

"I'm not just an agent," she reminded him. "I'm your sister. That should count for something."

"It does count for something with me, but the rest of the board will need more proof." He leaned against the porch railing and let out an exaggerated sigh. "Look, I understand you're probably still angry about

San Francisco." He shrugged. "To be honest, I'm still pretty upset about it too, but we can't let that cloud the waters this time."

Claire turned away from him, willing herself not to say what she was thinking. "You're wasting time," she said instead. "While you're retreading ground that I've already investigated, Philip is out there draining who knows how many more rogues."

Zach folded his arms across his chest. "I know you don't want to hear this, but the rogues aren't our top priority. No registered projections have gone missing to this point, so we're going to do this by the book, no matter how much time it takes."

"Are you going to try to get in touch with Philip?" Claire asked.

"And accuse him of what exactly? I won't risk exposing Bureau secrets to a non-agent."

Claire was about to point out that Philip already knew Bureau secrets, but the sight of Drew's truck pulling up in front of the house stopped her. In all the activity surrounding Zach's arrival, she had completely forgotten about her dinner date.

Her eyes grew wide in horror at the thought of Zach meeting Drew. There was no way her brother would miss the ghost hunter's sensitivity level. She hurried down the porch steps. At least she wouldn't have to worry about officially submitting his name to the Bureau. It was about be done for her.

Drew got out of his truck and looked at the fleet of SUVs. "Did the President come to town?" he asked with a chuckle.

"No," Claire said, meeting him in the yard and trying to redirect him back to his truck. "Just my brother and some friends."

Though Zach wasn't as strong a sensitive as Claire was, he had to already be sensing Drew's energy level, even from the porch. But maybe there was still time to minimize the damage.

"Claire Bear, aren't you going to introduce me to your friend?"

Claire cursed silently at the sound of her brother's voice behind her.

"Zach Abelard," he said, stepping around her and extending his hand in Drew's direction.

The two men shook hands.

"Drew Mitchell. It's nice to meet you."

"You, too." Zach turned his attention toward his sister, an amused look on his face. "So, I guess you're a friend of Claire's then?"

Claire could feel her face heating up. "Drew is one of the men who came to our rescue at the cemetery the other night," she said lamely.

Zach's expression grew serious. "Well, then, it looks like I owe you a huge 'thank you' for looking out for my baby sister."

Drew nodded, an unspoken acknowledgement of Zach's thanks. He turned to Claire and smiled. "Are you ready?"

Claire hesitated.

"Claire Bear," Zach said, clearly enjoying the moment way too much, "you didn't tell me you had a date tonight. Now I feel awful for disrupting your plans."

She wanted to punch him in the throat. Instead, she put her arm through Drew's and pulled him in the direction of his truck.

"See you guys later," Zach called out as Drew held the car door open for her.

Claire glared at her brother as Drew circled the car to the driver's side. In response, Zach simply smiled serenely and waved.

Drew slid in behind the wheel but didn't start the engine immediately. "Is everything okay?" he asked.

Claire nodded, fuming as she stared out the passenger window. "I'm fine. It's just brothers, you know." She turned toward him and forced a smile. "I promise I won't let this ruin our evening."

Drew started the car and backed out of the driveway. They had only driven a few houses down the block when he pulled the car over to the curb.

Claire stared at him. "What are you doing?"

He turned in his seat to face her. "Okay, look, I need you to tell me what's really going on here."

Claire opened her mouth to answer, but nothing came out. She wanted so badly to tell him everything, but years of agent training made any words of explanation stick in her throat. One misstep here and her entire life could implode.

"I'm not an idiot, Claire," Drew pressed on. "I know something's not right. The other night in the cemetery? I know that wasn't just a group of guys there to vandalize some gravestones. They did something to you and your friend. I could feel it." He shook his head. "You live in a house full of ghosts, which is unusual in and of itself, but then your brother shows up with the black SUV brigade and I'm supposed to think that's normal."

Claire took a deep breath and let it out slowly. She looked at Drew and a strange sense of calm came over her. Whatever the consequences might be, she couldn't keep lying to him.

"Okay," she finally said. "I'll tell you everything, but we need to go somewhere we can't be overheard."

"Seriously?"

She nodded solemnly. "Yes, seriously."

He thought for a second and shrugged. "Now you definitely have my attention."

Claire didn't doubt it. She swallowed hard as he put the car into drive and pulled away from the curb. Drew thought he wanted to know the truth. She prayed he wanted to stick around once he did.

Chapter 37

Thirty minutes later, Claire found herself sitting next to Drew on a bench on the Seawall, still unsure how to tell him the truth. They had pulled through a fast food drive-thru to get some burgers, but Claire didn't have much of an appetite. She had never had to initiate someone into the world of the Bureau for Historical Preservation before. It was a lot harder than she realized.

"Well," Drew said, holding up his hamburger, "this isn't exactly the romantic dinner I had in mind for our first date, but I guess it's better than no date at all."

He offered her a smile and she returned it halfheartedly.

"I'm sorry. I didn't mean to ruin our evening."

She took a quick look around. It wasn't the most secluded spot, but it was unlikely their conversation would be overheard by any passing tourists.

"You haven't ruined it," Drew assured her. "The point of a date is to get to know someone better, right?" He chuckled. "And it sounds like I'm about to learn a whole lot about you."

"Yeah, probably way more than you'd ever want to know."

"Don't be so sure about that." He took a bite of his burger and chewed it slowly. "My imagination has been going wild trying to figure out what's going on with you, so it'll probably be a relief to know the truth."

"Don't be so sure about that," Claire said with a hesitant smile.

"It can't be worse than the theories I've come up with so far."

"Like what?" She knew she was stalling.

Drew wiped his mouth with his napkin. "Well, at first I thought CIA, but I decided that would be too obvious and actually kind of boring. Then I thought maybe you were a member of a mysterious, ancient league of ninja assassins." He grinned at her. "But, again, too obvious."

She laughed despite her nerves.

"My most recently formed theory," he continued, "is that you're a princess from some small European country. You escaped your sheltered life and you've been living here incognito. I assume the black SUVs are your security team who has finally found you and they're here to take you home."

"Wow," Claire said, setting her hamburger aside. "You're really good at this."

He raised his eyebrows. "Really?"

She laughed again. "No, not at all."

"Okay," he nodded. "So, you're not a spy, a ninja, or a princess. What other possible explanation could there be?"

Claire took a deep breath. "Well, I could work for a secret organization that monitors and assists ghosts in an effort to preserve the history of significant locations around the world." She looked at him, waiting for his response.

He pointed a French fry at her. "No offense, but I think my ninja assassin theory is way more believable."

"Maybe." She looked out at the waves rather than making eye contact with him. "But I'm not joking." She took another deep breath. "In the Middle Ages, a group of scientists and philosophers discovered that all humans give off some amount of electrical current..."

Twenty minutes later, she had finished her history lesson. Drew didn't make any comments or ask any questions the entire time. She couldn't bring herself to look at him, so they sat in silence, staring out at the waves.

After what felt like an eternity, Drew cleared his throat. "So, what we call ghosts are really these energy projections that have been left behind."

Claire nodded.

"That makes sense when you think about how they interact with our ghost hunting equipment. We're just picking up on their energy."

At this point Claire mustered the courage to look at him. He seemed thoughtful, but not freaked out. "That's right," she said with a smile. "It's their energy."

"Honestly, that explains a lot." He looked a little sheepish. "I've always wondered why the EVPs only come through on electronic devices. It never made sense to me that we could only hear the communication on the recordings later and never in real time."

"Actually…" Claire began, still weighing how far she wanted to take him down the rabbit hole.

"What?" he pressed.

She looked down at her hands. "I suspect you probably don't need the EVP recordings, or any other equipment, to communicate with them."

His brow wrinkled in confusion. "What do you mean?"

She let out a heavy sigh. "Did you ever talk to your Blue Lady when you were a kid? I mean, have actual conversations with her?"

"Yeah, all the time. She used to tell me bedtime stories."

Claire smiled. "Well, then, you should definitely be able to talk to other projections as well." She shrugged. "And with your sensitivity level, you can probably talk to them all."

He frowned. "Then how come I haven't had any encounters like that since I was a kid? We've done dozens of investigations and none of the spirits have communicated with me directly."

"If you haven't done it since you were little, you've probably forgotten how." She picked up a French fry, her appetite slowly returning. "And most sensitives can't fully communicate with projections. It's actually a pretty rare ability, so the projections don't automatically assume people can. More often than not, it's a waste of their time and it just frustrates them, so they eventually learn not to try anymore."

"I'm definitely going to give it a shot on our next investigation," he said, grinning like a little kid. "What should I do to let them know I can talk to them without the equipment?"

Now it was Claire's turn to frown. "I honestly don't know. I've never had that problem."

She remembered they covered that in agent training, but she hadn't paid much attention. Since she had Attractive Acumen, the projections she had encountered over the years, even the rogues, usually initiated communication with her.

"I'll think of something," Drew said with a wink. A slow smile crept across his lips. "That would be so awesome though, to actually have a conversation with a spirit. Oops, I mean, projection."

Claire shook her head. "Maybe at first, but then the trick is getting them to shut up."

He chuckled. "I can imagine." He sat in thoughtful silence for a few seconds, then his face grew serious and he turned on the bench to look at her. "So, what really happened that night in the cemetery?" He pointed back over his shoulder. "And what's with all the SUVs outside your house?"

"Actually, those two things are connected." She felt exhausted just thinking about what was waiting for her at home. "The SUVs are for one of the Bureau's Paranormal Investigation teams. They're here to investigate what happened in the cemetery."

"Which was?"

She shook her head. "We really don't know. Several projections have gone missing on the island. Isabel and I were looking into it that night when we came across that group of men draining the energy from a rogue."

"Rogue?"

"A projection not under the jurisdiction of the Bureau." She looked out at the water. "Normally Bureau agents don't interact with them, but it's definitely a cause for concern when they start to go missing."

"What happened to Isabel that night?"

"Again, I don't really know." She frowned. "The tools that dispatch projections aren't supposed to be able to harm the living, but that one did. It was draining her energy, which shouldn't be possible."

He looked thoughtful. "So, it really is all about the energy then, for projections and for people." He paused. "Is that what you meant when you said I had a 'high sensitivity level'?"

She nodded. "Ever wonder why you seem to instantly connect with some people and not so much with others? Usually, it's because of energy connections."

"I know exactly what that's like." He gave her a smile that made her heart flutter. "That first day we met, it felt like there was something drawing me to the candy store. I don't usually eat sweets, so I know that didn't have anything to do with it. Then when we walked in the door, it felt like a wave hit me and almost knocked me off my feet." He paused. "Was that you?"

She nodded. "It hit me pretty hard, too. It's been years since I met another high-level sensitive, so it caught me completely off guard."

"How come it doesn't feel like that now?"

"Your body adjusts to the amount of energy around you and reaches a sort of stasis. We've been around each other enough the past few days that things have stabilized." She nibbled on a French fry. "Basically, we've gotten used to each other."

"I've got no complaints about that."

She could feel her face turning red, but she didn't mind.

He reached over and took her hand. "Okay, so, I get the bit about projections and I get the energy thing. But what is it that I see when projections are around?"

"You're actually *seeing* their energy." She turned to look at him. "Like I said before, not all sensitives can communicate with projections, but we all have different abilities and ways we can interact with them. Some sensitives can see the projections' physical forms while others can hear them. At the Bureau we call these kinds of abilities acumens."

"Okay," he said. "So, which acumen do you have?"

She looked back out at the water. "Almost all of them."

"I take it that's not usually the case."

She shook her head. "Usually a sensitive only has one, maybe two abilities. For obvious reasons, Bureau field agents have to have the Communicative Acumen or they can't do the job." She shrugged. "There are agents who can see the projections more clearly than I do, but they can't communicate with them or feel their emotions the way I can."

"Can you see the energy, too?"

"No." She bit her lip. "Actually, that's a very rare ability. It's called Force Perceptive Acumen, and I only know of a handful of agents who have it." She smiled at him. "And they're pretty much legends."

A smile played at the corners of his lips. "Well, then..."

Claire laughed, genuinely pleased at how well he was handling everything. They sat in silence for a few seconds.

"So, what happens now?" he eventually asked. "Do you have some special contraption that wipes my memory?"

She pulled her hand away from his and looked back out at the waves. "Actually, you'll most likely be approached by the Bureau for recruitment. There's no way my brother missed how strong your sensitivity level is." She cut a glance in his direction. "And like I said, your ability is very rare and would be highly sought after."

"Recruitment?" he repeated. "What would that mean?"

"Well, if you decide you want to join the Bureau, you'll go through agent training where they'll teach you how to take advantage of your acumens. After that, you'll be assigned where they think you're most needed."

He smiled broadly. "Will they teach me how to communicate with projections?"

"Definitely." She looked down at her burger, her appetite gone again. "In fact, you'll probably have instructors fighting over the chance to train you. Again, they don't see a lot of sensitives with Force Perceptive Acumen."

He studied her face for a few seconds. "You don't sound very happy that the Bureau might want to recruit me. It sounds like an awesome gig."

She could hear the hurt in his voice. "It is," she assured him, "and I think you'd make a great agent." She paused. "But we already have three agents here in Galveston. If you join the Bureau, we most likely won't be assigned to the same city. In fact, they'll probably want you to stay in Boston at headquarters."

He smiled. "And you don't want that to happen because...?"

She couldn't resist a smile. "Do I really have to say it?"

He shook his head then leaned forward and placed a gentle kiss on her lips. He pulled back a few inches to gauge her response but didn't have to wait long as she quickly closed the distance between them again. It was all the encouragement he needed.

By that time, the sun had already dropped to the horizon, setting the sky ablaze. Maybe the evening hadn't been a total loss on the romance front after all.

Chapter 38

Claire and Drew sat on the bench on the Seawall for another hour, neither wanting their time together to end. They talked about the Bureau and projections, but nothing more about the possibility of Drew's recruitment. Claire knew they'd eventually have to go back and face reality, but she was in no rush to make that happen.

After a few moments of comfortable silence, Drew lifted their joined hands to his lips and kissed the back of Claire's hand. "I guess I better get you home," he said with a tender smile. "I don't want a fleet of black SUVs hunting me down because they think I've kidnapped you." He let out a heavy sigh. "Plus, my phone has been vibrating in my pocket every five minutes or so. It's probably Spencer, freaking out because I'm not there helping sort through the data."

Claire nodded and stood up. "Yeah, and I really want to be involved with Zach's investigation. It's not that I don't trust them to be thorough. I just don't know how concerned they're actually going to be about the missing rogues."

Drew stood as well and together they walked slowly, hand-in-hand, back to his truck. They didn't talk much during the drive back to Claire's house, but it wasn't an awkward silence. When they finally pulled in Claire's driveway, the SUVs were gone. They sat in the darkness of Drew's truck, neither wanting to open the door and break the spell.

Drew leaned toward Claire and kissed her again, not as intensely as their kiss at the beach but still enough to leave her breathless.

"I'll call you tomorrow," he said, his lips inches from hers. "And don't worry, your secret is safe with me."

Claire smiled. She never doubted it would be. She gave Drew one more quick kiss, then climbed out of the truck.

When she opened the front door of her house, she was immediately greeted by three ripples of energy.

"Oh, Claire, I'm so happy for you!" Sarah told her.

"He's so dreamy!" Thelma concurred.

"Are you going to see him again?" April asked.

Claire smiled and nodded. "We've got one more tour tomorrow night."

"It's so romantic!" Thelma squealed, pretending to dance with a non-existent partner. "Every woman should have at least one fling in her life."

Claire frowned. "This isn't a fling."

Thelma stopped spinning and looked at her, batting her eyes innocently. "Isn't he leaving in a few days?"

"Thelma!" Sarah scolded. "She doesn't need you to remind her of that."

Claire wanted to be angry with them, but she knew it wasn't their fault. They were only voicing the truth she had let herself ignore for a few precious hours. Drew would be walking out of her life, one way or another, in a few days.

Claire walked through the three projections, shivering as she did so, and headed toward the kitchen. "Where are my parents?" she asked, desperate to change the subject.

"They went to the hospital with those people." Thelma made a face and pretended to vomit.

Claire rolled her eyes. "By 'those people,' I assume you mean Zach and his team."

Thelma wretched. "Yes. They can't blouse out of town soon enough for my liking."

"I agree," Claire said honestly, since their departure would hopefully mean the issue of the disappearing rogues had been resolved.

She went to the kitchen and got a soda from the refrigerator before returning to the living room. The house felt eerily quiet after the excitement of the past few days. She considered heading to the hospital to join her parents, but the introverted part of her personality was enjoying the solitude.

She spotted her laptop on the desk and realized the empty house afforded her an additional opportunity she couldn't afford to let pass by. Without any distractions or interruptions, this would be the perfect time to do a little research on Beguiling Acuity.

She crossed the room, opened the laptop, and pulled up the login screen for the Bureau's private server. Once the familiar home screen appeared, she accessed the Bureau's archives, entered the words "Beguiling Acuity" into the search bar, and clicked "Go." Almost instantly, a message appeared on the screen.

0 entries found for this category

She frowned. Her dad had said Bureau leadership didn't want agents dabbling with such a dangerous acumen, but how could there be no information about it at all? She nibbled at her bottom lip as she stared at the screen, considering her options. Maybe the Bureau didn't want agents to know the truth, but the information had to exist somewhere, and she knew exactly who would have access to it.

She maneuvered the mouse and moved the arrow slowly across the screen, logging out of her own account. She took a deep breath, hesitating before logging back in. What she was about to do would almost certainly get her fired if she were caught, but she needed to know the truth, and this was the only way.

With another deep breath, she entered Zach's username, which wasn't a secret since the Bureau followed a set pattern for all employees. Their passwords were supposed to be a secret, but Zach used the same one for everything, and Claire had figured out ages ago.

Once she was logged in as Zach, Claire easily accessed the information she needed from the archives. Any feelings of guilt quickly melted away as she uncovered a treasure trove of data about Beguiling Acuity. There were several accounts of unsuccessful attempts at mastering the skill with graphic descriptions of the negative consequences that followed. It was almost enough to convince her not to try again. Almost.

A tingle of excitement spread over her as she opened a research document that described how the acumen theoretically should work. She read through it twice, a confused frown creasing her brow. Was that all there was to it? The process seemed so simple.

"Claire," Thelma announced, breezing into the room with a sparkle of sequins.

Claire jumped in surprise, quickly closing the laptop before Thelma could see what was on the screen. "Don't sneak up on me like that," she scolded.

Thelma stared at her for several seconds, then shrugged. "Whatever." She placed her hands on her hips. "Jean Lafitte sent word through the Ghost Net that he's willing to talk to the P.I.D. team, but only if you're there, too."

Claire nodded. "Great. That's progress." She smiled at Thelma. "Thank you for letting me know."

"I live only to serve," Thelma said with a dramatic flourish as she faded out of sight.

Claire waited until Thelma's energy had completely left the room before opening the laptop back up and logging out of Zach's account. She picked up her phone and texted Zach the news about the meeting, as well as the details of the location where she usually met with Jean Lafitte.

She tapped her phone against the desk a few times, considering her options. She had no idea when Zach and his team would get around to meeting with Jean, and she didn't want him to get offended and change his mind. She sent Zach another text telling him she was on her way to the meeting place, then grabbed her purse and headed for the door.

Chapter 39

Claire drove straight to the Harbor House Hotel and found a parking place not far from the dock. She still hadn't heard back from Zach, and it was really starting to irritate her.

As she waited in the parking lot, she was keenly aware of the fact that Drew was probably somewhere inside the hotel, just a few yards away from her. She resisted the urge to call him. Of all the projections he could try to communicate with first, it would be fun to introduce him to Jean Lafitte. If the circumstances had been different, that's exactly what she would have done. Tonight, though, the last thing she needed was for Zach to show up and see Drew interacting with a projection.

She looked toward the pier where Jean should be waiting for her. A wise person would have waited for Zach and the P.I.D. team, but Claire didn't feel like she had that luxury. This conversation was too important to risk letting them screw it up.

After another look around the dark parking lot, Claire exited the car. As she made her way to the meeting place, she repeatedly checked her surroundings. The parking lot and dock both appeared to be empty. Breathing a bit more easily, she rounded the corner of the hotel and headed for the spot where she had previously waited for Jean.

She stepped into the shadows, but unlike the previous time, she didn't have to wait long before she felt a massive surge of energy coming toward her from the water. *The Pride* glimmered into view, with Jean and his crew standing proudly on the deck. As soon as the ship reached the dock, Jean materialized beside her.

"Your message has reached me," he said with a bow. "I have come as commanded."

Before Claire could thank him, a very real, solid human arm came from behind her and wrapped around her neck. For a second, she was too stunned to react, but then her Bureau training kicked in. She raised one hand up to her attacker's arm, jammed her other elbow back into the person's stomach and stepped hard on the instep of his foot. She heard a grunt and felt the grip loosen enough that she was able to duck out of his grip.

She had no idea who this person was or whether they had one of the energy-draining weapons, but she wasn't taking any chances. "Jean, get out of here!" she yelled.

She spun around to face her attacker. He was wearing a ski mask. If he was with Philip's group, they had learned a few things from their encounter in the cemetery.

"I can't leave a damsel in distress!" Jean called out.

Claire was touched by his concern, but the only way he could help was to go full-poltergeist, and that would deplete his energy, leaving him even more vulnerable to any weapons the attacker might have.

"He has a device that can drain your energy," she called out to Jean, not taking her eyes off the man who had grabbed her.

The man hadn't made a second attempt for her, and she wasn't going to give him another chance to do so. The fact that he wasn't completely freaked out by her conversation with someone who wasn't actually there confirmed he wasn't an average mugger looking for an easy target.

After a few agonizing seconds, Claire felt the energy around the dock ripple as Jean and *The Pride* disappeared. She breathed a sigh of relief. Now she could focus on her own safety.

She glanced toward the parking lot, preparing to make a break for it. As if reading her mind, the man moved to block her path, but still kept his distance. Claire frowned. What did he want from her?

With her path to the parking lot blocked, her only other means of escape was the dock itself. She turned and ran, the wooden planks creaking under her feet. The boards groaned a second time as the man took off after her. She had only taken a few steps when she felt a large hand wrap around her arm. She swung around, balling up her other fist and clocking her attacker upside the head. This time his grip didn't loosen. Claire struggled to get free, losing her balance in the process. The man was quickly on top of her.

"They told me not to hurt you," he hissed in her ear as he pressed his forearm across her throat. "But you're making me want to forget my orders."

Claire tried to summon up her energy to send out another blast like she had in the cemetery, but since she had no idea how she did it the first time, she had little hope of making it happen now.

She heard a car door slam somewhere in the parking lot. Her attacker stood up quickly and ran down the dock into the darkness. She raised her hand up to her bruised throat and tried to suck in several painful breaths. Footsteps quickly approached and a familiar voice spoke in the darkness.

"Claire!" Blake knelt down on the dock next to her. "My God, are you alright?"

She nodded and pointed down the dock. "The man ran off that way." Her throat felt like it was on fire.

"I'm not leaving you here like this," he told her. "We need to get you to the hospital."

She shook her head. "He'll get away."

"I'm not worried about him right now."

Claire grabbed hold of Blake's shirt. "Please, go after him. He might be our only way to find Philip and the people he's working with." When he hesitated again, she said, "I'll be fine. I'll call Drew. They're staying in this hotel. He'll be out here in a few minutes."

Blake helped her to her feet. "Come on. Let me at least get you into my car."

She looked around the parking lot as he led her away from the pier. "Where's Zach and the rest of the team?"

"He asked me to come by myself. He thought Jean Lafitte might feel more open to talking if it was just you and me."

Claire nodded. Despite her frazzled nerves and the pain in her throat, she was glad Zach had put his ego aside and considered the feelings of a projection for a change. "Would you please call him and get the team over here?" she asked. "We can't let that guy get away. He may be our only way to find Philip."

Blake opened his passenger door for her. "Don't worry about him." When she didn't immediately get in, he turned to look at her. "God, I forgot how stubborn you can be." He sighed loudly. "Get in the car and I'll go after him."

Claire leaned up on her tiptoes and gave him a kiss on the cheek before sliding into the passenger's seat. She pulled her phone out of her pocket and showed it to him, proof that she was going to call Drew. Blake let out another sigh and closed the car door.

Claire pressed the automatic locks and watched Blake trot off into the darkness of the dock before pulling up Drew's number on her phone. Her throat ached and her voice croaked, so she decided a text message would be best.

Within minutes, Drew bolted out the front door of the hotel. It was ridiculous how relieved Claire felt when she saw him. She opened the car door and stepped out where he could see her. As soon as he spotted her, he made a bee line for the SUV.

"Oh, my God, Claire," he said, wrapping her in a strong embrace. "You were attacked again? What happened?"

She didn't want to think about it. "Why are you so sweaty?" she asked instead, pulling back to look at his face.

He frowned. "I just ran down three flights of stairs to get to you. What happened?"

"It's a long story." She pointed in the direction Blake had gone. "Blake went after the guy, but I'm sure he's long gone by now." She shook her head. "Looks like I screwed that up, too."

"What are you talking about?" He took her face in his hands and examined her for injuries.

"The man got away because of me."

"I'm not even going to listen to that kind of talk," he said, taking her hand. She winced and he released his grip.

"Sorry." She cradled her wrist against her chest.

He set his jaw and took her by the elbow instead. "I'm taking you to the hospital."

Claire hesitated. "I need to wait for Blake to get back."

"You can call him. I'm sure he'll understand."

She was about to protest again when she spotted Blake jogging in their direction from the docks. "Did you find him?"

He shook his head. "I've called Zach. He's sending some agents." He looked at Drew. "Can you take her to the hospital?"

Drew nodded. "I was about to."

Claire shook her head. "I'm not going to the hospital." Blake and Drew shared a look, causing Claire to let out a heavy sigh. "I'm fine."

Blake raised his eyebrows. "I think your arm might not agree with you on that."

She shook her hear again.

"I don't want to be jerk about this," Drew said, "but I really think you need to go."

Blake gave her a stern look. "I don't mind being a jerk. You're going." He turned to Drew. "Where's your car?"

Drew pushed the button on his key fob and the lights on his truck flashed from a few parking spots away. Blake went to the truck, opened the passenger door, and waited for Claire to follow.

"And you call me stubborn," she grumbled as she started walking in his direction. She had enough experience with Blake to know that he would probably pick her up and carry her if she didn't cooperate, so there was no point in continuing to argue.

After she was buckled in, Blake reached out to shake Drew's hand. "Thanks." He leaned into the truck and kissed Claire on the cheek. "I'll call to check on you later."

Claire grunted and looked away, back in the direction of the docks where she had been attacked. Her wrist was screaming at her and her throat continued to throb, but she tried not to show it. Blake chuckled, then closed the passenger door as Drew made his way to the driver's side.

As they pulled out of the parking lot, Claire resisted the urge to cry. She couldn't help feeling that once again she was screwing everything up, this time by letting her attacker get away. She watched Blake head back to the dock, his cell phone to his ear. What difference did it make? The guy, and their only solid lead, had gotten away because she hadn't been strong enough to stop him.

Chapter 40

When Claire and Drew arrived at the hospital, Claire's parents met them at the entrance. She didn't want to go to the emergency room, but the others all insisted. Dr. Russell met them there and took Claire back to one of the examination rooms.

"Two visits in less than a week," the doctor said as she shined a light in Claire's eyes. "We've got to stop meeting like this."

Claire tried to force a smile as Drew handed her a cup of water. The stress of the past twenty-four hours and a serious lack of sleep were starting to take a toll on her.

"I don't think we'll need to keep you overnight," Dr. Russell told Claire. She had ordered a nurse to bandage the scrapes on Claire's arms and wrap her sprained wrist. "But I'd like for someone to keep an eye on you tonight all the same."

"Don't worry about that," Noah spoke up from the doorway. "She's got plenty of people looking out for her."

Dr. Russell smiled at Claire. "That's good to know, isn't it?"

Claire nodded again half-heartedly. She just wanted to go home and go to bed. It was almost three o'clock in the morning.

"We'll take her straight home," Leila said as she stood up and collected her purse. "First we need to go upstairs and tell Isabel what's going on." She patted Claire on the leg. "We'll be back in a few minutes."

"I can drive Claire home," Drew offered. "I really don't mind."

Claire's parents exchanged a look and Claire let out a sigh.

"That sounds like a great plan." She sat up and swung her legs over the side of the bed. Noah opened his mouth to protest as Claire stood up, but she held up a hand to stop him. "I just want to get some sleep, and the sooner that can happen the better."

She started toward the door, not waiting to see if anyone was going with her. When she felt a strong but gentle hand on her elbow, the mild jolt that shot up her arm assured her Drew had followed. They made their way to his truck where he opened the door and Claire slid into the passenger's seat. As she watched him circle the car to the driver's side, she again had to resist the urge to cry. Everything was such a mess, and it was all her fault.

Drew started the engine, then turned to look at her. "Are you sure you're okay?"

Claire nodded but didn't speak. He hesitated before shifting into reverse and backing out of the parking space. She was quiet the whole way home, certain that any attempts at conversation would only have resulted in uncontrollable tears, maybe even hysterics.

When they finally pulled into Claire's driveway, Drew put the truck in park and turned off the engine.

Claire forced a smile. "You don't have to walk me to the door. I'll be fine."

"Oh, I'm not walking you to the door," he told her as he exited the truck. "I'm coming inside to make sure the coast is clear."

She didn't have the energy or desire to argue with him. Even though her parents shouldn't be far behind them, Claire knew it would be smart to let him check everything out. She unlocked the front door and he entered the house first.

"Stay here," he told her with a kiss on her cheek.

A wave of exhaustion flooded over her as she waited for Drew to return. She leaned against the porch railing for support, the stress and emotions from everything that had happened over the past few hours finally taking their toll.

A few minutes later, Drew returned and gave her a thumb's up. "All clear."

Claire smiled unenthusiastically and thanked him.

He stepped aside so she could enter the house. "Are you sure you don't want me to stay until your parents get here?" he asked as she crossed the threshold. "I don't mind."

Claire set her purse on the table next to the door. "They won't be long, and honestly I'm going straight to bed. I wouldn't be very good company."

He nodded and turned to leave.

"I'm sorry I ruined your life," Claire announced suddenly, stopping him in his tracks. The thought had been eating away at her for a while and she couldn't keep it in anymore.

"What?" he said with a surprised chuckle as he turned back to face her.

"I'm sorry I ruined your life." She wiped away a tear that had escaped despite her best efforts to contain it. Closing her eyes, she let out a heavy sigh. "I never should have told you about the Bureau. Now I've ruined everything for you."

"Wow, that's really dramatic." He waited until she opened her eyes and looked at him. Claire could tell he was trying not to smile. "Don't take this the wrong way, but I think you might be giving yourself too much credit here. Ghost hunting was a hobby. It wasn't my whole life."

"Are you going to keep doing it, then?" He shook his head and Claire felt the tears threatening again. "Can't you just pretend? I have to do it all the time on my ghost tours. You get used to it."

He shook his head. "I know myself. There's no way I can keep up a charade like that, and I would feel like a complete dick not being able to tell the other guys the truth."

Claire bit her bottom lip to keep it from trembling. She knew he didn't mean it the way it sounded, but his words stung all the same. It didn't take long before he realized what he had said.

He closed the distance between them and took her face in his hands. "I didn't mean it like that. It's your job to keep secrets like that. It's not mine."

"One day it might be," she offered feebly.

"Maybe," he said with a gentle smile, "but until that day, I'll just have to do what I have to do." He kissed her on the tip of her nose. "Honestly, I'm glad I know the truth. And I promise no matter what happens, I won't tell anybody about the Bureau."

Claire wrapped her arms around his waist and rested her head on his chest. "I thought my brother would have recruited you by now. I know he's had a lot on his plate since he got here, and I haven't told him you're a Force Perceptive yet, but he knows you're a level 5. I thought that would be enough."

Drew squeezed her tighter. "It's okay. I don't know if I even want to join the Bureau anyway, so it's kind of a relief that I don't have to make any decisions right now."

Claire didn't know how long they held each other, but eventually she leaned up and gave him a kiss. "Thank you for everything tonight. I promise I'll call you tomorrow, okay?"

He hesitated at first, but eventually nodded. After one more lingering kiss, he made his way to the door, pausing on the threshold.

"Good night, ladies," he said to the empty room, giving Claire a wink at the same time.

Claire chuckled. He was already a favorite with the house projections, but that just sealed the deal. She watched him trot down the porch steps and cross the yard to his truck, then closed the door.

"Such a nice young man," Sarah said as she materialized next to Claire.

"Yeah," Thelma agreed, materializing on the other side, "it's too bad he's a ghost hunter."

"Not anymore," Claire sighed, making her way to the couch. She really wanted her bed, but she was too exhausted to make it that far.

"I'm sure he'll be an agent soon enough," April said, making her appearance behind the other two projections.

Claire collapsed onto the couch. "I hope you're right." She closed her eyes and the let the exhaustion take over.

Chapter 41

Claire had no idea how long she slept before a sound woke her. She briefly opened her eyes to see her parents tiptoeing into the house, then drifted off to sleep again.

When she finally woke up in earnest, the sun was already high in the sky, showing it was at least late morning or early afternoon. Whatever the time, Claire was sure she had just gotten more sleep than at any one time in close to a week.

She sat up on the couch and stretched, noticing for the first time that her dad was asleep in the armchair across the room. The chair was comfortable, but not built for sleeping. All the same, his chin was resting forward on his chest and he was snoring. Claire couldn't help but smile despite her grogginess.

She stood up as quietly as she could, trying to remember what she had done with her phone the night before. Despite her best efforts, Noah stirred from his watchful post in the chair.

"What time is it?" he asked, rubbing his eyes.

"I was about to go look."

Noah picked up his phone from the end table and sat up straighter in the chair. "Good Lord, it's almost noon."

"That would explain why I'm so hungry." Claire shuffled toward the kitchen. "I'll see what I can scrounge up for breakfast, or I guess it would be lunch, wouldn't it?"

Noah stood and stretched again. "I can go get something, if you don't feel like cooking."

Claire stopped in the doorway to the kitchen. "You know what? I think I'll let you."

"I wouldn't turn down a burger," Leila's voice broke in from the hallway to the bedrooms.

Noah began checking his pockets, presumably looking for his keys, wallet, or glasses, or all three. "Burgers sound great." He finally found his keys on the end table along with his wallet and glasses. With a firm nod, he headed toward the front door. "I'll be back in no time."

Claire smiled at him, but her smile faded when he opened the front door and froze. He stared at the ground in front of him for several seconds before bending over and picking something up. When he turned around, he was holding a medium-sized envelope in his hand.

"It's got your name on it," he told Claire, closing the door.

Claire couldn't imagine what it could be, though she had a few ideas who it could be from. She stepped forward and carefully took the envelope from him. It wasn't very heavy but there was a slight bulge in the middle of it.

"Be careful," Noah cautioned as Claire started opening it.

Claire nodded. She doubted there was any danger, but Ann's warnings about the Syndicate rang in the back of her mind. She let out a breath and dumped the envelope's contents into her hand. There was a USB drive and a folded note. She checked the envelope again to make sure there wasn't anything else, then set it on the table before opening the note.

"It's from Ann," she told her parents.

Dear Claire,

I've thought a lot about what you said the other day and, of course, you're right. Peter would want me to do whatever I can to stop the Syndicate, and it looks like the Bureau is my best chance to do that. I still don't know if I can trust them, but I do trust you, and that will have to be enough for now.

As for me, I'm through chasing the Syndicate. I know this won't end with me finding Peter, so there's no point continuing the search. I'm leaving town today, and then I'm going to do what Peter told me to do all those years ago. I'm going to disappear.

I've copied all the information Peter collected about the Syndicate onto this USB drive, but I'm keeping the original drive for myself as protection.

I caution you to be careful who you trust. There's a good reason I have my doubts about the Bureau. They may be more closely tied to the Syndicate than you want to believe.

I wish you well and pray that you're able to stop them before it's too late.

Sincerely,

Ann

Claire re-read the note then handed it to her dad. He and Leila read it together as Claire opened her laptop and inserted the USB drive.

"Now she's saying the Syndicate and the Bureau are connected?" Noah said with a snort of derision. "It sounds to me like she's grasping at straws to make her story sound more believable."

"Let's wait and see what's on the drive," Leila suggested, pulling a chair over to join Claire at the desk. Noah pulled a chair over as well and they all three waited in silence as the computer ran through its start-up sequence.

When the computer was finally ready to go, Claire took a deep breath and clicked on the folder to open the USB drive. There were several files and documents, so she just opened the first one on the screen. It contained copies of several emails. Claire was too curious about the rest of the information on the drive to spend too much time reading them, so she opened the next folder.

The first document in the folder seemed to be a written summary of all the information Ann's husband had been able to discover about the Syndicate. *Well, that's convenient,* Claire thought. This would be the best place to start. They could work their way through the rest of the evidence later.

Claire quickly scanned the document, but then slowed down when she reached a paragraph about halfway down the page.

"Woah." She pointed at the words on the screen. "This says the Syndicate was founded by surveyors who were dismissed during the Schism of 1955." She turned to look at her dad. "How could Ann know about the schism if this isn't legit?"

For the first time since learning about the possible existence of the Syndicate, Noah looked uncertain. "That's an excellent question." He clearly wasn't happy with the implications.

"Did anybody keep tabs on those dismissed surveyors?" Claire asked.

Noah stared at the computer screen with a serious look on his face. "I couldn't say. I don't know that anyone thought there would be a need." After a few seconds, he cleared his throat and rubbed his chin. "I guess I could make some calls and see if there are any records from that time."

"If this is true," Leila said, "then the Syndicate really is linked to the Bureau, at least to some degree."

Noah stood up and took his phone out of his pocket. "Maybe they were at the start, but that doesn't mean there are still ties today." He shook his head again and began scrolling through the contacts list on his phone. "None of this makes sense to me." He selected a number and stood up. "I can promise you I'll get to the bottom of it though."

Claire turned back to the computer and opened another folder, too impatient to wait for her dad to finish his call. "It looks like this one has all the information Peter collected on the man Ann was telling me about," she told her mom. "She's been following him for the past several years because she thinks he's responsible for her husband's disappearance."

Claire opened one of the files and gasped. It was a surveillance photo taken outside a well-known restaurant that she remembered from San Francisco. The man's face was easily recognizable. Though Claire wasn't surprised that it was a picture of Philip, her heart began to pound all the same as the pieces began to fall into place.

"That's Philip," she told Leila. "He's the one Ann's been following this whole time."

Noah returned to the living room, his cell phone still pressed against his ear. "Your brother is on his way over. He wants to check out this information for himself."

"Did you learn anything about the dismissed surveyors?" Leila asked.

Noah placed a hand on her shoulder. "I've asked some people to look into it. Harlan has me on hold right now."

Leila patted his hand. "I think I'll go grab a shower then."

She and Noah left the room together and Claire turned her attention back to the computer screen. It would take weeks, or even months, to thoroughly comb through all the folders and documents on the drive.

With a quick glance over her shoulder to make sure she was alone in the room, she opened one of the desk drawers, removed a second USB drive, and slipped it into the laptop. Zach had made some steps in the right direction over the past twenty-four hours, but Claire still wasn't ready to leave the entire investigation up to him.

As she waited for the files to copy over, she studied her investigation board. If the information contained on the USB drive was accurate, there was so much more to this mystery than Claire possibly could have imagined.

Chapter 42

"This is all very interesting," Zach said with a sigh. He had been sitting at Claire's computer for over an hour, opening one file after another. "We'll definitely need to look into this further, though, before I can say whether or not I believe any of it."

It wasn't an unreasonable reaction for someone in his position, and it certainly wasn't unexpected, but still it irritated Claire. "But you *are* going to take this seriously, right?"

"Seriously enough to look into it." He turned around to face her. "If this is all true, then it's a potential powder keg. I can't just accept everything that's on this drive as fact without further investigation."

Claire leaned over and opened the file with the surveillance photo of Philip. "Look at this, though. This is Philip. We've got photographic evidence he was in San Francisco when all those rogues went missing before. It can't be a coincidence that he's here now."

Zach sighed. "I know Claire, but we still don't know what all this means. Just because there's a connection with this Philip person, that doesn't prove the existence of this other organization."

Claire let out a frustrated growl and stood up, fully intending to leave the room. Zach leaned forward and took her unbandaged hand, catching her off guard and stopping her.

"Please, Claire, for the love of God, give me some time to look into this so I can actually do my job. If there is something to these claims, we'll take whatever steps are necessary to deal with it." He let go of her hand and turned back to the laptop. "I don't want you to do anything that would jeopardize your career again. I can only go to bat for you so many times."

Claire stared dumbly at the back of his head as he ejected the USB drive and removed it from the computer. Everything reasonable inside of her had to admit he was right. This was his job and she needed to trust him enough to let him handle it. But that didn't mean she had to like it.

He stood up from the desk and put the USB drive in his pocket before turning to face her. They looked at each other for a few seconds without saying anything. Finally, he leaned forward and gave her a kiss on her forehead.

"I promise we'll take this seriously."

Claire nodded and wrapped her arms around his waist. It was the first genuine, heartfelt hug they had exchanged in years. For the first time since the fiasco in San Francisco, Claire believed it was possible things could get back to the way they used to be between them.

She heard a sniffle from the direction of the living room and didn't even have to look to know it was her mom. Zach chuckled and they stepped away from each other. *Thanks, Mom, for making it weird*, Claire thought.

Zach's cell phone chimed, indicating he had a text message. He removed the phone from his pocket and frowned as he read it. "It's Blake," he said to no one in particular. "The team has picked up some strange readings at the cemetery."

"What kind of readings?" Claire asked, trying not to seem overly concerned.

Zach returned the phone to his pocket. "He didn't say. I'm going to head over there now." He crossed the room to the front door and opened it before turning back to face Claire. "Why don't you join us at the cemetery? After all, you *are* the only witness we have access to right now."

Claire shrugged. "I don't know what else I can tell you. My memories of that night are still pretty fuzzy."

"All the more reason to get back to the scene of the crime," Zach said. "Maybe it will help shake something loose."

Claire smiled hesitantly. "I guess it can't hurt."

"Great." Zach nodded good-bye to both of his parents. "Get dressed and I'll see you there."

Claire glared after her brother, and continued to even after the door had closed behind him. Who did he think he was bossing her around like that? Then she realized that in that moment, he was in fact her boss. He wasn't her brother. He was her boss.

"Well," Noah commented with a chuckle. "I guess it's back to business then."

"Yeah," Claire said with a scowl as she headed to her room to change clothes. "Lucky me."

Chapter 43

Resigned, but still irritated, Claire drove to the cemetery. The sun was just beginning to set, so she felt right at home pulling up to the gate.

As she got out of her car, she was greeted by one of the P.I.D. agents and not the night watchman. After locking the gate behind them, the agent accompanied Claire to the scene of the "accident," where Zach was waiting. The rest of the P.I.D. team seemed to be hard at work, though Claire had no idea what they were doing. They had various instruments out, most of which she didn't recognize and could only imagine what purpose they served.

"How's the investigation going?" she asked as she approached.

Zach looked back to where her car was parked. "Mom and Dad didn't come with you?"

"No," she told him. "They went back up to the hospital to stay with Isabel. When Mom found she doesn't have any family to sit with her, she went into full-on maternal mode."

Zach smiled. "I'm sure." He motioned to one of his team members. "We need you to walk us through the events of the other night. Maybe that will help explain the strange readings we've picked up."

Claire looked around the cemetery. "What kind of readings?"

"We're picking up an unusual amount of residual energy," Blake told her as he approached with another P.I.D. agent. "The readings all seem to be emanating from near that mausoleum." He kissed Claire on the cheek, then took a tablet from the other agent, frowning into the screen. "This doesn't read like anything we've seen from a projection before, and it certainly shouldn't still be registering if a projection had been the source. Can you remember who, or what, was there that night?"

"Which mausoleum?" Claire asked, though she knew exactly which one he was talking about. She had been standing right next to it when she sent out the energy blast.

Blake led the way and Claire followed. When they reached the mausoleum, Claire noticed several grave markers lying in pieces nearby. It was safe to assume they had exploded when she sent out the energy blast. She instinctively touched the bandage on her forehead.

Claire looked around and shook her head. "Sorry," she lied. "I just don't remember if there was anything here." She decided it would be wise to deflect. "I was more focused on what was happening to Isabel."

"That's what I'm most concerned about, too," Zach said with a deep frown. "Who were these people, and how could they drain Isabel's energy? That's what we need to figure out first."

Claire clinched her teeth. "We know who it was."

"We have a theory about who it *might* be," Zach pointed out. "A theory, but no evidence, based solely on what some random lady told you about her husband."

"And what about the rogues being drained?" Claire asked.

He gave her a stern look. "You already know the answer to that question. They aren't the priority here. But a device with the ability to drain energy from a living human, now that's something that should have us all concerned."

Claire decided to let the matter drop rather than start another argument with her brother. They had just begun to mend their relationship. Was it worth messing things up again?

"Well," she said, "I'm sorry I can't be more help to your investigation."

"That's okay," Zach told her, completely unfazed by the bitterness in her sarcastic tone. "We'll start with what you do remember." He turned to the agent next to him. "Let's re-create the scene and see if that will jog her memory."

Claire resisted the urge to scream. Instead, she took a deep breath and crossed to where Isabel had been kneeling in front of the hooded man Claire now knew to be Philip. She pointed out where the others had been standing, then waited while the P.I.D. agents furiously entered the data into their tablets.

When they had finished, she shrugged her shoulders. "And that's all I can remember."

"And what about you?" Blake asked. "Where were you standing?"

"Right over there," she lied again, pointing to the walkway farthest away from the mausoleum that was giving off the strange readings.

"Did they use the device on you as well?" Zach asked. "The police report said you were unconscious when the EMTs arrived."

Claire shrugged again. "I guess they must have. What other explanation could there be?" She could feel Blake looking at her but didn't make eye contact with him.

"This investigation would be much easier if both our main witnesses didn't have selective amnesia," Zach grumbled.

"I'm sorry I couldn't be more help." Her tone was sarcastic, but her regret was genuine. She wanted to help them figure out how Philip had managed to drain Isabel's energy, and more importantly how to stop him from draining anyone else, but she wasn't ready to be completely honest with her brother yet.

"It's okay," Zach assured her with a curt nod. "We'll figure it out, one way or another." He turned and spoke in hushed tones to one of the agents standing near him.

Claire glanced at Blake, unnerved to find him studying her intently. "What do you think we're dealing with here?" she asked as casually as she could. She turned her attention back to Zach and the other agents as she waited for Blake's response. When no answer came, she turned to look at him.

"Are you sure you're telling us everything?" he asked her once their eyes met.

Claire shrugged. "I don't know what else you think I can tell you." She looked away. He didn't seem convinced, so she decided to try another tactic. Addressing Zach, she asked, "Maybe I should go up to the hospital and talk to Isabel tomorrow? Maybe between the two of us we can figure out some more details."

He didn't answer immediately, but eventually he nodded. "Sure, that's probably a good idea. Blake will go with you."

"Great," Claire said, forcing a smile. She didn't really want anyone else to be there, just in case Isabel actually remembered more than she had let on, but she couldn't tell them that without raising suspicions.

Relieved that this part of the interrogation was over, Claire patted Blake on the shoulder, gave Zach and his team one last look, then headed back to her car.

Chapter 44

Early the next morning, Blake showed up at Claire's house in one of the black SUVs.

"You couldn't have brought something a little less conspicuous?" Claire asked as she slid into the passenger's seat.

Blake frowned. "We haven't had much time to go out and look for rental cars. Sorry if this is inconvenient for you."

Claire glanced over at him but didn't ask what bee had gotten into his bonnet. She could probably guess. Having grown up with Zach, she could only imagine how irritating it would be to have him as her direct superior.

"Thanks for coming to pick me up," she said instead as Blake backed out of the driveway.

"Of course," was all he said.

"If you've got something else you need to be doing," she told him, "I can drive myself."

"It's fine." He let out a sigh and looked over at her. "I can think of worse assignments right now."

Now it was Claire's turn to frown. "And that would be?"

"I could be out interviewing rogues." He scowled as he focused on the road ahead of him. "We're having a hard time making contact with them, and the ones we are finding aren't exactly being helpful."

Claire resisted the urge to laugh. "Are you surprised? They're all well aware of the Bureau's policies. They don't have any more obligation to help you than you do to help them."

"I know that," he said, "but we're trying to help them now, and things would go a lot more smoothly if they would cooperate with us."

Claire looked out the window. "Do you think it would help if I came along on the interviews?" She knew Zach would never ask her to, but he might go along with it if the suggestion came from someone else.

Blake frowned again. "I already thought of that and it was shot down." He glanced over at her again. "Why do you think I'm in such a pissy mood?"

Claire didn't push the issue. "Well, I've already asked the house projections to get word to Jean Lafitte that we'd still like to talk to him. Hopefully he hasn't gone back to New Orleans yet."

They drove the rest of the way to the hospital in silence. The heavy awkwardness between them felt completely foreign to Claire and she hated it. Maybe it was paranoia, but she couldn't shake the feeling Blake knew she wasn't being completely honest with them. That wasn't going to change anytime soon, though, so that left them at a stalemate.

After Blake had parked, they entered the hospital and rode the elevator to the fourth floor, still in silence.

When they reached Isabel's room, Blake stopped right outside the door. "I'll wait for you in the hallway." He put a hand on Claire's shoulder and looked her in the eyes. "You have to promise you'll tell me if you two remember anything important."

"Of course," Claire assured him before pushing the door open and stepping inside.

When Isabel saw Claire, she smiled. "Another Abelard. How lucky for me! That makes a full set."

Claire's parents had stayed with Isabel until earlier that morning. Since Claire was coming to see Isabel, they had gone home to get a few hours of much-needed sleep. And of course, Zach had already been to see her the day before.

Claire approached the bed. "If you ever had any doubt how special you are, there's your answer."

Isabel's face grew serious. "Or at least it proves how big of a deal this all is."

Claire sat down in the chair next to the bed. "How're you doing?" She put her hand on top of Isabel's where it was resting on the bed. "I mean, really?"

"I'm fine," Isabel assured her. Apparently, Claire didn't look convinced because Isabel squeezed her hand and added, "Really."

Tears began to fill her eyes. "I'm so sorry, Isabel. This is all my fault. If I hadn't dragged you into this investigation, you wouldn't be lying here right now."

Isabel laughed good-naturedly. "Claire, you didn't force me to go to that cemetery with you. You were right. It was our responsibility to look into the disappearances." She waved her free hand around the room. "And I'm sure you couldn't have predicted any of *this* would happen."

Claire smiled weakly, but she couldn't shake the guilt.

"And what about you?" Isabel asked, nodding toward Claire's bandaged wrist. "Your parents told me you were attacked again."

Claire put her hand in her lap. "I'll be fine. It's just further proof of how dangerous these people are. We need to figure this all out before anyone else gets hurt." She glanced over her shoulder toward the doorway. "Have you remembered anything else from that night in the cemetery?"

Isabel nodded. "The more my energy returns, the more I remember. A lot of the details are still fuzzy, so I didn't totally lie to Zach and his team yesterday."

"You've been under a lot of physical stress," Claire reminded her. "It's completely understandable that things would get muddled."

Isabel closed her eyes and thought for a few seconds. "They're becoming clearer though." She opened her eyes and looked at Claire. "I think I saw his face."

Claire sat forward in her seat. "Whose? The man who was draining your energy?"

Isabel nodded. "I woke up in the middle of the night from what I thought was a nightmare," she began, "but then when I was awake, I couldn't get the man's face out of my mind."

"Isabel, this is huge," Claire told her, taking her phone out of her pocket. "Do you think you could remember well enough to have someone draw it?"

Isabel nodded and Claire immediately dialed the number for Deputy Martens. "This is great news," she said with a genuine smile. The call connected, and Claire explained the situation to the deputy.

"I'll get someone over there as soon as I can," Martens told her.

Claire tried to contain her excitement as she hung up the phone. Though she already knew whose face would emerge in the drawing, it would still be nice to have confirmation, especially when it came to convincing her brother that she wasn't crazy.

"Martens is sending someone over," Claire told Isabel as she stood up and headed out to the hall. She filled Blake in on the new development then returned to Isabel's bedside.

Once Claire was seated again, Isabel gave her a serious look. "There's something else I remember." She met Claire's gaze. "I didn't tell your brother because I wanted to talk to you first."

Claire's stomach dropped. She suspected Isabel was waiting for her to speak first, but when she didn't say anything, Isabel continued.

"At first, I thought I was dead and an angel had come to take me away. I may have been delusional, but that's what you looked like. You had this intense glow all around you, then there was this bright flash of light." She searched Claire's face. "What happened?"

Claire feigned innocence. "What do you mean? The ghost hunters scared the men off. Maybe someone's flashlight shined in your eyes."

"Maybe after the fact," Isabel conceded, "but that's not what stopped those men from draining my energy."

Claire shook her head. "I'm afraid I can't help you much here. My memories of that night are a little fuzzy, too."

Isabel smiled at her then leaned her head back on the pillow and closed her eyes. "You're a horrible liar."

"I'm not lying," Claire tried to sound convincing. "There's nothing to tell."

Isabel opened one eye and looked at her. "It's okay. I won't tell anyone about it if you don't want them to know."

Claire wanted to protest again but decided it was pointless. "Honestly," she said with a sigh, "I don't know what happened that night. I've never done anything like that before, so I can't even begin to explain it."

Isabel opened both eyes. "Well, whatever you did, it saved my life, so thank you. Keeping this secret for you is the least I can do."

Claire stood up and kissed her friend on the forehead. "Thank you."

She didn't have a chance to say anything else before Aaron entered the room. Claire's parents had told her how much time he'd been spending up at the hospital, so she wasn't exactly surprised to see him there.

"How's the patient today?" he asked.

"Feeling almost like my old self," Isabel said. "The doctor said if I keep improving like I have been, they'll send me home in a day or two."

"That's great news." Aaron looked around the room. "Where are your parents, Claire?"

"They went home to get some sleep, but they'll be back in a few hours." She turned her attention back to Isabel. "I'm glad you're doing so much better. I need to get back to help with the investigation, then I'm taking the ghost hunters on a tour of the Galvez tonight."

"Another tour?" Isabel asked. "At a time like this?"

Claire shrugged. "I felt like it was the least I could do after the dud of a lockdown they had at Bishop's Palace. Plus," she said with a wink, "it'll give me a chance to make contact with some of the projections there without my brother and his team getting in the way."

"Good luck with that," Isabel said.

"You know it." Claire patted her hand. "Let me know when you've finished with the sketch artist. I'll get Deputy Martens to text me a copy."

"Sketch artist?" Aaron asked, confusion clearly written on his face.

Isabel nodded. "I got a good look at the man who drained my energy. I just remembered it this morning."

Aaron raised his eyebrows. "Well, that's an interesting development."

Claire nodded as she turned to leave. "Definitely."

She glanced back over her shoulder as Aaron sat down in the chair next to Isabel's bed.

She was surprised by how attentive Aaron was being. Other than Claire's parents, Aaron had spent the most time by Isabel's bedside. Claire couldn't help but wonder if there might be something more to Aaron's behavior than friendly concern.

She shook her head and chuckled. It must be Monica's influence. Why else would she be seeing romantic intrigue in every relationship around her?

When she exited Isabel's room, Blake was waiting for her in the hall. As they made their way back to the elevators, Claire had a thought. She heard Ann's voice in her head, telling her how dangerous The Syndicate could be. Most likely she was being paranoid, but at this point she'd rather be safe than sorry. She called Deputy Martens again.

"Hey, Rick," Claire said when the call connected. "It's me again. Is there any way you could get a protective detail for Isabel's room while she's here at the hospital?"

"Why?" he asked. "Has something happened?"

"No." Claire hated to admit it. "I just worry there might be trouble, especially now that she remembers what the man looked like."

"I'll see what I can do," he said after a short pause.

Claire hung up the phone and boarded the elevator. Maybe she was being overly cautious, but with everything that had happened over the past few days, she wasn't about to take any more chances with Isabel's safety.

Chapter 45

Blake dropped Claire off at her house then went to join Zach and the rest of the P.I.D. team at the hotel where they were staying. Apparently, Zach wanted to strategize before moving forward with the next stage of the investigation. Claire's parents had returned to the hospital to sit with Isabel, so it was just Claire and the house projections, and for once they weren't feeling very talkative.

Claire tried to take a nap so she'd be refreshed for the tour that night, but her thoughts wouldn't slow down enough to give her a moment's rest. Her investigation board seemed to be taunting her from across the room, no matter how much she tried to ignore it. With a resigned sigh, she crossed the room and examined the pieces of paper for what she was sure was the hundredth time.

Out of the corner of her eye, she spotted a piece of paper sitting on her desk. It was the note Deshaun had given her, the one with Philip's phone number written on it. Claire had told Zach about it, but he didn't seem interested in making contact with Philip until they had a better idea of what was happening on the island. So, there the paper sat.

Claire picked it up and returned to the couch. There were so many reasons why she shouldn't dial the number, but then there was an equal number of reasons why she should. After debating with herself for several minutes, she took a deep breath and punched in the numbers.

"Hello," the familiar voice said when the call connected.

Claire didn't respond. She couldn't respond. She had no idea what to say to him.

"Claire?" he said after several seconds of silence.

She swallowed hard. "How did you know it was me?"

He chuckled. "I can practically feel your apprehension through the phone line." He paused. "There are only a few people who have this number, and you're the only one who might have any trouble finding any words to say to me right now."

"Are the other people part of the Syndicate?"

Now it was his turn to be silent. "You shouldn't know about that," he eventually said.

"Why not?"

"Because it's dangerous for you." He cleared his throat. "If they knew that you knew about them, it would change the game entirely."

Claire laughed bitterly. "So, this really is a game to you?"

"Far from it. I just meant you need to tread very carefully down this road. These are very dangerous people, and the less you know about them the better."

"Yes," she spat into the phone, "I've got a pretty good idea how dangerous these people can be."

"I'm very sorry about that." He sounded sincere. "I tried to shield you as much as I could, but some things are out of my control."

She gritted her teeth. "I'm not a child that needs to be protected."

"I wish that were true."

She leaned her head against the back of the couch. She wasn't sure what to believe anymore. "My father admitted to me that Beguiling Acuity is real," she told him, unsure why she had felt the need. "He also told me the Bureau has kept it a secret because it's so dangerous."

"If the sensitive isn't strong enough, yes, it is very dangerous, but I doubt you'll have any problems with it."

"Why do you say that?"

"Because you're the strongest sensitive I've ever met. I knew from the moment I met you that you were special, and your performance at the cemetery confirmed it."

"How am I special?" Claire hoped she didn't sound as desperate as she felt. Something inside her screamed a warning that she couldn't trust this man, but she wanted answers.

"I don't know," he admitted, "but I'd like to help you find out."

"And how would you do that? Run tests on me?"

"I wouldn't do something like that to you." He sounded genuinely hurt. "I want to help you reach your fullest potential. With your energy level, I'm certain there's so much more you can do if you would just break free of the Bureau's restrictions."

Claire didn't want him to know her resolve was wavering, so she decided to change the subject. "Isabel saw her attacker's face." Again, she had no idea why she felt the need to tell him. She wanted to say something that might set him off balance. She didn't want him to think he was the one in charge of the situation, though she suspected he really was. "They're going to have her sit with a sketch artist. Am I going to be surprised by how it turns out, or do you want to go ahead and turn yourself in now?"

He chuckled again. "I think we both know the answers to those questions."

"We're going to stop you," she told him. "We won't let you keep draining rogues. It won't be like it was in San Francisco and New Orleans."

"I should have known you were the one who put them on my trail in San Francisco." It might have been her imagination, but Claire thought she detected a smile in his voice. "After all, how many other Bureau agents would care enough about missing rogues to give it a second thought?"

"And New Orleans?" she said. "What made you stop draining the rogues there?"

He cleared his throat. "I don't know what you're talking about. I never drained rogues in New Orleans."

Claire gave a disdainful laugh. "I don't believe you."

"That's your choice, but it doesn't change the facts." He paused as if considering his words carefully. "If rogues went missing in New Orleans, I'm not the one who drained them."

"Then who could it have been?"

"That's a very good question, and one I very much intend to find the answer to."

"I guess life with the Syndicate isn't as rosy as you thought it would be, huh?" It was childish to taunt him, but she couldn't help herself.

"They definitely have their secrets, but then again so does the Bureau." After another pause, he added, "But I guess that's to be expected from secret organizations, isn't it? It's in their nature."

"I still don't know that I believe the Syndicate exists. I can't imagine they could exist without anyone at the Bureau knowing about them."

"Who says nobody at the Bureau knows about them?"

Claire sat up straighter. "What do you mean? My dad said he's never heard of them, and he was high up in Bureau leadership for years."

"There would be no reason for your dad to know about them, but that doesn't mean nobody else does."

Her heart pounded in her chest as she considered the implications. "Are you telling me there's a Syndicate spy in the Bureau?"

"That would be a stupid thing for me to admit to," he said, "but I will tell you to be careful who you trust. Sometimes the people closest to us can hurt us the worst."

Claire had no response for him.

"I meant what I said before," he continued. "You don't want to go too far down this road. You might not like what you find."

With that, he disconnected the call. Claire dropped the phone on the couch next to her as if it had some kind of disease. If what Philip said was true, her whole world had just been turned upside down. If there was a Syndicate spy in the Bureau, how could she possibly know who she could trust anymore?

Chapter 46

Claire met the ghost hunters at the service entrance of the Hotel Galvez just after sundown. Though they had gotten permission to shoot an episode of their show there, the management of the high-end hotel was still very protective of its image and wanted to avoid any kind of spectacle. The team didn't mind. As long as they were able to have an investigation, they didn't care how they got into the building.

Claire smiled at Drew as he approached. "Hey."

He returned her smile and kissed her on the cheek. "Hey, yourself." He took a step back to let Keith bring in the camera equipment. "How's Isabel doing?"

"Better and better. They're probably going to let her go home soon."

"That's great."

He nodded toward Claire's bandaged wrist. "And how are you?"

"I'm fine," she assured him. She closed the door behind them after the last ghost hunter had entered then turned to address the group. "Let's get started then, shall we." She motioned for them to follow her out of the kitchen and into the ballroom. "There's been a lot of activity reported on the ground floor of the hotel over the years, so I think that will be the best place to start. After that, we can go upstairs and see if Audra feels like interacting with us."

"Let's hope we have more luck than we did at the Bishop's Palace," Spencer mumbled as he set his equipment against the wall.

Claire chose not to respond, primarily because there wasn't anything for her to say. She agreed with him, but with the atmosphere among the projections being so tense, she certainly couldn't make any promises.

"So, what kind of activity has been reported here?" Keith asked.

"Well, in this room people have reported hearing sounds of a party taking place, even though the room is empty. Plates and tables have been said to move on their own, and several dishes have mysteriously broken." Claire pointed toward the hall. "In other parts of the ground floor, employees have reported seeing a little girl bouncing a ball down the hall before disappearing into a wall."

She took a deep breath and let it out slowly as Keith lifted the camera and pointed it in her direction. Considering how horribly their lockdown at the Bishop's Palace had flopped, she decided not to protest this time.

"The Galvez was finished in 1911," she told them. "Along with the construction of the Seawall and the raising of the island, it was hoped that this new luxury hotel would lure visitors back to Galveston, and it did. During the course of its history, the Galvez has hosted Dean Martin and Frank Sinatra from time to time, and even served as a temporary White House for FDR when he was on vacation here."

"Impressive," Luke said. "Who knew?"

Claire stood against the wall as the ghost hunters conducted their investigation, taking readings around the massive ballroom and recording data. She could tell they weren't getting many hits, but she hoped that would change when they got to the fifth floor. Even if Audra didn't feel like communicating that night, maybe Claire could get some of the other projections to slam a few doors for them.

A persistent beeping sound filled the room and Claire sensed a change in the energy around them. She looked in Drew's direction and caught him smiling at her. He gave her a wink and set the device on the table next to him.

"Would you like to talk to us?" he asked the air around him. This was the first chance he had gotten to try to communicate directly with a projection and he wasn't going to let it pass him by. "I'm here to listen if you have something you want to say."

"Get the spirit box," Spencer told Luke. "In case they want to talk to us."

That wasn't what Drew meant but Claire wasn't about to tell Spencer that.

"Claire!" a soft voice whispered in her ear.

The air rippled next to her. Since Isabel was primarily responsible for the projections at the Galvez, Claire wasn't as familiar with them as she was with many of the others on the island. Plus, the projection hadn't fully materialized, so she had no idea which of the Galvez ghosts it was. All the same, she tilted her head slightly in the direction of the energy disturbance so they would know she was listening.

"How could you bring these people here at a time like this? You know it's not safe for us."

Claire let out a heavy sigh and moved toward the exit, hoping the projection would follow. At that time of night, there would probably only be a few hotel guests in the hallway, and Claire needed to get away from the ghost hunters' instruments. Once she was out of the ballroom, she took her phone out of her pocket and put it up to her ear as if taking a call.

Claire waited for the familiar shimmer of energy indicating the projection had followed her. "You've got nothing to worry about from these men," she said once she sensed the projection's presence nearby. "They're just ghost hunters doing an innocent investigation. They're not going to harm you."

"I'm not talking about *those* guys," the projection told her. "They're clearly no threat. It's the other ones that are skulking around the hotel that have us worried."

Claire felt her blood run cold and swallowed hard. "Are you telling me there's another group of hunters in the hotel?"

"They don't have a bunch of equipment like this group does, but they definitely seem to be looking for projections."

A million thoughts ran through Claire's mind. "Is it possible they're P.I.D. agents?" Zach hadn't told her he was sending any agents to the hotel, but that didn't mean he hadn't done it.

"They could be, but I can't say for sure," the projection said. "I've been staying as far away from them as possible." There was another pause. "So, those other men aren't with you?"

Claire shook her head. "No, and I think you're right to be worried about them. Where are they now?"

"I don't know. Like I said, we've been keeping our distance."

"Good, keep doing that, and make sure everyone knows to do the same." She thought for a few seconds. "Do you think you can find out where they are without getting too close?"

"I can try."

Claire nodded again. "Great, but only if you can stay safe in the process. See what you can find out, then meet me on the fifth floor."

The air rippled again as the projection left the room. Claire and the ghost hunters spent another fifteen minutes in the ballroom without picking up any other readings, so Claire suggested they head upstairs. In the elevator, she filled the group in on Audra's story and more of the hotel's haunted history.

"Will we be able to go into room 501?" Keith asked.

Claire nodded and held up a room key.

"Awesome!" was his response.

Claire wished she could share his enthusiasm. As the doors to the elevator slid open revealing the fifth floor hallway, she said a silent prayer that this wouldn't be a huge mistake. She could sense multiple energy signatures in the rooms around them, which she took as a good sign that the other group of hunters wasn't anywhere nearby. At least these projections should be safe for now.

To her surprise, it only took one attempt to open the door to room 501. Clearly none of the projections were in the mood to play around with the electronics. She pushed the door open and motioned for the team to go inside.

She stood by the door for a few seconds then made an excuse about needing to check a few other rooms on the floor. She headed back toward the elevators, then rounded a corner so she would be out of sight if any of the ghost hunters left room 501 for any reason. She didn't have to wait long for the projections to find her.

"Claire, you can't really expect us to put on a show for them at a time like this?" Audra began before she had even fully materialized. Her usual melancholy mood had been replaced by genuine fear. "Preserving the history of this hotel is not on the top of our lists right now. We've got to be concerned about our own survival."

Claire looked at the frightened, translucent faces around her. She felt all of their anxiety as if it were her own, which made it even more difficult to try to convince them to remain calm.

"I understand that," she assured them, "but there's no reason for everyone to freak out. My brother and the P.I.D. agents are looking into everything that's been happening, so hopefully we'll have some answers soon." She looked at Audra. "Was anybody able to locate the other men?"

Audra nodded. "They're in the basement museum."

"Okay." Claire took a deep breath and again tried to calm her own emotions. She was about to tell them she was going to go check things out when Drew rounded the corner.

He stopped dead in his tracks when he saw her. Claire could only imagine what the scene looked like to him, a group of colorful mists with Claire in the center. The look on his face made her chuckle despite the seriousness of the situation they were facing.

One by one, the projections faded out of sight until only Audra was left, hovering a few feet away, studying Drew.

"He's not like the others, is he?" she asked.

Claire shook her head. "He's a Force Perceptive."

Drew's eyes grew wide. "Are you talking to it right now?"

Audra huffed. "It?"

"Don't be offended," Claire told her. "He only sees you as a mist." She crossed to where Drew was standing and took his hand. "Drew," she said, gently leading him back down the hall, "this is Audra, the ghost bride of the Hotel Galvez."

Audra looked at their joined hands and smiled. "He's very handsome. You'll have beautiful children."

Claire chuckled then turned to Drew, relieved he hadn't developed his Auditory Acumen yet. "I wish we had time to work on honing your communication skills, but I need to go look into something right now. I'll be back in a few minutes." She looked at Audra. "You and the others stay up here with Drew and his friends. You should be safe near them." She took a few steps toward the elevator then turned back around. "And, Audra, tell the others to at least give them a little something to work with, please."

Drew followed Claire to the elevator. "Something tells me I shouldn't let you go wherever you're going alone." He stepped between Claire and the elevator doors, so she had no choice but to look at him. "Does this have anything to do with what happened in the cemetery the other night?"

Claire frowned. "Possibly, but I need to know for sure."

"We got a hit!"

Spencer's excited voice drew her attention back down the hallway to room 501. She smiled faintly.

"I guess your pep talk did the trick." Drew stepped to the side as the elevator doors slid open.

"The projections are really on edge right now. There's a lot going on in their world."

"Their world," he repeated thoughtfully. "It feels weird doing an investigation now that I know about 'their world'."

"I can imagine." She wasn't sure what else to say.

"So, where are we going?" he asked as they stepped on to the elevator. He seemed almost excited at the prospect of getting another glimpse into this new reality Claire had introduced him to.

"The basement."

He raised his eyebrows. "Well, that should be creepy enough."

Claire shook her head. "It's not as creepy as you might think. There's a small museum down there."

"And... we're checking out a museum, why?"

She wasn't sure how much she should tell him. Though she had already spilled the beans about the Bureau, he wasn't an agent, and he certainly wasn't ready to deal with the Syndicate, if they even existed. She wanted to tell him to go back upstairs, but she knew he wouldn't go.

"The projections have spotted some suspicious-looking men in the hotel," she admitted. "They're really nervous about it, so I told them I'd go look into it."

Drew frowned. "If it's the same group that attacked you and your friend in the cemetery, don't you think it's pretty dangerous to go chasing after them like this?"

Claire sighed. "I'm just going to look into it. I'm sure it's nothing." She kept her eyes on the elevator's floor indicator so she didn't have to meet his gaze. If he knew she was lying, he didn't call her on it.

When the doors opened onto the basement, she immediately felt a low hum of the strange energy signature that had unfortunately become all too familiar to her. They stood by the entrance to the museum for several seconds as she tried to get her bearings.

Drew took a few steps into the room then turned back to look at her. "I don't like this."

Claire studied him for several seconds. "What?"

He shook his head. "I don't know. Something's not right."

She looked around the room but saw no signs of the men the projections had described. As much as she hated to do it, she knew she needed to get away from Drew if she was going to conduct a proper investigation. Even if he didn't directly hinder her job, the strength of two high-level sensitives would be more than enough to alert another sensitive to their presence, making it impossible to sneak up on anybody.

"I know you aren't going to like this," she said, "but I think we should split up. The basement isn't very big, but we could still miss them."

"Are you serious?" he asked. "If these are the same men that attacked you, they've already proven they're dangerous. Do you really expect me to let you go after them alone?"

Claire sighed. "That's exactly what I need you to do right now." She refused to look him in the eyes. "We don't know for sure if they're the same guys. They could be a part of my brother's investigation team. If they are, this is Bureau business, and if anyone found out I brought a civilian into this, I'd lose my job."

He frowned but nodded. "Okay. I get it. I don't like it, but I get it."

She gave him a kiss on the cheek. "I'll keep my cell phone on vibrate. If you find anyone down here, text me and I'll come check it out." He hesitated, and Claire felt absolutely awful for putting him in that position. "If anything happens, I promise I'll yell really loud."

He nodded grumpily. She wanted to apologize, but she had a job to do, and until Drew was an agent, or even an agent in training, this wasn't something he could help her with.

She turned quickly and moved deeper into the museum. As best she could tell, the irregular energy signature was coming from somewhere to the left, so that was the direction she headed. The more distance she put between herself and Drew, the more she was able to tune in to it. The signature was nowhere as intense as it had been that night in the cemetery, but she still had no trouble following it.

She reached the last display case of the small museum without finding anything, though she could still feel the energy signature pulling on her. She looked around and noticed a maintenance door. Certain it would be locked, she decided to try the handle anyway.

The knob unexpectedly turned, and Claire briefly questioned the wisdom of going in without back-up. She knew she should probably call Zach, but by the time he and his team got there, if they came at all, the other men would probably be gone and they'd be no closer to finding out who they were and what they were doing to the rogues.

Claire took a deep breath and opened the door. The energy signature was stronger without the door to act as a barrier between them. She paused for a few seconds to let her eyes adjust to the dim light. Somewhere to her left, she heard voices, so she took a few cautious steps into the room.

Thankfully, between Claire and where the voices seemed to be, there was a tall storage shelf full of random objects. She crept slowly along behind it, peering in between the items, trying to get a look at the men who were talking.

The two men were standing about ten feet away from Claire's hiding place. To her dismay, there was a projection hovering not far from them. Claire recognized the blank stare and listless posture as an indication she was under the control of Beguiling Acuity. Claire's heart sank, and even more so when she realized one of the men was holding a familiar and very unwelcomed object.

"I don't *know* if she's a rogue or not," he told his companion with an exasperated sigh. "But since she's literally the only projection we've come across all night, I really don't care."

The other man shook his head. "I'm not comfortable moving forward if we don't know for sure. I'd rather go back empty handed than risk drawing the Bureau's attention."

Claire held her breath. She had to do something before the man with the weapon changed his mind.

She cleared her throat loudly and stepped out from behind the shelf. "Excuse me, gentlemen," she said in what she hoped was an official tone, being careful not to look in the direction of the projection. "I don't think you're supposed to be in here. This area is for hotel personnel only."

The man without the weapon looked at her with an amused smile on his face. "I'm sure you're right, Ms. Abelard. Which makes me wonder why you're here."

Claire was completely caught off guard. Whatever response she had expected from them, that definitely wasn't it. "Have we met?" she asked with a frown.

"Well, not exactly, but we definitely know who you are." He looked at his partner. "Why am I not surprised she's interfering again?"

The second man shrugged. "I guess she didn't learn from her friend's example."

The first man gave her a look as if he were scolding a child. "If she keeps this up, she's going to find herself in serious trouble."

Claire's confusion quickly turned to anger. "Who do you think you are?"

The man with the dispatching tool glared at her. "I really don't think you want to find out."

Claire realized there was no point pretending anymore. "Why are you doing this?"

"It's a necessary evil." The man looked at the projection floating a few feet away. He removed a ring from his finger, and immediately the energy level in the room increased. He turned his attention back to Claire. "Let's see how keen you are to protect them once they become a threat."

Claire noticed movement from the corner of her eye and turned to see the beguiled projection moving in her direction. She took a few steps back, bumping into a stack of boxes. The two men moved behind the projection and toward the door, but Claire didn't look at them. She kept her attention on the projection, who was still slowly moving toward her.

"I wish we could stay and see how you get yourself out of this one, but unfortunately, we have other things to do."

Claire knew from the small amount of research she had been able to do on Beguiling Acuity that once the men were a sufficient distance away, their hold on the projection should break. However, with the massive amount of energy the one man was emitting without his energy dampening ring, Claire had no idea how far that distance would have to be.

The projection continued moving toward her, though nothing about her behavior was particularly threatening. Claire wished she had brought a set of energy cuffs with her and made a mental note to get some from Zach when she saw him again. She had never needed to use them before, but she wouldn't be caught without them in the future.

Claire knew she needed to stall until the men were out of range, so she decided it couldn't hurt to try a little Beguiling Acuity of her own.

She took several deep breaths and tried to calm her pounding heart. She focused her thoughts and energy toward the projection.

The projection stopped moving, but Claire couldn't tell if she had had anything to do with it or if the men had gotten out of range. A few seconds later, the projection shook her head and looked around the small storage room.

"What happened?" she asked when she saw Claire. "Where am I?"

Claire tried to keep her emotions even. "You're in the basement," she told her. "Do you remember anything?"

The projection shook her again and frowned. Claire wanted to ask her more, but she heard Drew calling her name. She left the projection in the storage room and went back out to the museum.

"I was starting to get worried," he told her, pulling her into an embrace. "You weren't answering when I called you."

"Sorry," Claire said.

"Did you find who you were looking for?" he asked.

She nodded, not wanting to tell him another lie. "They got away." She took a step away from him. "Did you see anybody leaving this area?"

Drew shook his head. "I felt some weird energy, but I didn't see anybody."

Claire looked back toward the door of the storage room. She wanted to stay and look for clues, but she couldn't do that with the ghost hunters in the hotel. "We better get back upstairs," she told Drew. "The others must be wondering what happened to us."

As they waited for the elevator doors to slide open, Claire took out her cell phone and saw that she did in fact have missed calls – three from Drew and seven from her dad. She listened to the first voicemail and her face went white.

"Claire, you need to get back up to the hospital as soon as you can. Isabel's been attacked again..."

Not waiting to hear the rest of the message, Claire bolted toward the stairwell.

"What's wrong?" Drew asked as he followed her out of the basement.

"We've got to cut the tour short," she called back over her shoulder, taking the stairs two at a time. "I have to get back to the hospital."

Once they reached the ground floor, Drew reached out and took Claire's uninjured hand, pulling her to a stop. "Hey, talk to me. What's going on?"

Claire fought back tears. "Isabel's been attacked again."

"What?" He let go of her hand and took a step back. He thought for a few seconds then nodded his head. "Okay, you go. I'll go back upstairs and tell the others."

"Tell Spencer I'm sorry," she said, though honestly Spencer's feelings were the least of her concerns at that moment. "You guys can probably hang around the hotel a little longer, but I don't think the management will be very happy if they find you here without me."

"I'll take care of it," Drew assured her. "You go do what you've got to do."

She gave him a quick kiss then headed toward the hotel's front entrance, dialing her dad's number on the way.

Chapter 47

The elevator dinged to indicate Claire had reached the hospital's fourth floor. The doors had barely parted before she pushed through them into the corridor and practically sprinted toward Isabel's room. Claire's parents were standing in the hallway with Deputy Martens while Aaron sat in a chair next to them, holding an ice pack to the back of his head.

"Oh, Claire, honey, I'm so glad you're here," Leila said, wrapping her arms around her daughter.

Claire quickly stepped out of her embrace. "Tell me everything," she said to no one in particular.

"Well," Noah began, looking to Deputy Martens for confirmation that he should be the one to fill her in. The deputy nodded and Noah continued. "We were all here with Isabel, and we decided that since she was resting so peacefully, we would go get something to eat. The cafeteria was closed, so we had to go in search of a vending machine. When we got back, the lights were off, and there was someone in Isabel's room. Apparently, we startled him. There was a scuffle, and then he left."

Leila took her husband's hand. "Your dad got in a couple of good licks, though."

He smiled at her appreciatively. "I don't know how much good it did. It was too dark to really see what was happening."

Claire stared at her parents. "I can't believe you guys would leave her all alone like that."

"We didn't," Leila assured her. "Aaron was with her."

Claire looked at Aaron. "How did someone get in her room then?"

"I got a call from a blocked number," he said sheepishly, avoiding eye contact with her. "I thought it might be Isabel's parents calling me back since I had called them for her earlier in the day. There was a lot of static on the line and I couldn't hear the person on the other end of the line, so I stepped out in the hall to see if I could get a better signal." He shook his head. "I was only gone for a few minutes."

"Apparently that was all it took," Claire fumed, her anger directed more at herself than anyone else. "What happened to your head?" she asked Aaron.

"When the guy ran out of the room, I was down the hall. I saw him and started chasing him, but he got the jump on me when I came around the corner."

They heard the elevator ding and looked down the hall just as Zach was exiting with a couple of P.I.D. agents in tow. Claire resisted the urge to roll her eyes. The last thing she needed right then was to deal with her brother's condescending attitude.

She felt a hand on her shoulder and looked to see Deputy Martens smiling at her. "It's not a totally lost cause. The person left behind a syringe. They were apparently planning to use it to inject something into Isabel's I.V. I've already sent it off to the lab for processing."

Claire nodded, feeling more optimistic. "That's great."

"Don't get your hopes up. This isn't a TV show. I can put a rush on this, but it'll still take some time to get any results back. Even if there are prints on the syringe, the person might not be in the system."

"It's better than nothing," Claire told him.

"If they find prints," Zach said as he approached the group, "we'll want to run them against the Bureau's database as well. Considering the device used in the cemetery, it's possible we're dealing with a former agent here."

Deputy Martens nodded and made a note on a small notepad. Claire looked down the hall toward Isabel's room. There were two armed officers standing by her door.

"Wait a minute," she said, turning back to face the deputy. "Where was Isabel's protective detail when all of this was happening?"

Deputy Martens looked confused. "She didn't have one." He looked from Claire to her brother. "We sent an officer over, but Zach told me it wasn't necessary. He said you guys had her security covered."

Claire glared at Zach. "Could I talk to you in private, please?" she said through clenched teeth.

"Of course," he replied evenly.

Claire stormed down the hall and mashed the button to call the elevator. The farther they were away from everyone else, the better. Since Zach was her boss in that moment and not her brother, it would be a bad idea to call him out in front his subordinates.

As the elevator doors slid closed behind them, Zach started in. "Look, we had no reason to think something like this would happen."

"Are you kidding me?" Claire asked him, fighting not to completely lose her temper. "I *told* you what Ann said about the Syndicate and how dangerous they are."

He let out an exasperated sigh. "We have no evidence that there even *is* a Syndicate," he reminded her, "much less that they're behind any of this. We had every reason to think the attack in the cemetery was an isolated event."

The elevator reached the ground floor and the doors slid open. Thankfully at that time of night the lobby was deserted.

Claire stormed out of the elevator and Zach followed her. "You never take anything I say seriously," she accused, heading across the lobby. "You discount everything I say because I'm your baby sister and there's no way I could possibly know more about something than you do."

Zach had to jog to catch up to her. "Oh, please. You're just upset because I don't worship at your feet like everyone else in our family and in Bureau circles does. 'Oh, look, there goes Claire'," he said in a mocking voice. "'She's a Level 5 and she interacts with projections like they're real people'."

Claire spun around to face him. "Seriously? You ignore what I say because you're jealous?"

He scoffed. "I am *not* jealous of you. I just refuse to cater to your every whim." Now it was his turn to storm away. He shoved the lobby doors open and stepped outside. "You have *no* idea how hard I've had to work to get where I am in the Bureau." He stopped and placed a hand on his chest dramatically. "*I* wasn't blessed with Level-5 sensitivity and every acumen in the book. *I* had to actually put in some effort to be good at this job. Everything comes so easy for you. You have no idea what it's like to have to prove yourself every single day."

"Easy?" she threw the word back at him with a bitter laugh. "You think my life has been *easy* because I'm a Level 5?" She shook her head. "You're the one who has no idea. You can't even begin to imagine how horrible it was to find out at the age of *seven* that your best friend is actually dead. That was devastating to me."

He had the decency not to respond.

"And you know what else?" she said, pointing a finger at him. "You may have had to work at this, but I've been an agent my whole life. I just didn't get paid for it until I joined the Bureau."

He scowled. "What are you talking about?"

Claire could feel tears building but fought them back. "There has never been a time in my entire life when I haven't had projections bothering me everywhere I go." She swallowed hard. "Do you remember when I went to college and I didn't even make through one semester? It wasn't because I was stupid or because I couldn't handle the workload. It was because everywhere I turned there was a projection trying to get my attention and tell me their story or ask me to handle some kind of Bureau business for them. In class. In the library. In my dorm room. It didn't matter where I went on that campus. There was always a projection vying for my attention."

She took a deep breath and let it out in a puff, willing her emotions to get under control. She waited as a hospital employee walked past them into the building.

"I never wanted to be an agent," she told him. "I love it now, but I certainly didn't when I was younger." She spread her hands wide. "All I wanted was to lead a normal life. To get married and have kids and have a normal life and be normal like everyone else. But that's impossible for me because projections won't leave me alone. They never have."

She turned away from him and paced a few steps. She had never admitted any of these thoughts or feelings to anyone before, not even to herself. Finally, she turned back around to face her brother.

"Despite what you seem to think, I'm not trying to do your job for you or undermine your authority. I can't help but feel passionately about things that put these projections in danger, whether they're rogues or not."

They didn't speak for several seconds until eventually Zach cleared his throat. "I never knew that about your time in college," he said softly. "Honestly, I've never considered how hard it might be for you to be so in tune with them."

Claire let out a bitter laugh. "Of course not. Why would you?"

They stood awkwardly on the sidewalk, neither of them knowing what else to say. Eventually, Zach cleared his throat.

"Well, now that that's all out in the open, I guess we better get back upstairs."

Claire chuckled bitterly. Her brother had never been big on talking about emotions. Why should this be any different?

Zach took a few steps toward the hospital entrance then turned around when Claire didn't follow. "Are you coming?

She shook her head. She had no intention of following Zach back into the hospital where she would just disappear into his investigation again.

"I'm going to head home," she told him. "With everything that's happened over the past few days, I think it's really starting to get to me."

Zach took a step toward her and kissed her on the cheek. "Just be careful, please. Go straight home and stay there."

Claire nodded, touched by his concern, but still not willing to give in. She watched him go back into the hospital, then turned on her heel and headed toward the parking lot.

****

Once she arrived home, Claire took a quick shower before settling in at her desk. She opened her desk drawer and removed the copied USB drive from where she had hidden it under a stack of papers. All three house projections materialized around her.

"Do you really think that Ann person knows what she's talking about?" Thelma asked.

Claire frowned as she opened one of the files. "I don't know," she admitted. "She sure seemed convinced that it's all true."

Claire was determined to keep her promise to Zach and let him officially handle the investigation, no matter how hard it was for her to stand down. Still, she wanted to know as much as she could about the Syndicate.

She moved her mouse arrow over one of the documents in the folder, but her phone chimed a text message notification, stopping her mid-click. She looked at the screen and frowned. The message was from Aaron.

"There's something wrong with Bettie. You need to get to Ashton Villa ASAP."

A million questions ran through Claire's mind, only the least of which was what Aaron was doing at the Villa that time of day in the first place. She relayed the message to the three house projections as she grabbed her purse and keys off the kitchen counter.

"I'll go check it out," Thelma said.

Before Claire could tell her to stay put and let her handle it, Thelma disappeared.

Claire felt sick to her stomach as she hurried out the door. It was bad enough to think about something bad happening to rogue projections. Bettie was a whole different story.

Chapter 48

As soon as Claire pulled into the parking lot behind Ashton Villa, she sensed something wasn't right. The amount of energy coming from the mansion was almost overwhelming. Whatever was wrong with Bettie, Philip had to be behind it. Claire couldn't get out of her car fast enough.

She approached the building cautiously. Aaron's car was in the parking lot, so he had to be somewhere nearby. Whether he was in the house, and whether he was in danger, remained to be seen.

She entered the mansion through the back entrance. The amount of energy in the building made it hard for Claire to discern Bettie's energy signature. She could sense the projection was still there, but she had no idea where she was or if she was safe.

Philip would be easy to find. She just had to follow the source of the energy.

Claire made her way to the Gold Room and spotted Bettie, hovering next to the piano, a serene but vacant look on her face. Philip was standing a few feet away from her, with Aaron on his right. Aaron didn't seem to be in any distress, and for a second Claire wondered if Philip was somehow controlling him, too.

"I'm glad you decided to join us tonight," Philip said. "I was beginning to worry you hadn't gotten Aaron's message, or that you had chosen to ignore it."

Claire stared at him. She knew how to talk to Philip, the regular at the candy store, but what was she supposed to say to the stranger standing before her now?

Philip, on the other hand, was at no loss for words. "In case you're planning to do anything drastic..." He brandished a dispatching tool and motioned toward Bettie. "Don't."

Claire glared at him but still said nothing. The last time she had seen him, it was clear they both knew she had no idea how she had shot out the energy blast. But he couldn't be certain if she had figured it out since then. Unfortunately, she hadn't.

"I told you Bettie was the key," Aaron told Philip with a satisfied nod. "She's her favorite."

Claire stared at Aaron in disbelief. "You're *helping* him?"

"I like to think it's more than that," Aaron said. "We're more like partners."

He looked at Philip, but the older man's face remained neutral. Claire wondered how much Philip shared his understanding of their arrangement.

"How could you do this?" she asked Aaron. "You're a Bureau agent. We're supposed to protect projections."

"Not the rogues," he pointed out. "I don't owe them anything."

"And what about Isabel?" Claire wanted to know. "Are you okay with what they were planning to do to her?" When Aaron didn't respond, she realized the truth. "You were the person in her hospital room, weren't you?" She laughed bitterly. "Isabel's attacker didn't injure you. My dad did."

"I didn't want to hurt Isabel," Aaron insisted. He looked at Philip. "It was just supposed to be about the rogues, but The Syndicate can be very persuasive when they need to be."

"How did you even get involved in all this?"

"He didn't need much convincing," Philip assured her.

Aaron shrugged. "When Philip told me his plan to start dispatching rogue projections, I just couldn't resist joining him."

"*You* approached him about this?" Claire directed the question at Philip.

"I needed to make sure I didn't drain any Bureau projections," he explained. "And who better than a Bureau agent to let me know which projections were rogues and which ones weren't?"

"How did you know Aaron was an agent?"

Philip smirked. "When I first arrived on the island, I took a few ghost tours to learn as much as I could about the projection activity on the island." He chuckled. "During one of the tours, Aaron said 'projection' instead of 'ghost.'"

Claire gave Aaron a scathing look. "How could you even think about doing this? The rogues you've been draining were innocent. They hadn't hurt anybody. They didn't deserve to be dispatched."

"You're the only person I know who would think like that." Aaron's face hardened. "We're doing the world a favor by getting rid of these before they actually did start hurting people."

A warm tide of anger was beginning to build inside her. "You can't blame every rogue for what happened to your brother."

He clenched his jaw muscles. "It's not about that."

She took a step toward him. "Isn't it?"

Philip sighed heavily. "Can we finish the therapy session later? We've got a timetable here."

Claire turned her attention back to Philip. "Why have you brought me here?"

"We want you to convince the P.I.D. team to drop their investigation and go back to Boston. Tell them it was a false alarm and the rogues moved on or re-tethered themselves someplace else."

Aaron folded his arms across his chest. "It shouldn't be too hard for you to convince them. They're only here because of you in the first place. They don't care about missing rogues and you know it. If you weren't related to Zach, nobody would even have given this a second glance."

Claire didn't take her eyes off Philip. "I don't think anything I say to them at this point will make any difference. You made this about more than just rogues when you tried to drain Isabel's energy. Zach isn't going to let that go. They want to know how you did it."

Philip smirked. "I'm sure they do. Now."

Claire studied his face. "How come your friends in The Syndicate can't bail you out? If they're as formidable as you say they are, I'm sure one little P.I.D. team would be no match for them."

He frowned. For the first time since she had met him, he appeared uncertain. "I can't depend on their help with this."

"What do you mean?"

He waved his hand as if shooing a fly. "There's no need to concern you with Syndicate politics. There are much more pressing matters to attend to."

Claire thought for a second. "If I can convince the P.I.D. team to leave, will you stop draining rogues?"

"I can't do that," he said with a sad smile. His thoughts seemed to be elsewhere for an instant, then he sighed. "I wish I could lie and tell you I'll stop, but the simple fact of the matter is I *have* to continue draining rogues. I just won't do it here anymore."

Claire's body had begun to adjust to the force of Philip's energy in the mansion. The more she felt like herself again, the more her courage grew. "You know I'm not going to let you do that, right? I can't just drop this and let you keep hurting projections."

"Actually, I think you will," Aaron said. He nodded to Philip. "Go ahead. Tell her."

Philip rolled his eyes but maintained his composure. "We've planted devices in strategic places around the island. They're a little invention of mine I like to call 'dispatchment bombs.'" He seemed genuinely pleased with himself. "When these devices are detonated, they will dispatch any projection within a fifty-foot radius of their location." He held up what appeared to be a can of mace. "I can set them off or disarm them remotely. Or, I can disarm them with a code. Once we're safely out of town, we'll text you the locations and codes for all the devices."

"If anyone follows us," Aaron finished for him, "we'll set off all the bombs remotely...Starting with this one."

He stepped to the side to reveal a black box sitting on the chair behind him. It was roughly the size of a shoebox and had a blinking red light on top.

Claire stared at them both in disbelief. "How could you even think of doing something like that?" she asked Aaron. "Your job as an agent is to help preserve history. If you wipe out the projections, their history will go with them."

Claire knew Aaron answered her question, but another powerful energy source in the area caught her attention. Drew. But why would he be there? She tried to keep her expression neutral so as not to give anything away, but the tilt of Philip's head told her he already knew.

"Actually," Philip said, interrupting whatever Aaron had been saying. "I think you should come with us, Claire. I think we both know your abilities are wasted babysitting projections for the Bureau. You're capable of so much more than you realize."

"You mean like controlling projections the way you do?" Claire shook her head vigorously. "Not interested."

"Manipulating the projections is just the tip of the iceberg. I can help you figure out how you projected that wave of energy the other night, and maybe even harness it."

Claire hesitated. She desperately wanted answers, but not enough to sacrifice more projections to get them. "I don't care about any of that," she lied. "You have to know I'm not going to help you hurt projections."

He thought for a second. "Would it help if you knew their sacrifice was for a noble cause?"

Claire frowned. "What cause could possibly be noble enough to justify that?"

"What if their dissolution provided a way for diseases to be cured?" He paused. "Or death to be forestalled?"

Aaron turned to face him. "What are you talking about?"

Philip didn't take his eyes off Claire, and she returned his gaze. An impossible idea began to form at the edges of her mind. Pieces began to fall into place, but the implications were too overwhelming to take it all seriously.

She could feel Drew getting closer, and his nearness empowered her. She took a step in Philip's direction. "Do you realize that I can feel all of their emotions when it happens? They die all over again, and I get a front row seat. To me, what you're doing is murder, no matter what you plan to do with their energy."

He looked genuinely sad. "That's your gift and your curse, Claire. You're too emotionally connected to them. Your grandfather was the same way."

Claire took a step back. "My grandfather? How do you know what my grandfather was like?"

He studied her for several seconds, clearly weighing his response. Claire could see a war of emotions on his face. Eventually he took a deep breath and forced a smile. "You might as well come out and join us, Mr. Ghost Hunter," he finally said, avoiding Claire's question altogether. "We all know you're here."

Drew stepped out of the shadows leading into the hallway.

"What the hell is going on here?" Aaron yelled, clearly sick of being left in the dark.

Philip glanced over at him and frowned. "Correction, not all of us knew you were here."

Drew crossed the room to where Claire was standing.

"Sensitives can sense other sensitives," she told him quietly.

He nodded. "Yeah, I get that now."

"How did you know to come here?"

"It's a long story. I'll just say 'Jean Lafitte' and leave it at that for now."

Claire smiled despite the seriousness of their situation. If Jean was involved, it was sure to be a great story, but it would have to wait. She turned her attention back to Philip.

"How do you know what my grandfather was like?" she pressed, determined not to let that detail slide. He had mentioned him before, but then it was more in a historical context. This time it felt much more personal.

"He was a great man," Philip said, "and my mentor. I was devastated when he had me dismissed from the Bureau."

Claire froze. The truth she hadn't wanted to acknowledge slapped her in the face. "So," she eventually said, "using the rogues' energy to forestall death, that isn't just a theory of yours."

Philip shook his head. "I owe them my life. Literally."

"Wait," Aaron said, his face turning redder by the minute, "you told me we were getting rid of the rogues. But really you've been using their energy for yourself this whole time? Like some kind of twisted Dr. Frankenstein?"

Philip, who Claire finally knew to be Werner Vogel, didn't bother to hide his irritation. "I needed their energy, and I needed your help to get it. Only a fool would let all that energy go to waste."

"Go to waste?" Aaron repeated, clearly not following Philip's train of thought.

"Yes, you idiot. You can't destroy energy. It can never be destroyed." Vogel paused and looked at Claire. "It's a scientific fact the Bureau knows all too well."

Claire frowned. "What does that mean?" She had never even considered what happened to energy from dispatched rogues. She had always assumed it was released back into nature, like when a projection moves on.

"Ask your brother," Vogel said, "or better yet your father, about it." He chuckled humorlessly. "I'm sure they know all the Bureau's dirty little secrets."

"Hey!" Aaron said loudly, drawing everyone's attention back to himself. "That can wait." He stuck his finger in Philip's face. "I want to know exactly what you've been doing with all that rogue energy you've been draining."

Philip batted Aaron's hand to the side. "We are not equals in this. I don't owe you any explanation." He glared at the younger man. "I couldn't care less about what happened to your brother or about your little crusade to rid the world of rogues. My purposes are far too lofty. Someone with so narrow a focus as yours could never understand."

Aaron's face turned bright red. "You don't care about my little crusade, huh?" He reached into his pocket and pulled out a remote detonator exactly like the one in Vogel's hand. "How about now?"

Before anyone could make a move to stop him, Aaron pressed the button.

Claire's heart leapt into her throat. She had no idea what to expect from a dispatchment explosion like the one Vogel had described. She looked at Bettie. To her relief and amazement, the projection was still hovering next to the piano, exactly as she had been.

Confused, Claire looked at Vogel. Had he been bluffing about the bombs?

He let out an exasperated sigh. "Did you really think I would trust you with something as important as this? You're too volatile. I would never risk letting you displace all that energy."

Claire had never seen Aaron as angry as he was at that moment. He fumed silently for several seconds then reached out and yanked the dispatching tool out of Vogel's hand. Again, Claire was worried for Bettie's safety, but the projection wasn't Aaron's intended target. Vogel responded quickly and attempted to retrieve the weapon, but Aaron resisted.

"We need to get Bettie out of here," Claire told Drew. She pointed to the device on the chair. "If that thing goes go off, she'll be dispatched."

Drew studied the scene on the other side of the room. "I can see his connection to her," he said, almost more to himself than to Claire. "I think I can break it."

"How?"

"I'm not sure," he admitted, "but Jean Lafitte told me to trust my instincts. He said I'd know what to do when the time came."

Claire smiled. Clearly, she had seriously underestimated Jean.

Drew focused on Bettie, while Claire kept her eyes on Vogel and Aaron. Neither man was ready to concede to the other, so the struggle continued. Eventually Aaron got control of the weapon and turned it on Vogel.

"I got it!" Drew said, going down on one knee.

Claire could only imagine the amount of energy he had exerted to free Bettie. She looked across the room to find Bettie staring at her, clearly confused but thankfully no longer in a trance.

"Bettie, you have to get out of here!" she told her as she knelt down to check on Drew.

Bettie looked at Aaron and Vogel, then took one look at the weapon in Aaron's hand and disappeared.

With Bettie out of immediate danger, Claire turned her attention back to Drew.

"I'm fine," he assured her, breathing heavily. "I just feel really hungover."

She kept her hand on his shoulder but turned her attention to the two men on the other side of the room. Claire could feel the energy in the room decreasing by the second as Aaron continued to drain Vogel's energy. The older man had apparently been injured during his fight with Aaron, so he wasn't able to put up much resistance to what was happening to him.

Despite everything Vogel had done, Claire couldn't help feeling sorry for him. "We have to stop Aaron," she told Drew.

"Then stop him."

Claire frowned. "How?"

He smiled weakly at her. "Trust your instincts."

Claire focused her thoughts and energy on Aaron, but nothing happened. "It's not working."

"Keep trying," Drew said as he reached out and took her hand.

As soon as their hands touched, Claire felt a surge of energy flow through her. Gradually, the room began to take on a strange green glow, and it seemed to be emanating from where Philip was kneeling on the floor. Claire knew instinctively she was seeing his energy signature. She was also keenly aware that it was fading quickly.

Claire couldn't explain how, but she immediately knew what she needed to do. She focused on Aaron and thought about how she wanted him to drop the dispatching device. With only a few seconds of hesitation, he let go of the weapon. Claire could feel his surprise and confusion as he watched it fall to the ground. He wanted to pick it up again, but she wouldn't let him. So, he just stood there, staring dumbly down at the weapon.

"You did it," Drew said, squeezing her hand. "I knew you could."

As Claire held Aaron in place, Vogel gradually regained his energy. The green glow surrounding them steadily intensified. Since he had possessed such a huge reserve of stolen energy before being drained, he was recovering quickly. He got to one knee, then reached over and picked up the weapon before standing all the way to his feet.

"You little cockroach," he said, raising the weapon and pointing it at Aaron. With his other hand, he held his side where he had been injured during their fight.

Claire felt a wave of panic sweep over her. "I can't control them both," she told Drew. "Vogel's too strong."

Drew slowly stood to his feet. "Not for both of us."

Claire smiled up at him. "Not for both of us."

They held hands and Claire focused on Vogel. She immediately felt his resistance, but she held on. Her grip on Aaron began to weaken, but she couldn't worry about that. She forced Vogel to throw the dispatching tool across the room, hoping the impact might break it. Even if it didn't, at least it would be well out of his reach.

"Leave me alone, Claire!" Vogel yelled from the other side of the room. Despite his efforts to resist, with a grunt of frustration, he threw the weapon as hard as he could against the wall.

Claire could feel Aaron slip free of her control as she focused all their combined energy on Vogel. She glanced quickly at Aaron and saw the look of sheer terror on his face. He was only a Level-3 sensitive, so there was no way he could understand what was really going on around him. With one final wide-eyed look at Claire, he turned and ran out of the room.

With all Claire and Drew's energy focused on Vogel, he remained frozen in place. "You can't hold me here forever," he said.

Claire knew he was right. She felt strong now with Drew holding her hand, but she had no idea how long it would last. And once Vogel was free of their control, there was no telling what he would do.

"We don't have to hold you forever," Drew replied. "The Bureau guys should be here soon."

Claire looked up at him. "How did you get word to them?"

Drew smiled again. "Jean Lafitte."

Chapter 49

"Where are the other devices?" Claire asked Vogel. "You need to shut them down now."

She could feel him resisting, but her determination grew. If even one of those devices went off, it would be disastrous for any projections nearby. She held her breath as Vogel reached into his pocket and pulled out the detonator he had shown her earlier.

"Shut them down," Claire repeated.

He reluctantly pressed a button on the device. The box on the chair made a whirring noise then went silent. Philip's frustrated growl let Claire know the devices had been disarmed. She nodded to Drew and breathed a sigh of relief. She made Philip throw the detonator across the room, like he had done with the dispatching tool. She wasn't taking any chances.

A few minutes later, Claire heard the sound of screeching tires outside the mansion. For the first time since their arrival on the island, she desperately hoped it was Zach and his team.

"Claire," Vogel said, now down on one knee.

Claire felt a pang of guilt. She couldn't tell if he was exhausted from his efforts to resist the combined strength of their Beguiling Acuity or from his injury. Either way, she couldn't allow herself to feel sympathy for him now.

Vogel let out a heavy breath but maintained Claire's gaze. "Don't tell them what you can do."

Her resolve wavered. "What do you mean?"

"The Bureau. I worked for them, remember? If they find out what you're capable of, there's no telling how they'll use you."

Claire didn't want to trust him, but deep down inside she suspected he might be right. Why else would her parents have kept their secret for all these years?

The front door to Ashton Villa flew open. Zach and his entire P.I.D. team flooded into the room, followed closely by Claire's parents. Claire and Drew stepped out of the way, still holding hands, and let them get to work. There was a bustle of activity, and eventually Vogel was taken into custody. Claire didn't release her hold on him until one of the agents had clamped a set of energy-dampening cuffs on his wrists. Under different circumstances, Claire might have chuckled at the irony. The cuffs were one of Vogel's own inventions.

Noah and Leila rushed over to Drew and Claire, pulling them both into a large group hug.

"Honey, we were so worried about you," Leila said. "When Jean Lafitte found us at the hospital, he made it sound like you were in mortal danger."

Noah shook Drew's hand so hard Claire thought he might squeeze it off. "And we have you to thank for it. Jean said you're the one who sent him to find us."

"Well, he's the one who got me mobilized in the first place," Drew said, "so it's all thanks to him really."

"Apparently, it's a long story," Claire told her parents. She looked at Drew. "I can't wait to hear it."

They all turned their attention to the flurry of activity surrounding Vogel.

"His weapon is over there," Drew told the agents, pointing at the broken pieces next to the wall. "Or at least what's left of it is."

Noah turned to Claire. "Is he Vogel's son?"

She shook her head. "You're not going to believe it. I think you'll definitely want to sit in on the debrief."

As if on cue, one of the P.I.D. agents came to escort Claire and Drew out of the room to get their statements. Claire's dad followed, his curiosity piqued. Since Drew was a civilian, the agent tried to separate them for their debriefings.

"He already knows about the Bureau," Claire told the agent. She looked at Drew and smiled. "And he's a prime candidate for recruitment, so there's no point separating us." The agent protested, but Claire insisted. "If you want my cooperation, he's going to be in the room or you don't get my statement, and you can take it up with my brother later."

The agent reluctantly agreed and they all sat down around the antique dining room table. Claire and Drew held hands as the agent set a digital recorder on the table and pushed record. Claire started from the beginning, and two hours later they were finished.

The most amusing part of the interview was Drew's account of Jean Lafitte's appearance in his hotel room at the Harbor House.

Apparently, Thelma had gotten word through The Ghost Net that Claire was walking into a trap. Jean found out about it and learned from other rogues where the ghost hunters were staying. He had no trouble figuring out which ghost hunter was Drew, and then it was just a matter of making himself known in an unmistakable way.

With their interview completed, Claire and Drew returned to the Gold Room where the P.I.D. team was leading Vogel away. Claire briefly met his gaze and offered him a sad smile, wishing she could still think of him as Philip, one of the regulars at the candy shop.

As Vogel was led out the back door, Claire felt Drew squeeze her hand. "Let's get you home," he said with a warm smile. "I don't know about you, but I'm beat."

Claire nodded and returned Drew's smile. She looked at her parents and they were both smiling as well.

"I think they can handle it from here," Noah said, putting his arm around Leila's shoulders. "If they have any other questions, they know where to find you."

While Claire was more exhausted than she ever thought it was possible for a person to feel, for the first time in days she felt hope. The sun had just begun peeking over the horizon, and Claire couldn't wait to see what the day had in store.

Chapter 50

The next afternoon, Claire was sitting out on her porch with her parents and Drew, enjoying the cool autumn weather. Another cold front had come through the night before, dropping the temperatures into the fifties, practically an arctic blast for the Texas Gulf Coast at that time of year. They had all managed to get a few hours of sleep after the events at Ashton Villa. Now they were waiting for Zach to stop by with an update.

"I bet Spencer was pretty mad at you for running out on them last night," Claire said to Drew.

He shrugged. "Spencer's usually upset about something, so I'm not too worried about it."

"What excuse did you give him?" Noah asked. Always the agent, Claire was sure he was worried about Bureau secrecy.

Drew smiled. "I claimed I was having digestive distress. I told him I drove myself to a pharmacy and then to a quick care clinic."

Claire smiled, but she hated the fact that now Drew was having to lie to the people he cared about as well.

"I hope he bought it," Noah said.

"Honestly," Drew told him, giving Claire's hand a squeeze, "I'm not in the least bit worried about it if he didn't. My days as a ghost hunter are numbered anyway." He shook his head. "I don't think I can go back to the way things were before. Doing the show seems so ridiculous now that I know the truth about what we're actually investigating."

Noah smiled at him. "Well, I'm pretty sure you won't have any trouble finding ways to fill your spare time."

"If the Bureau even lets him have any spare time," Leila pointed out.

Drew looked from Claire to her parents. "Do you really think they'll ask me to join the Bureau?"

Claire nodded. "I've got no doubt they will, given your sensitivity level. And since you already know about the Bureau, that's one less hurdle for them to clear."

"And when they find out you have Force Perceptive Acumen..." Noah motioned with his hand as if there was nothing more to say about it.

"Well then," Drew said. "I guess I've got a lot to think about, huh?"

Claire was dying to know what direction he was leaning, but at the same time she was terrified to find out. She didn't have the chance to ask, though, as a black SUV pulled up in the driveway. Zach climbed out of the passenger's side while the driver remained in the vehicle.

As Zach made his way across the yard, they all stood up to greet him. Claire wasn't looking forward to the conversation she knew was coming. She didn't know if she should expect a reprimand for involving a civilian in her investigation, or much worse.

Zach climbed the front steps and headed straight for Claire, wrapping her up in a big bear hug. "I owe you a huge apology," he said in her ear. "You were right all along."

Claire was speechless. As far as she could remember, her brother had never admitted he was wrong about anything, and he had certainly never apologized to her. "Apology accepted," she eventually said.

Zach released her from his embrace and took a step back, shaking his head. "He confessed to it all. I mean, we'll still need to conduct a full investigation, but he admitted to draining the rogues."

"Did he tell you everything?" Claire asked.

"You mean that he's actually Werner Vogel?" Zach shook his head. "Crazy, huh?"

"That's not exactly the word I'd choose to describe it," Noah said.

Zach chuckled. He looked at Drew, then extended his hand. "Thank you so much for looking out for my little sister again."

Drew shook the offered hand. "My pleasure." He put his arm around Claire's shoulders. "Anytime."

Zach looked at Claire. "So, clearly he knows about the Bureau." Claire nodded, though it hadn't actually been a question. "And we don't really need to have him tested to know he's a Level 5, do we?"

Claire smiled broadly. "And he's a Force Perceptive."

Zach stared at her. "Are you serious?"

"Yep."

Zach frowned. "And you're just telling me this now?"

Claire shrugged.

Zach nodded several times, deep in thought. "Alright then," he eventually said, motioning toward the house. "Shall we all go inside and finish this conversation?"

Once they were all settled in the living room, Claire spoke up. "What's going to happen to Vogel, now?"

"I can't say," Zach admitted. "This kind of crime is totally unprecedented in Bureau history, and quite honestly, it's way out of the range of the standard punitive inquiry committee. With Vogel's use of Beguiling Acuity, only members of the chief governing council can be privy to the truth about what's happened."

"What do you think his punishment will be?" Noah asked.

"I don't have a clue. It's not like he can go to a standard prison, and we certainly don't have any kind of holding facilities for offenses like this." Zach shook his head. "I honestly don't know what they're going to do with him."

"Have you found the other one?" Drew asked. "The Bureau agent?"

"No, Aaron is still in the wind. We've got eyes on every aspect of his life that we know about, though, so if he surfaces, we'll get him."

"That's what has me worried," Claire said. "Clearly there's a lot we didn't know about him. He and Vogel weren't working alone. There were at least six men in the cemetery that night."

Zach frowned. "Vogel won't give up the identities of the other men, so there's only so much we can do. Every Bureau agent in the country has been put on alert to be on the lookout for Aaron. We'll have to hope that's enough." He cleared his throat. "Okay, now I've got a few questions for you two."

"Shoot," Claire said, feeling very proud of how confident she sounded. Drew's grip on her hand tightened. She didn't know if he was anticipating the question she was dreading or if it was just a gesture of encouragement.

"How did you two manage to subdue Vogel? He didn't offer us many details about that, but with the amount of energy he had consumed over the years, he would have been very powerful."

Drew looked at Claire then held up their joined hands. "But he wasn't more powerful than the two of us together."

Claire smiled, but Vogel's warning still rang in her ears. There was no way she was going to tell Zach she had figured out how to use Beguiling Acuity, and especially not that she had been able to use it on a living.

"It must have been our combined energy levels and abilities," she told him instead. "When we were holding hands, I had Force Perceptive Acumen, too." She looked from her dad to her brother. "Have any agents ever combined their energies like that before?"

Noah answered. "Not that I know of. In hundreds of years of Bureau history, I don't think it's even been tried."

"I bet it will be now," Drew said proudly.

Zach smiled. "I can assure you we'll definitely look into the implications as well as the possibilities." He turned his attention back to Claire. "So, any details you can give me about what you did and how you did it will be extremely helpful moving forward."

"I don't know how we did it," she said, giving Drew's hand a squeeze, "I think Vogel got injured when he was fighting with Aaron. I'm sure that weakened him."

Zach studied them both for several seconds. Claire could tell he wasn't satisfied with her answer. He sat back in his chair and shook his head. "Vogel had absorbed a *lot* of energy over the years from thousands of dispatched rogues. Even with the energy-dampening cuffs we put on him, his energy output was still off-the-charts."

"I know," Claire agreed. "I've never met any sensitive as strong as he was without his energy-dampening ring."

Zach frowned. "Energy-dampening ring," he repeated. "Vogel wasn't wearing a ring." He took out his phone and sent a text. "I'll have the team do another sweep of Ashton Villa and look for it."

Claire waited until Zach slipped his phone back into his jacket pocket. "Now I've got a question for you," she said, releasing Drew's hand and leaning forward in her seat. "Vogel suggested I ask you about what happens to all the energy that's syphoned off rogues when they're dispatched. I've always assumed it's released back into nature, but he hinted that isn't the case."

Zach laughed and exchanged a look with their dad. "Claire Bear," he said, back to his usual condescending tone, "Vogel hasn't worked for the Bureau for over seventy years. How could he possibly know what we do with the energy?"

"Clearly, he had his own ideas about how it should be used," Noah pointed out, "but that doesn't mean the Bureau actually followed through with them."

Claire studied them both for several seconds. She could tell they weren't being completely honest with her, but she decided not to push the issue since she was keeping secrets of her own.

"Well, I've got a lot of work left to do before we head back to Boston tonight," Zach said, standing up suddenly.

He gave Leila and Claire hugs then shook hands with Noah. When he turned and extended his hand in Drew's direction, Claire felt her heart stop. As the two men shook hands, Zach uttered the words she had been dreading.

"So, what do you say, Drew? Are you interested in joining the Bureau?" Claire had to resist the urge to cry, but then Zach added, "After all, we're going to need a third agent here in Galveston."

A word from the Author

Thanks for reading *Ghost Agents.* I hope you enjoyed it!

Would you like to know what happens next? Stay tuned as the adventure continues with the 2nd book of the trilogy - *Ghost Agents: Revelations* (due for release in December 2021).

In the meantime, keep reading for a teaser!

And don't forget, you can sign up at the link below to be notified of giveaways and pre-release specials – plus, you'll receive a free scene that bridges the gap between the 2 books!

https://BookHip.com/SWNAPZX

If you loved *Ghost Agents* & and have a little time to spare, please help other readers find it by leaving a short review on the product page where you purchased the book, as well as on Goodreads. Reviews make a huge difference in spreading the word!

Thanks!

About the Author

Nita DeBorde is a published author and teacher from Houston, TX. Writing and teaching are her two major passions, though traveling and being dog-mom to a crazy Staffordshire-Boxer mix named Mabel are high on the list as well.

Nita has taught high school French for more than 20 years and absolutely loves her "day job" (about 95% of the time). She loves to travel, and not surprisingly, France is her favorite destination, though her home state of Texas runs a close second.

She is also a huge history buff, which comes through in her fiction writing, and particularly in her latest novel, Ghost Agents, a genre-defying, cozy paranormal mystery with a little sci-fi and romance thrown into the mix.

Excerpt from Ghost Agents: Revelations

"I know those men," Aaron said from behind Claire as they entered the room. His voice was barely above a whisper. "They're the Syndicate operatives I've been working with the last few weeks. The big one is named Draper and the other one is Galvan." He frowned at Claire. "They're bad news."

Claire studied the two men. There wasn't anything particularly menacing about them or their demeanor. If it wasn't for the oily feel of the projection energy surrounding them, Claire wouldn't have known there was anything unusual about them at all.

"Miss Abelard," the man named Draper said. "We were hoping you'd find your way here tonight."

Claire kept her distance. "You've been waiting for us?"

The other man nodded. "Well, we've been waiting for you." He smiled at Aaron. "Thank you for bringing her to us."

Claire whirled around to face Aaron. "You ass!" she hissed.

Aaron threw his hands up in a defensive gesture. "I swear, I didn't set you up. I had no idea they were going to be here." He motioned to the Syndicate operatives. "Draper, tell her!"

The two men looked at each other. "As much as I hate to let this little weasel off the hook," Draper said, "it's true. He didn't know anything about our plans tonight."

Galvan smirked. "And that wasn't by accident." He looked at Aaron. "We knew once you had made contact with her, it would only be a matter of time before you led her to us."

"Beyond that," Draper added, "you're really of no use to us whatsoever."

Aaron glared at him. "I told you everything I know about the Bureau."

Draper laughed. "You don't even know enough to know how much you don't know about the Bureau."

Aaron looked confused, but he didn't have long to figure out what the man meant. Claire watched in horror as Galvan removed a handgun from a shoulder holster and shot Aaron in the stomach.

Claire gasped. Drew took a step toward the two men but stopped short when a half dozen translucent forms floated into the room. It was Jean Lafitte and his pirate crew. Their energy carried that oily feel Claire was becoming accustomed to, and their vacant expressions confirmed they were clearly under the influence of Beguiling Acuity.

"Well, we wanted to find Jean Lafitte," Jeff said unenthusiastically.

"Their energy is gray," Drew said as he took a step back so he was standing directly next to Claire.

"And you must be Drew," Draper said, his eyebrows raised. "We've heard about you as well. Not as gifted as Miss Abelard, I think, but potentially still useful in your own way." The man turned his attention to Jeff. "This one, however, is of no use to us."

Without any warning, Jean Lafitte floated across the room, closing the distance before any of them could react. He wrapped his hands around Jeff's neck and began to squeeze. Jeff had no way to defend himself against the attack.

"Jean," Claire yelled, hoping her years of friendship with the pirate would somehow get through to him.

Jean didn't loosen his grip. He didn't even respond to Claire's voice.

She tried to use Beguiling Acuity, but quickly realized it was no use. Whatever they had done to him, she couldn't reach him.

She turned her attention back to the two Syndicate operatives. "Stop it!"

The two men simply smiled at her, clearly enjoying themselves.

She took a step toward Jean but stopped short when the remaining pirates began moving in her direction. They slowly encircled her and Drew but didn't attack. Without needing to speak, she and Drew instinctively stood back-to-back, the best way to keep their eyes on all the pirates.

"I'm going to try to manipulate Jean's energy," Drew whispered over his shoulder.

Claire nodded. He had been able to free Bettie from Vogel's control at Ashton Villa. She prayed it would work now.

Drew extended his hand slightly in Jean Lafitte's direction. Claire could sense the moment he made the connection and for a brief instant she felt hope that they could get Jean back. Her hopes were quickly dashed, though, when Drew doubled over in pain.

"Drew!" She bent down next to him, careful to keep her attention on the pirates slowly closing in around them. "What is it?"

"There's something wrong with their energy," he told her through gritted teeth.

She reached out to touch him but pulled her hand away quickly once she did. The malevolent chill that went down her spine told her all she needed to know. "You can't manipulate it."

Drew shook his head. "Not without it affecting me, too."

Claire didn't ask him to elaborate. He didn't need to.

She glared at the two Syndicate agents. They seemed almost amused by the scene playing out in front of them.

She looked across the room to where Aaron was lying against the wall, a dark crimson pool forming on the wooden floor beneath him.

A wave of anger began building inside her.

She looked at Jeff, slowly having the life choked out of him by Jean Lafitte.

She looked at Drew, who was now on one knee, doing his best to fight against whatever effects the strange energy was having on him.

Finally, she looked back at the two Syndicate agents with their smug expressions.

A familiar sensation began to stir inside her. This time, she was prepared for it. Remembering the advice Vogel had given her only days before, she closed her eyes and allowed the emotions and adrenaline to flow through her.

A warm glow began in the middle of her chest and grew.

Claire embraced it. She allowed all of her fear and frustration to well up inside of her until finally it forced its way out through every cell in her body.